every bell that *rings*

every bell that rings

TALENA WINTERS

Published by My Secret Wish Publishing
www.mysecretwishpublishing.com

Every Bell that Rings (Peace Crossing Book 2)
Copyright © 2024 by Talena Winters. All rights reserved.
Contact the author at www.talenawinters.com.

Summary: Stephanie Neufeld's bah-humbug ways have met their match when her old crush decides to make her fall in love with Christmas. But while Noel Butler slowly melts her reserve, will she ever unwrap the secrets in his fiercely guarded heart?

ISBN (eBook): 978-1-989800-14-0
ISBN (digital audiobook): 978-1-998164-08-0
ISBN (paperback): 978-1-989800-15-7
ISBN (hardcover): 978-1-989800-16-4

Cover design by Talena Winters
Developmental editing by Jennifer Lindsay, thewriterswellspring.com
Author Photo © Amanda Monette. Used with permission.

Printed in the United States of America, or the country of purchase.

*To my husband, Jason,
who loved me back to life.*

Content Warning

T HIS BOOK IS WRITTEN using Canadian English, spelling, and idiomatic or regional language. It also includes references to domestic violence and accidental death, and themes of addictions and trauma recovery.

So be prepared, eh?

T. W.

Chapter One

STEPHANIE NEUFELD HAD A love-hate relationship with Christmas. Mostly hate.

It wasn't the season's fault, exactly. This time of year was simply haunted by too many ghosts of Christmases past. But if Steph could, she would cancel the whole thing.

Which left her wondering what, exactly, she was doing in the cozy confines of Cool Beans coffee shop on the night of the Peace Crossing Santa Claus Parade, wrestling with candy canes and juggling glitter balls. And why she'd agreed to attend the parade itself afterwards.

Oh, right . . . Sisterly duty and a guilt trip from her childhood chum. How festive.

Stephanie kept her annoyance to herself while she scanned the fake twelve-foot spruce tree for a good spot to hang the candy cane she held. Seeing a space near the top of the tree with no candy canes close by, she hung the treat, then bent to the sad-looking cardboard box near her feet for another ornament.

"Look!" came Autumn's voice at her elbow, "It's snowing!"

Steph straightened and glanced through the large glass window beside her with chagrin, a sparkling silver globe ornament hanging from her fingers. Her sister was right. Fat, fluffy snowflakes floated gently from the sky above, which was already pitch black at four-thirty in the afternoon. The snow dusted the hats, hair, and coats of the people gathering on the shovelled sidewalk beyond and glinted in the orange glow of the street lamps.

Steph cringed and wrinkled her nose. *Bad enough I have to go to the Santa Claus Parade. Now I'll be standing in the cold, wet snow too?*

"Huh." Autumn put her hands on her slender hips, one hand grasping the end of a fake evergreen garland she'd been tacking along the top of the window. "I guess the forecast was wrong. Glad I told Mom to have Julien wear his snowsuit."

"Can she bring an extra for me?" Steph thought of her energetic three-year-old nephew's toothy grin framed by a fur-lined hood, smiling to herself at the image of the two of them in matching poofy one-piece snowsuits. "I wasn't planning on snow when I came down here this afternoon."

Autumn let out a disbelieving puff of air, crossing her arms and cocking her head at a saucy angle that made it look like she were looking down at Steph, though she was a good six inches shorter. The garland trailing around her body made it look like she was decorating herself, not the shop.

"What?" Steph demanded.

Autumn dropped the garland, letting it hang from the last tack she'd placed, and moved her stepladder down to the far end of the row of picture windows.

"I'm not sure what's more unbelievable—that I finally convinced you to come to the Santa Claus Parade, or that you aren't prepared for something. Haven't you lived in Peace Crossing your whole life? She asks, rhetorically." Autumn shook her head, her wavy brown bob swaying next to her chin. She retrieved the end of the garland swag with an amused grin. "And you haven't learned yet that it almost *always* snows on the Santa Claus Parade? It either snows, or it's twenty-five below. Seriously, I don't know why they don't change the date."

She climbed the stepladder, eyeballed the garland swag to match the rest of the row, held it to the top corner of the window, and lined up the staple gun she'd left on the top tray of the ladder to place the final tack. She squeezed the gun, grunting with the effort, and a loud *whap* echoed through the shop.

"I'm prepared," Steph said, trying not to sound defensive. "I brought my winter coat and boots, obviously. But the weatherman made snow seem highly unlikely." She glared out the window and muttered, "I should have bought myself some snow pants anyway."

"You should call him up and give him a piece of your mind," Autumn said. "That'll teach 'im."

Steph made a face at her sister, then turned back toward the tree and surveyed it for another empty branch. It wasn't tough to find a vacancy. The hard part of this job would be making the coffee shop's slim stash of decorations look like they were filling out the entire tree. She found a gaping hole and hung the ornament with grim satisfaction, then glanced at the milling crowds outside the window.

"I bet it's going to be a busy night, though."

Autumn grinned. "See? Even you gotta admit that snow isn't all bad."

Stephanie chuckled. "The only good thing about snow is getting to wear cute hats and having a guilt-free excuse to drink hot chocolate. And Cool Beans is the best source of hot chocolate around. Especially tonight."

Every year, the Santa Claus parade signalled the kickoff of Peace Crossing's seasonal Christmas events. The parade was followed by the annual Midnight Madness event, when all the shops around town would stay open late and offer special deals and bonuses to encourage residents to shop local. While Cool Beans closed by mid-afternoon most of the time, catering only to the morning and lunch crowd, it always hosted a hot chocolate-and-cookies night as part of the event. Given the shop's location near the beginning of the downtown parade route, their winter warmers were always in high demand. The Cool Beans baker, Ellie, had been elbow deep in cookie dough since three, pumping out batches of fresh ginger snaps, chocolate chip cookies, and peppermint sugar cookie twists for tonight. Heavenly sweetness permeated the entire shop.

"Besides, you know I haven't gone to the parade in years," Steph added.

"No," Autumn said, "you usually work. Which is why I thought you would know about the snow, what with all the fender-benders that usually keep you so busy in Emergency."

She had a point. At this time of year, what with icy roads and nothing much for folks to do on the weekend except ski, snowmobile, or get into trouble at the bar, the hospital always had a higher number of patients in the ER. Snowstorms meant busy nights at the hospital. But Steph had never taken particular note of the Santa Claus Parade date—unless it was to avoid downtown that night. Just like she typically avoided all reminders of this so-called festive season.

Autumn paused, catching her eye. "Hey. You know I'm teasing, right? I'm really glad you agreed to do this."

At the look in her sister's eyes, Steph's annoyance softened. "Of course. You know I'm always here for you."

Autumn gave her a grateful smile, then went over to a box against the wall and rummaged through it for the end of another evergreen garland.

Earlier in the week, several of Autumn's staff had come down with a cold that had been making the rounds. Between covering for the absent staff and missing a day of work to take Julien to a medical appointment in the city—a full-day event when Autumn had to travel two hours to the nearest major medical centre—she hadn't had time to decorate the shop. Since it was Steph's day off, she'd agreed to help. After the morning staff had gone home at the regular closing time that afternoon, Steph and Autumn had set to work decorating the place. Other than Ellie, they were the only ones there.

Steph stepped back to survey her work while smoothing her long mahogany curls off her warm forehead, bunching it into a hand-held ponytail at the nape of her neck. The results weren't half bad, especially considering she and Autumn had discovered that a leak in the storage room had ruined at least a third of the decorations when they'd dug out the boxes that afternoon. Still, the sparkling white lights glinting off silver stars, pointed swirly baubles, enormous glitter-encrusted blue balls, and the wrappers of the candy canes they'd used to fill some gaps, all with a red plaid ribbon winding throughout was . . . pretty. If you ignored how much space remained between each ornament.

The last time she'd decorated a Christmas tree, there had been even bigger gaps—mostly in the top third, which had been out of her and her sisters' reach. Had that been nearly sixteen years ago? Steph blinked at the realization. As the oldest, she'd always been the tallest of her sisters, but at twelve, she'd still been shorter than Autumn's current five-foot-three-inch frame. The top of the tree hadn't been completely bare, though—eight-year-old Melody had made sure of it. Steph and Autumn's littlest sister had handed their dad ornaments and then pointed to where she'd wanted them hung. When it came time to put up the angel tree topper, Eddie had swung a giggling Melody onto his shoulders so she could reach. He'd zoomed her around the room, making her fly like an angel to reach the top of the tree, while Steph, Autumn, and their mom had looked on and laughed. Later, Eddie had pulled out his guitar and they'd sung "Jingle Bells", his strong baritone carrying the sweet voices of Steph and her sisters, with their mom adding a sweet contralto harmony.

That had been a good Christmas.

Unlike so many others since.

Stephanie crossed her arms, her stomach roiling and her shoulders tight. Ever since she'd received the unexpected voice mail from Eddie a few days ago, old memories had been coming back unbidden. Most of them weren't nearly as pleasant as that one.

"What's wrong?" Autumn asked softly. She stepped away from the antique upright piano near the hearth, which now sported an evergreen garland swag accented with white twinkle lights along the top edge.

Blinking, Steph snapped out of her reverie, deliberately relaxing her frown. "This tree. It's half naked. I know I'm no expert, but aren't Christmas trees usually a bit more . . . dressed?"

Autumn's worried face relaxed. She surveyed the tree and its red, silver, and blue decorations from top to bottom, then sighed. "I suppose I'm going to need to replace the decorations we lost. Hopefully with something that has more personality. This stuff came with the place, and I've never bothered to replace any of it. Do you think I could find coffee-related decorations online?"

Steph shrugged. "You can find pretty much anything online. Or check at Pearl's Petals. She might be able to order something in for you."

"Great idea. I'll have to get her to put a rush on it." Autumn tapped her lip in thought, spinning to take in the room. "Well, that's all the decorations. Just in time, too. Thanks again for helping me out with this. It turned out amazing."

Steph glanced around the inviting coffee shop, now be-garlanded with strings of white lights and fake pine boughs and glittery garlands to within an inch of its life. Small snowmen and reindeer statuettes peeked from between the plants and antique coffee grinders tucked in the cubbies between rustic square wooden tables. A miniature nativity perched on the mantle above the gas fireplace. A few fuzzy red-and-white stockings labelled with staff members' names in puffy gold fabric paint added a homey touch to the hearth. And the tree that had replaced two of the tables near the front door still drew the eye, even if the decorations *were* a bit sparse and generic.

"Any time," Steph said.

And, despite her distaste for this particular holiday, she meant it. Ever since Autumn's husband, Denis, had died in a quadding accident two years ago, Steph had been helping her sister out more than ever, filling in behind the coffee shop counter or babysitting Julien almost every day she had off from the hospital. No, that didn't leave much room for a personal life—but her relationship with romance was almost as complicated as her relationship with Christmas. It was hard to miss something that had never been that exciting in the first place.

"Besides," she added, "Delanie's been bugging me to get together, and I didn't have a good reason to say no again."

Autumn quirked her brow. "Why would you want to? I thought you and Delanie were good friends."

Steph sighed and shrugged. Ten years ago, she and Delanie Fletcher had been more than *good friends*. They'd been inseparable. But times changed. And Steph was tired of being ghosted by people she thought cared about her.

"We used to be, back in high school. But then she went off to film school in Vancouver and kind of faded away. I don't know how I feel about her trying to pick up where we left off when she didn't want to be friends while she was gone."

Autumn gave her an askance look. "You don't know she didn't want to be friends anymore. She probably just got busy. Relationships often change when circumstances do."

"I was busy, too, going to nursing school and interning, but I still reached out."

"True. I get it. Still, you never know unless you try, right? She's probably different than she was when she left."

Steph twisted her lips. "Maybe. But I'm not sure how invested I want to get to find out."

Autumn pursed her lips as if she wanted to say more, but she didn't. Steph was glad she dropped it.

Since Delanie had returned to Peace Crossing only a few months before, she'd managed to produce the local kids community musical and reignite her romance with her high school boyfriend, single dad Caleb Toews. Even though it seemed that Delanie was putting down roots in the community, Steph couldn't help feel the actress might disappear again as soon as the right opportunity came along. Which was why she'd already declined several of Delanie's previous attempts to reconnect. But when Delanie had asked Steph to meet her, Caleb, and Caleb's daughter, Emma, at the parade, Steph had felt obligated to say yes this time. Besides, Autumn and Julien would be there, too, and Julien had been over the moon when she'd told him she would be coming tonight.

So here she was. Regretting her life choices.

It's been sixteen years. Maybe it'll be okay.

And maybe reindeer actually could fly.

She huffed in dry amusement.

"You know," Autumn added slowly, "I thought maybe you were thinking about Dad earlier. Eddie, I mean."

Steph tensed. She understood why Autumn had specified—they rarely talked about Eddie. Not that she would have been confused about who Autumn meant when she'd said it like that.

"Why would I be thinking about him?" Even though she had been. Autumn had a sixth sense about these things.

Autumn glanced away, busying herself with packing up the ornament boxes as she spoke. Swallowing, Stephanie bent to help, nesting empty boxes inside larger ones with jerky movements.

"He asked me for your phone number. He says he has something he wants to talk about."

Stephanie froze with a box in midair. "And you gave it to him?" She'd wondered how he'd been able to reach her.

"I did." Autumn met her gaze. "He's different, Steph. I think you should hear him out."

"Hear him out?" Stephanie had been reaching for a stack of empty boxes, but she missed, accidentally knocking the top several off the stack. She bent to pick them up, keeping her face averted from her sister. "There's not a thing that man can say to make up for what he did. Melody's *dead*, Tum."

"Yes, she is." Autumn laid a hand on Steph's arm, halting her frenetic movements so Steph met her gaze. "But we aren't. Which means there's still a chance for us to repair what's broken between us and those we love."

"I don't love Eddie."

Autumn's expression grew sorrowful. "You don't mean that."

"I do. Why wouldn't I?"

Autumn studied her for a moment. "Please call him back. Give him a chance."

"No. He's dangerous. I can't believe you're willing to talk to him, especially with Julien to be concerned about." The thought of the unpredictable alcoholic who had kept her and her sisters' lives in a constant state of turmoil until she was fourteen being in proximity to her darling, innocent nephew made Stephanie's shoulders tense. That couldn't be allowed to happen. She wouldn't let it.

Autumn sighed. "Eddie's not dangerous."

Stephanie gritted her teeth, drawing a deep breath. Her sister always saw the best in people, even to her own detriment. It was one of her best and most irritating qualities, and why Stephanie had so often had to protect Autumn from herself. And now Julien, too.

"Just be careful, okay?"

"I will. But, Steph, have you considered that holding on to the past isn't hurting anyone but you?"

Stephanie's annoyance sprang back to life, defensive words rushing to her lips.

Her protest was cut short by the chiming of the bell above the front door.

Chapter Two

Steph and Autumn glanced toward the door to see Julien burst into the coffee shop in a flurry of snowflakes, followed by their mother and stepfather. The little boy barrelled toward Steph's legs, the hard soles of his snow boots clacking against the tile floor as he ran. In his snowsuit and mittens and with his rosy pink cheeks and glittering brown eyes, he looked like a snow baby miniature.

"Auntieeee!" he cried, throwing his arms around her knees and nearly bowling her over.

Pushing aside her tension, Steph swung him up into her arms, gripping tightly to keep his over-padded, wriggly little body from slipping from her grasp as she planted a kiss on his pudgy cheek. She pushed his hood off his head, revealing a mop of fine dark brown hair sticking up in all directions from the static. "Hi, munchkin. Did you have fun with Grandma and Grandpa today?"

"Uh-huh. We made weindeer cookies! An' I bwought you an' Mommy some. Gwandma has dem."

"Grandma Jill's shortbread?" Autumn asked their mother.

Angelica nodded with a wide grin as she moved toward the counter with a sealed semi-opaque white plastic tub with a red lid in her hands. The reusable container she set near the till held shapes that looked vaguely cookie-like.

Steph grinned at Julien. "Oo, Grandma Jill's cookies are my favourite. I can't wait to try them."

She waggled her fingers against his ribs. Even though he could probably barely feel them through his winter gear, her nephew still rewarded her with an uproarious giggle and a squirm. His unhindered joy melted the last of the coldness that had clamped her heart, and she laughed along with him.

"No kiss for Mommy?" Autumn asked, planting a zerbert on her son's chubby cheek and making him giggle even more.

"Mommy, *stop*," he wheezed through his gasps.

"Yes, please," added Steph, who'd been holding the squirming child with difficulty.

Autumn relented with a tweak of Julien's nose. "That's what you get for going to auntie first," she whispered.

Julien wrinkled his nose, looking not the least bit sheepish.

"Who found the barrel of Christmas cheer and dumped it all over this place?" boomed Reuben Neufeld's baritone.

Steph glanced up to see her stepfather taking in the Christmas decorations, an appreciative expression on his broad, friendly face.

"You girls did a stellar job," he said, moving toward Autumn and encircling her in a bear hug. "You want to come and decorate the Ferryman next?"

Reuben released Autumn, then came over and side-squeezed Steph's shoulders from the side opposite the little boy who still rested on her hip. Angelica was right behind him, ready for her turn.

"Hi, girls." She hugged Autumn, then Stephanie, her hazel eyes crinkled from the affectionate smile she wore on her round, lovely face, which was framed by long, dark brown hair streaked with caramel that floated down her back beneath the cable-knit hat she slipped off her head. The highlights were preference instead of a bid to prolong the appearance of youth—at forty-seven, Angelica was the youngest grandmother Steph knew, with hardly any grey to cover. Angelica took off her coat and hung her winter clothes on the back of a chair.

"Down, auntie," Julien said, bouncing his pointing finger toward the floor.

"Sure, bud, as soon as you say the magic word." Steph raised her eyebrows.

"Pwease," Julien added impatiently, already trying to wiggle out of her grasp.

Steph held back a grin. Relieved to let the heavy toddler go, she allowed him to slide to the floor so he could run over to the cookie tub and proudly carry it to his mother. Autumn opened the container and oohed and aahed over the sugar cookies decorated with messy icing antlers and misaligned red gumdrop noses. She made a show of pulling one out, taking a bite, and exclaiming how delicious it was, much to Julien's delight. He soon repeated the process with Steph, who managed to match her sister's enthusiasm. The cookies *were* quite tasty, even if the decorations were a bit wonky, so it wasn't hard.

"What happened to the doves you had on here last year?" Angelica asked, inspecting the Christmas tree.

"Jack Frost, I think," Steph said.

Angelica gave her a quizzical look.

Autumn sighed. "All the boxes of decorations have water damage. We must have had a leak at the back of the storage room last spring and no one noticed." A flash of sadness crossed her face, then faded as quickly as it had come. Since Denis had died, lots of things had gone unnoticed. Steph had been glad to see her sister coming back to her old self more and more in the past year, but it was no wonder a few things slipped through the cracks.

"The roof's pretty bad, too," Steph added while she snagged another cookie from the plastic tub.

Reuben nodded. "I'll take a look at that leak later. We can't let that go through another spring."

"Thanks, Dad," Autumn said, a relieved smile on her face. "I know you have a lot to do, but—"

"For Pete's sake, m'girl, I ain't gonna do it myself! I'll call Derrick Butler—he did some great work for me at the Ferryman this summer. I'd rather spend that time on other things. Like my restaurant. And my grandson."

He winked at Julien, who giggled before stuffing another bite of cookie in his face.

"Speaking of whom," Autumn said, giving her son a chagrined look and closing the tub, "that's the last cookie for you, mister. You'll be bouncing off the walls all night, and what would Santa say about that?" She secreted the tub somewhere behind the counter.

At the mention of Derrick's name, anxiety had seeped through Steph once more, and she slowly chewed her last bite. Derrick and his older brother, Noel, co-owned Butler Bros Construction, one of the highest-rated construction and repair companies in town. Noel Butler's darkly handsome face smiling at her beneath the mistletoe in the middle of the dance floor flashed through her mind, and she scowled. That had been four years ago, and she'd long since realized that night hadn't meant anything to him—he'd likely been caught up in the moment. That didn't make the fact he'd ghosted her after that sting less, or the thought of seeing him again any less awkward. She'd known the guy since ninth grade—she should have known better than to let down her guard with him.

Thankfully, despite how small this town was, encounters with him since that fateful night at the community Christmas party had been rare and brief. But she definitely hoped Derrick would be the one to fix the leak at Cool Beans.

Angelica walked around the tree, pursing her lips. "We'll have to find more decorations than this. You both did a wonderful job with what you had, but it looks kind of . . ."

"Sad," Reuben supplied, coming to stand beside his wife.

Angelica swatted his arm playfully.

Reuben chuckled. "It does, though. We had a few trees that looked like this back on the farm in the eighties, except without all those artificial branches to give it fullness. All you need is some of that tacky tinsel and some home-made construction paper chains and they would be a match."

"Ugh. Tinsel." Angelica shuddered.

Autumn smiled. "I have the paper chains on my tree at home—I made them for my first Christmas with Denis. But I know we need more decorations, Mom. And maybe a few plastic tubs to store them in, even though we'll be fixing that leak soon. In this old building, we're better off safe than sorry."

Angelica's face lit up. "Maybe we'll find some decorations when we go to the Christmas Craft Fair."

Stephanie blinked. The Peace Crossing Christmas Craft Fair was legendary. People travelled for hours from all over the region to get a start on their Christmas shopping at the event, which hosted some of the most unique crafts and gifts the Peace Country had to offer. But the last time Steph had gone, she'd been put in charge of making sure her two younger sisters didn't get into any trouble. As far as she knew, Angelica hadn't gone since then, either.

"You and Autumn are going to the craft fair this year?"

"Actually," Angelica said, turning slowly toward Steph, "I was hoping all three of us could go. You know, have some girl time. We're overdue."

Reindeer cookies, the craft fair . . . When did Mom start celebrating Christmas again?

Autumn, she could understand. Denis's family had had deeply ensconced Christmas traditions, and Autumn wasn't the type to rock the boat too much. Besides, there was something to be said for providing a wonderful Christmas experience for Julien while he was young enough to believe in magic. But Angelica? After Melody had died, the darkness of northern winters had stretched long in their home, unbroken by mid-season lights and festivities—which was just how Stephanie had wanted it. Christmas had become a painful reminder of the scars they all carried. Why was Angelica suddenly resurrecting old traditions after all this time?

"I'd love to, Mom," Autumn said.

"Can I go?" Julien begged. "Pweeease?"

Autumn ruffled his hair. "It would be pretty boring for you, squirt. Although . . ." She glanced at Steph, a troubled expression on her face. "If you're both there, I won't have a babysitter. Oh, gosh. Maybe he *will* have to come."

"Nah," said Reuben with a dismissive wave before Steph could interject. "He can come hang out with me. I'll put him to work doing dishes at the restaurant."

Julien wrinkled his nose. "I have to do dishes?"

"Sure," Reuben said with a deadpan expression. "After that, I'll have you clean out the storage room."

Julien's small forehead bunched in a worried frown.

Autumn laughed. "Grandpa's kidding. I think." She gave Reuben side-eye, and he betrayed his prank with a mischievous grin. Autumn chuckled. "Thanks, Dad. That would be great."

"And since it's on a Sunday, you won't even have to worry about the shop," Angelica added in a satisfied tone. "How about you, Steph? Do you want to join us?"

Stephanie's neck stiffened. All her excuses had been erased for her. "Um, I don't know. You know how I feel about Christmas . . ."

"Oh, come now," Angelica said. "You helped decorate the coffee shop and didn't melt into a puddle, and you're going to the parade with all of us in an hour. I thought you'd finally gotten over all those hang-ups about Christmas."

"I did those things because of the people involved, not because I've changed my mind about Christmas." *And there* were *some painful moments, thank you very much.* But she kept that last bit to herself. She didn't need to be snippy and bring down the mood any more than she already had.

"Well, isn't going to the craft fair with me and your sister about the people too?" Angelica's eyes glistened.

Steph swallowed. She knew she was being manipulated, but she could see Autumn over her mother's shoulder, looking at her with a hopeful expression and mouthing *Come*.

"Yes, of course, Mom. I . . . I suppose I can go with you. I'll just have to trade a shift with someone."

Angelica's face split in a grin, and she blinked away the moisture in her eyes. "Thanks, dear. I'm sure you'll have a good time once you get there."

Steph wasn't so sure about that. Her envelope had already been pushed so far that she was feeling a little torn at the edges. This time of year had been nothing more than the anniversary that had ripped their family and her life apart for so long, she'd stopped believing it could be anything else. But her family obviously didn't feel the same way, and she didn't want to be left out of family events just because she was the only one who still couldn't move on. Not that she thought they *would* leave her out. Would they?

For the first time, she felt like the lone grinch in the group. To cover her discomfort, she went to get a glass of water from behind the counter while Autumn talked to their mother and Reuben about her preparations for the cocoa-and-cookies event.

When the door chimed again, Steph turned in relief at the distraction from her circling thoughts. Caleb Toews held the door open for Delanie and his daughter, Emma. With the snowflakes caught in Caleb's dark brown beard and dusting Delanie's long golden locks and Emma's dark brown braids beneath their warm winter beanies, they looked like a family from the poster of a Hallmark Christmas movie. The three of them blew into the shop in a flurry of snow, Delanie holding an insulated travel mug that probably contained one of Caleb's homemade lattes. Steph supposed Delanie could be excused for bringing coffee to a coffee shop since her boyfriend made it—and since Cool Beans was technically closed right now.

"Guess what?" Emma said to the room at large. "Daddy and Delanie are engaged!"

Stephanie blinked. A glance at the consternation on Delanie's face confirmed Emma's news.

"Emma!" Delanie exclaimed, but her smile belied her tone. She pulled off her left glove, her gaze finding Steph's as she came over to show off the glittering diamond on her ring finger. "I was going to tell you myself, but she's just so excited. I made Caleb a surprise birthday supper, but he was the one who surprised me."

Angelica hustled over to admire the ring and congratulate the happy couple, and Reuben clapped his hand into Caleb's for a firm shake. Autumn's smile and wishes were as warm and genuine as her heart, as always.

Stephanie forced a smile and murmured her congratulations, adding a suitable exclamation for the ring. It's not that she wasn't happy for them. After ten years apart, they deserved to find their happiness. She just wasn't as expressive as Delanie. That was all.

Her phone buzzed in her back pocket, and she moved away from the exclaiming group to check the text. Kate Thomson from work needed someone to cover her shift for that night. Her babysitter had cancelled, and she had no one else to watch her three-year-old son, Tristan. Steph's chest pinched with guilt. Normally, as the one person in the unit who didn't care if she missed out on a single Christmas activity, she would be the one on shift tonight. By asking to have it off, she'd upset the balance. Yesterday, she'd overheard Kate mention how disappointed she was to not be able to take Tristan to the first Santa Claus Parade he was likely to remember. But Steph had already promised Delanie and Julien. She bit her lip. Maybe she could offer to babysit Tristan for the night . . .

Her mother's voice floated into her consciousness, and heat rose through her chest.

"It's about time you two got together," Angelica gushed to Delanie. "Gives me hope for my girls. Autumn still needs time, of course, but Stephanie hasn't been on a date for years—longer, if you don't count that Noel fellow. I don't suppose you have any eligible single friends, do you, Caleb?"

"Other than Noel?" Caleb chuckled nervously and glanced at Steph, rubbing his well-trimmed beard. "I don't know, Mrs. Neufeld. If I was any sort of matchmaker, I'd have set my buddies up already. I'm just glad I finally found my own happily-ever-after. Second time's the charm, I guess."

"Or first time, depending on how you look at it," Reuben said. "Stephanie told me you two were destined for each other since high school. When it's right, it's right." He took Angelica's hand. "And sometimes, you have to give it more than one go to find it."

Angelica smiled warmly at her husband. But Stephanie's heart thumped in her throat. All the anxiety and tension of the afternoon piled up on her at once, and her head swirled with thoughts of Melody and Eddie and Noel. She couldn't do the parade, not after all this. She would only ruin it for everyone. Shooting a text to Kate that she would take the shift, Steph went to the table where she'd left her coat and purse.

Autumn noticed and followed her. "Where are you going?"

"I'm covering a shift at work. Last-minute babysitter emergency." Steph adjusted her coat collar, then pulled on her toque—a chunky-knit cream hat with a faux-fur pom-pom—and hit the remote start on her key fob so her car would warm up.

Autumn frowned, then glanced at the happy, bubbling group still fawning over Delanie's ring. She turned back to Steph with an understanding look. "I'll tell them."

Steph cast her sister a grateful smile. They didn't agree on everything, but she could always count on Autumn to support her, no matter what. Steph didn't know what she would do without her.

"Thanks, sis. See you tomorrow."

And with that, she made her escape to the one place in her life where she felt safe, where everything was always unpredictably predictable—the Peace Crossing Hospital Emergency Ward.

No matter what surprises the rest of the night threw at her, she'd be prepared for them. Because that's what she was trained to do.

My ghosts will simply have to call it a night.

Later, she would remember thinking that. If only her ghosts hadn't had other ideas . . .

Chapter Three

Noel Butler crouched in the new bell tower on the recently restored roof of the quaint St. John's Cathedral, ignoring the cramped quarters. He'd certainly experienced worse during his army days. Still, he kept a firm grip on a nearby support beam with one gloved hand while he gingerly twisted his ratchet back and forth with the other, his progress illuminated by the lights beaming down from the rafters above. A few fat, fluffy flakes drifted through the openings of the belfry—the beginnings of a storm he'd been sure would come, despite the low probability in the forecast. The Santa Claus Parade would begin in thirty minutes, and the weather was almost up to freezing. Of course it was going to snow.

But he hadn't foreseen hauling himself onto a church roof to repair a bell that hadn't even officially made its debut. Thankfully, the fix had been as simple as he'd hoped—a loose bolt on the small motor secured to the floor had caused the tension to slack off on the belt that moved the metal hammer-like striker. At least, he prayed that's all that was wrong.

Once the bolt had been snugged tight, he stood and leaned through the opening of the small belfry, keeping a tight grip on the frame with both hands as he hollered at the short man in the grey parka standing in front of the church below.

"Try it now, reverend!"

"Yes, okay," Reverend Adelike Olowe said in his strongly accented English, the pompom on top of his toque bobbing as he nodded. "Are you sure you're okay up there?"

Noel gave a thumbs up, suppressing an eye roll—and a twinge of guilt. When the reverend had called him, he'd been nearby and had most of the tools he'd needed in his truck . . . except his roofing harness. The pitch of the roof was steep, but the asphalt tiles were still ice-free. Since he had his roofing boots with him, he'd decided to take a look and assess the situation. Driving to the shop on the other side of town just to grab his harness had seemed like a waste of time. But he supposed it was understandable that the minister might worry, however unwarranted. He was fine.

The squat man nodded before disappearing from view beneath the roof overhang. Seconds later, the church door squeaked and slammed.

Noel pulled the fleece liner on his hard hat a little lower over his ears, wishing he'd been able to grow his springy black curls enough to give him a little more insulation before it had gotten cold. In truth, every time he grew his hair long, he got annoyed with how much work it was and shaved his head again, which meant winter headgear was a necessity from early in the season. Didn't mean he would have passed up the ability to grow an instant Afro between sweltering August and frigid November if God had seen fit to grant him that superpower.

You know what would be a cool superpower? Being able to make fireballs with my hands. Then I wouldn't be freezing my digits off up here.

Or super strength. Because, c'mon. It's super strength.

How long does it take to push a button, anyway?

He sighed, bouncing his knees to get his blood flowing and ward off the early December chill, his back to the three-foot-tall refurbished cast bronze bell he'd installed earlier in the week. Up here on the roof of the historic Anglican cathedral, there was no hiding from the biting wind that shot down the Peace River valley like a luge and turned the snow into stinging pellets against his skin.

This was hardly the time of year for this type of work. Of course, it should have been finished weeks ago. When Derrick had taken the contract, there had been plenty of time left before winter. But the delivery of the bell had been delayed, which had left Noel in a bind, rushing to finish the project before winter arrived in earnest—and before the Peace Crossing Christmas season started up.

Across the street in Riverside Park, sheltered somewhat by the dike and evergreen trees, families milled beneath the orange street lights, setting up lawn chairs along the freshly cleared sidewalks. The parade always wrapped up with a tree lighting event in the park, and crowds were gathering in preparation. Not even the snow and the stiff breeze could keep Peace Crossing-ites away tonight.

Noel didn't bother looking for the group he was supposed to meet when he finished here—Caleb had said he, Delanie, and Emma would set up near the other end of the parade route outside of Cool Beans. Noel had been disappointed that he wouldn't get to see the grand finale from there, but he figured it was more important to spend time with his friends than witness every tree being set ablaze in a splendour of light and colour.

Besides, the coffee shop was staying open late to serve hot chocolate. And after spending a half-hour on this roof in below-freezing temperatures and the beginnings of a snow flurry, Noel thought hot chocolate sounded like a stellar idea. He could always drive by the park later to take in the view.

If he was lucky, he might even run into Stephanie Neufeld tonight. Though she mostly worked at the hospital, the pretty brunette sometimes helped her sister out in the coffee shop for special events like this. He knew, because he'd seen her there plenty before the community Christmas party three years, eleven months, and ten days ago, and a handful of times since. He'd only gone in for coffee, of course. Cool Beans was one of exactly two coffee shops in this town, so of *course* he went there sometimes. It would be weird not to. And *sometimes*, she was there too—though not as often as he might like.

At the memory of that epic night at the party that had nearly ended in so much tragedy, he frowned. That night could have been game over for him and his sister both. Instead, it had been the reason he'd started turning everything around. Reflexively, he stuck his hand in his pocket and fingered his sobriety chip. He'd be earning another one soon.

That didn't mean he was ready to tempt fate by getting romantically involved with anyone again. Some old habits died way too hard, and he didn't want to hurt anyone else. He'd already callously handled enough hearts to last two lifetimes.

Still, that didn't mean he couldn't enjoy a cute smile once in a while. Even if Steph never seemed to be on the till when he went in anymore—seeing her from a distance was close enough.

A familiar woman pushing a wheelchair along the sidewalk below caught his eye. She wore a quilted white parka and white cable-knit cap over long strawberry-blond curls he would know anywhere.

Madeleine Kennedy.

Maddie looked both ways along the street, then stepped onto the blocked-off River Road to cross to the park. The woman in the wheelchair was bundled in winter clothing, a brightly coloured blanket across her legs.

Seeing Maddie triggered a knee-jerk rush of heat and a tightening in Noel's gut. He felt bad for Maddie's mom—his own mom had told him Rose Kennedy's multiple sclerosis had advanced to the point where she was now wheelchair-bound. Violet and Rose had called themselves the "Flower Girls" back in school, and their friendship had never died. But Noel and Maddie hadn't spoken in years, though he'd seen her around town on occasion since graduation. She was even lovelier than when they'd dated in high school. A little more hardened, maybe. He regretted his part in that—but then again, he was harder too.

Harder, but not unhappy. He'd long since decided he was better off alone—which was why he was spending one of his favourite annual events with his twitterpated friends instead of bringing someone special of his own.

He frowned and turned away. Maybe it would be best if he *didn't* run into Stephanie tonight. Seeing Maddie had reminded him of why he'd never let his relationship with Steph get anywhere, no matter how well they'd hit it off at that party. There were too many unknowns when it came to love. The only sure way to protect himself from disappointment was not to let himself be vulnerable in the first place. Maddie had taught him that. And he'd passed that same lesson on to far too many others—which was why he'd officially taken dating off the table. Not only did he not trust his heart to anyone, he was pretty sure he couldn't be trusted with anyone else's.

Noel glanced back across the street in time to see Maddie's gaze skip away from him as though she didn't want him to know she'd been looking directly at him seconds earlier. He watched her for a moment in case she looked back to show her that he, at least, wasn't going to look away. But she studiously ignored him, and he finally glanced away in annoyance. Yep, avoiding Stephanie was definitely for the best.

He looked over his shoulder at the silent bell. The reverend had to have gotten to the switch by now, which meant the bell must not be working yet. Maybe there was a problem at the electrical panel inside. He could call Caleb to take a look so he could get an electrician's input. At this rate, he'd miss the whole parade anyway. Which *would* give him a built-in excuse to just head home when he was done and avoid Cool Beans—and temptation—altogether.

"Now I don't know if I'm grumpy you decided to ditch your job at the last minute or not," he muttered at the uncooperative bell.

The bell had rung perfectly well when he'd tested it Tuesday morning. He'd already left a message for the bell company consultant, but since Ohio was several time zones ahead of Alberta, Noel probably wouldn't hear from Molly until at least tomorrow, maybe even Monday. Maybe he *should* call Caleb. He knew his friend would be happy to help, and Caleb was only a few minutes away . . .

Nah. He could handle this. As long as his fingers didn't freeze into icicles while he waited. Maybe he should go inside and find out what was going on . . . but despite how good his boots were, he didn't want to be climbing up and down this roof without safety gear any more than necessary. He decided to wait a few more minutes.

When Reverend Olowe had called to tell him that the new bell wasn't working, Noel had assured the distressed minister that he would definitely have it fixed before the parade. Its first official chime would be in sync with the lighting of the trees in the park across the road—a significant celebratory event the good reverend obviously felt strongly about, despite only having lived in Peace Crossing for the past three years. Noel understood. There was something about the community that made people want to participate and give back. Which was probably why the congregation of one of the oldest churches in town had decided to add a bell tower to their aging cathedral while doing roof repairs in the first place. It was hard to deny the special charm of hearing church bells ringing out over the snow on a winter night. Noel smiled at the thought of it. He hadn't thought it was possible to make Christmas better, but this bell might do just that.

While he waited, he started another visual sweep of the bell and striker setup, just to make sure he hadn't missed any other problems. Maybe there was a loose wire? But until he knew the reverend had tried to ring the bell and failed, he wasn't about to do a manual check of the belt or striker apparatus. The last thing he needed was to get injured while doing this. Derrick would never let him hear the end of it . . . and Noel liked his hands, numb as they currently were.

His phone vibrated against his chest. Maybe Reverend Olowe was calling from inside, which probably meant he'd tried to ring the bell with no result.

Rats.

Noel glanced at his smart watch to check the caller ID before answering, but it wasn't the minister calling. The display read *Jared Larson*, and Noel's guard went up.

Normally on a Friday night, Noel would be helping Jared run the youth group at Peace Crossing Christian Assembly. His friend had stepped in as interim youth pastor there a few months ago, despite also working a full-time job at the local boys' group home. When Jared had asked Noel to split the huge time commitment, Noel had reluctantly agreed. To his surprise, he'd discovered he enjoyed working with the teens.

Still, he sometimes wondered if his and Jared's roles should be reversed—Jared had an incredible heart the kids responded to, but he lacked the decisiveness the group needed. Noel would have taken over long ago if he hadn't been so busy with work projects and making sets for the local kids' musical earlier in the fall. But once the play had wrapped up, he'd made it to every Friday youth event. And, more and more, he found that having to prop up Jared's scatter-brained leadership rankled. The guy was so disorganized, Noel sometimes wondered how he managed to function as an adult.

Jared had said tonight would be free so kids could watch the parade with their families, but that didn't mean he wasn't calling to have Noel help him solve some other minor crisis. Normally, Noel would love to jump in and troubleshoot, but he was kind of busy at the moment.

And also kind of not.

Steeling himself, he touched the button on his ear piece to answer the call.

"Hey, Jared. Everything good?"

"Yeah, yeah, it's fine," Jared said, and Noel relaxed. "I'm over at Riverside Park. Is that you freezing your cheeks off on top of the Anglican church?"

Relieved, Noel laughed and squinted across the street to the people setting up camp chairs in the snow under the street lights. Sure enough, there was Jared, waving at Noel from the sidewalk. He was only several people over from Madeleine Kennedy.

"Yeah, you got me." He waved back.

Jared chuckled and let his arm drop. "Don't you ever stop working? When the scaffolding came down from the church earlier this week, I thought you were finished that job."

"I did, too. Then Reverend Olowe called me in a panic this afternoon, saying he'd tested the bell again and nothing happened. So I'm here doing warranty work. Can't have the guest of honour be late to her first outing." Noel glanced over his shoulder at the bell, which still taunted him with its silence. "And it looks like she's still being stubborn. I better go down and see what's happening." He swung his leg through the arched belfry opening, steadying himself with a hand on the frame until he was certain he'd found his balance on the roof.

"Hey, quick question before you go," Jared said. "Did you get a hold of the Andersons about the sleigh ride?"

Noel paused, keeping his grip on the tower.

"Yeah, I talked to Heath earlier today but got distracted by the bell issue. He said his parents were happy to be on board. Said there would be no charge. We're booked in for two weeks from tomorrow."

"They're doing it for free? That's nice of them."

Noel smirked. He'd fully expected as much from that family. The Andersons owned a ranch not too far out of town where they raised draft and quarter horses and gave occasional old-fashioned sleigh rides in the winter. When Noel had called his old friend Heath to ask for his parents' number, Heath had voluntarily arranged a sleigh ride event for the youth group instead. And, Noel was pretty sure, it was actually Heath who was covering the cost, though the architect hadn't said it outright. His parents were generous, but the last few years had been tough on everyone, and Heath was the type to sneak one like that in to help his parents and the youth group out at the same time.

Noel resumed his progress toward the ladder while he talked. Leaning back, he kept his core engaged and arms held out for balance while he carefully scooched down the steep roof.

"Paul and Brenda are nice people," he agreed. "But, uh, maybe don't mention the 'free' bit to them."

"Ah. Will do."

Jared was no dummy.

A teenage boy's excited voice seeped through the line. "Do we get to go on a sleigh ride?"

"Yes, Trevor," Jared said, a smile audible in his muffled voice. "In two weeks."

"Cool!"

Noel glanced across the street again and saw round-faced fourteen-year-old Trevor Harris, an Indigenous kid who used to live at the group home where Jared worked, standing between Jared and Trevor's adoptive dad, Gary. Gary's wife, Lou, sat wrapped in a warm blanket on a chair next to her husband, chatting with Rose Kennedy, who sat on her other side. Gary and Lou's older two boys—also former foster kids from the group home—must have been elsewhere, because Noel was certain he'd have been able to pick out Byron's lanky height and Lionel's barrel-chested bulk if they'd been with their family. As a senior, Byron was too busy with work and other activities to come to youth group much, but Lionel and Trevor were regulars. And at last week's event, Noel had discovered that he and Trevor shared a mutual love for Christmas—Trevor's very much inspired by his adoptive parents.

"Say hi to Trevor for me," Noel said, his attention on his footing, "and Gary and Lou, too."

"Will do." Jared's voice became muffled as he passed the greeting along. "They say hi back."

Noel grinned. He probably shouldn't have favourites among the youth group kids, but he did, and Trevor was one of them. The kid had a soft heart and a tenderness that his difficult upbringing hadn't managed to strip from him.

Ryker Dyck's pale, gaunt face and shock of black hair flashed into his mind—the youth group's most recent addition, along with his twin sister, Ryleigh. Ryker was another foster kid who'd found a special place in Noel's heart. He couldn't help hoping he and his sister got a similar happy ending to Trevor's, especially after the twins' recent separation. They'd certainly experienced enough tragedy already.

Reaching the aluminum extension ladder, Noel grasped the posts in relief. He swung himself onto the rungs with the confidence of long practice, carefully balancing his weight to keep the ladder steady. The snowy ground was a good twenty feet below, but he'd climbed up and down so many ladders, he barely had to think about how to do it safely. The hard part was behind him now.

"I better let you get back to work," Jared said. "Unless, of course, you—"

Jared's words were drowned out by an ear-splitting clang from the bell. Noel jumped. The ladder trembled in response, and his foot slipped off the icy rung. He tried to break his fall with his grip on the ladder rails, but his stiff fingers lost their grip. He twisted in the air to minimize injury as he'd learned during his long-ago karate lessons, but as he hit the ground, his leg folded under him with a *crack* and he gave an involuntary yell—or he would have, if all the breath hadn't been evicted from his body. He lay gasping for air, staring up at the starry sky, barely registering Jared's alarmed voice in his ear piece before the line beeped and went silent.

As soon as he could draw half a breath, he attempted to push himself upright—then froze when shooting pain seared up his leg and black stars filled his vision. Deciding he needed a minute, he eased himself back onto the snow.

Eons later, Jared's face came into his field of view, right next to Reverend Olowe's. Jared was still on the phone, but not with Noel. It sounded like he was talking to emergency services.

Adelike bent over Noel with a worried expression, taking in the length of Noel's body before focusing on his face.

"How . . . bad . . . is it?" Noel choked out.

"I believe your leg is broken, brother. Lie still. The ambulance should be here soon."

Noel gave a minute nod, then stared skyward once more, focusing on the cold wetness of thick, wet flakes melting on his exposed skin. The bell tower appeared upside-down in his field of vision, the bell still giving off faint undulating vibrations. He glanced back at the minister.

"I told you . . . I'd fix . . . the bell," he said through gritted teeth.

Reverend Olowe chuckled, his teeth white against his night-black skin. "You did indeed. Thank you."

Noel gave another weak nod before the pain made him decide he had nothing else to say.

So much for the parade. He pushed aside his surge of disappointment, closing his eyes to focus on managing his pain through breathing while he waited for the ambulance. He could hear the wailing siren crossing the bridge now.

At least he wouldn't have to worry about running into Stephanie.

That thought comforted him until he was wheeled into the Emergency ward and the first face he saw approaching his gurney was Stephanie Neufeld's.

Chapter Four

NOEL LAY ON THE exam room table in the somewhat spacious casting room of the Peace Crossing Community Hospital, his injured leg protruding from his cut-open jeans. His leg felt odd, like a lump of wood where his flesh would normally be. After arriving at the hospital, his leg had been X-rayed, injected with a local anaesthetic, set, and X-rayed again, and he had been wheeled in here to wait for the results. His mind wandered as he stared through the window at the snow falling from the night sky. The light cast by the white flood lights outside the hospital made it look like he was trapped in a snow globe—minus the Christmas cheer.

At a gentle knock at the door, he turned to see the slender frame of his mother, Violet, coming into the room. She looked as elegant as ever, with a purple streak in her silver bangs and a wedge cut that framed her creamy-skinned, youthful-looking face. When she saw him, her expression changed from worry to a warm smile of relief.

"Hey, Mom," he said sleepily. "What are you doing here?"

"Seeing if all the king's horses and all the king's men can put you back together again, of course." She unbuttoned her long deep purple woollen coat while she walked over, then bent and planted a kiss on his forehead before sitting on a hard plastic chair across from him, sitting erect and crossing her legs. "When Jared called, I just about had a heart attack. Haven't I told you not to scare me like that?"

Noel chuckled. "I'll try to do better."

"See that you do." She gave him a mock glare, her lips pressed together in a chagrined line.

Noel strained his neck to see the door. "Did Dad come?"

Violet shook her head. "He said he'll come by in the morning . . . and that he'll bring a ladder to give you a proper demonstration how to use one."

Noel gave a snort of mirth. Carl Butler was nothing if not sardonic. But Noel had always appreciated his father's ability to find the humour in any situation.

"Jenny said to get well soon," Violet added. "And your brother wanted me to tell you if you wanted an early Christmas vacation, you could have just said so."

Of course she'd told both his siblings already. And their reactions were exactly what he'd expected. Glancing at his mother's face, Noel noted the exhaustion around her eyes. Visiting her injured son in the hospital was probably the last thing she needed after a busy day with her music students.

"You didn't need to come up here, you know," he said.

She smiled gently. "I didn't want you to be alone."

"I would have been fine."

"I know," Violet said, her warm smile tightening around the edges. "You haven't needed me since you were a preteen."

Realizing she was here as much for her sake as for his, he regretted his flippant dismissal. He gave her a grin that he hoped was reassuring. "I do appreciate that you came."

"Thanks, honey." Violet tilted her head and smiled. "So, how bad is it?" She indicated his leg.

"I'm still waiting to find out. Definitely broken. The X-ray tech said the doctor would come see me as soon as he'd had a chance to look at the images. Doesn't feel too bad, though, all things considered." He wasn't even exaggerating. It hurt, sure, but not as bad as it had a couple of hours ago.

She arched a brow. "Are you on painkillers?"

"Yeah," he said sheepishly. "But still . . ."

She chuckled and shook her head.

A tall, athletic man in his early thirties holding a clipboard entered the room. Noel recognized him from a few brief encounters while they'd both been jogging on the dike-top riverside trail downtown. He wore a dress shirt and dark slacks—no white coat in sight—and his light brown wavy hair and square jaw suggested he wasn't a real doctor, only playing one on TV. He introduced himself as Doctor Ross and gave Noel an empathetic nod.

"Well, Mr. Butler, it looks like you've managed a pretty clean break. After we cast it, you can head home. You'll be off that leg for about six to eight weeks."

Noel clenched his fist. "Six to eight weeks? I can't be off work that long. My business—"

"Will have to manage without you for a bit," Doctor Ross said firmly. "You need to let this heal properly, or you risk a much longer recovery."

Derrick's gonna love this. But, in truth, he was more worried about what he'd do to occupy his time than his brother's annoyance. *I'm just going to have to find a project I can tackle while I'm recovering.*

But what could he do while he was flat on his back for two months during what was normally his most social time of year?

"I'll send in a nurse to apply the cast. It should only be a few minutes." The doctor levelled a stare at Noel, as though he could tell exactly what he was thinking. "Do try and stay off your feet, Mr. Butler."

Noel gave a snort of mirth. "I'll do what I can."

Doctor Ross gave him a knowing look, his brow arched, and then left.

Violet came to stand by the exam table. "That sounded like good news." She gave him a cheerful smile.

"That's one way to look at it," he muttered. "You know how terrible I am at sitting still."

He hadn't been sick much as a child, but when he was, he'd driven his mother crazy by refusing to rest like he was supposed to. He was pretty sure she'd always been relieved when he'd been well enough to go back to school.

Violet tilted her head and rested one hand on his forearm. "It could have been a lot worse," she said quietly.

"I'm aware." He supposed he ought to be thankful it hadn't been. Mostly, he was irritated that he'd let himself fall from the ladder at all. All because he hadn't wanted to drive across town for a harness.

Violet took his hand in hers, her skin pale against his warm brown fingers and her thin shoulders drooping with exhaustion.

"Mom, what time is it? You should go home."

She gave him a tired smile. "No, no. I'm fine. Don't you worry about me. I'll wait and give you a ride home."

He snorted. "I'm twenty-eight, not ten. Besides, I've seen the doctor version of *a few minutes* before—it could be half an hour or more before a nurse gets in here. At least. A lot longer if they're dealing with other emergencies in the meantime. Then however long it takes for them to give me the all-clear to leave. I can take a cab home. No sense in you losing more sleep for this."

Violet glanced toward the door. "There *were* quite a few people in the waiting room. And I have to be at handbell choir practice early tomorrow." She sighed. "If you're sure, honey."

"You bet. Go get some sleep."

She smiled at him, stroking his forehead as though he *were* still ten. "Okay. I'll come by your place with your dad tomorrow." She bent to kiss his head and then gathered her purse from the chair where she'd been sitting. "Jared's been waiting too. I'll let him know you're fine and he can go home."

Jared had come all the way to the hospital? Noel repented of his unkind thoughts from earlier. Despite the guy's faults, Jared Larson was one of the most caring people Noel had ever met. "Yeah, that sounds good."

His mom said goodnight and sailed out of the room.

Noel stared at the pockmarked ceiling tiles, replaying the events that got him there to distract him from his throbbing leg, his gut roiling at his own carelessness. How could he have been so stupid? He'd always told himself he'd never be one of *those guys* whose construction careers—and sometimes their lives—were cut short in a tragic accident. Yeah, it sounded like he would recover from this to climb another ladder, but what if things had gone differently? He hadn't been following all the safety protocols he should have, and he knew whatever earful he was giving himself now, Derrick would give it to him worse. Still, better an earful for what could have happened than not being around because of something that actually had. Once again, he'd been miraculously protected, despite his own stupidity.

He was suddenly overcome with gratitude, and wiped a drop of moisture from his eye.

I don't know what you've got planned for me, he thought toward the heavens, *but I hope it's worth all the effort to keep me alive until then.*

At a firm knock on the open door, he raised his head, expecting to see a nurse. Instead, a small tank-like man with short stick-straight hair stood there—Jared. Noel thought Jared would have done well in the military—it might even have helped with his organizational skills—but Jared always dismissed such comments with a self-deprecating wave. *I guess God had other ideas*, he'd say. *He knew I wasn't tough enough for combat.* Noel wasn't so sure—it took a special blend of toughness and tenderheartedness to work with the teenage boys in the group home full time, never mind being a youth pastor. Jared embodied it well.

When Jared saw Noel looking at him, he came to stand by the bed. "Your mom says they're sending you home tonight. You need a ride?"

Noel suppressed a surge of irritation at the offer. Jared was just trying to help, as per usual. It wasn't Jared's fault Noel actually needed it.

Instead, he grinned. "Nah, I'll call a cab. But thanks for coming up here."

"Anytime." Jared looked around the room, then back at Noel. "Actually, don't ever do that again, okay? Poor Trevor thought you'd died."

Noel chuckled. "It'll take more than that to bring me down. Tell the kid I'm sorry I scared him, and I'll be back in action in time for the sleigh ride."

Jared rubbed the back of his neck. "You sure about that?" He gave Noel's leg a pointed look.

"Is snow cold?" Noel harrumphed. "I'm sure. I'll have a cast on. That'll make me practically invincible."

"If anyone could be, it'd be you." Jared chuckled. "But I *can* find someone else to chaperone."

Noel frowned. He knew Jared was right, but he'd really been looking forward to the sleigh ride. Besides, Trevor would want him there, and so would Ryker Dyck. Heaven knew there were few enough people who were there for kids in Ryker's situation, as his foster parents had recently proven.

"Trust me, bro. I'll be there," he said.

"Alright." Jared shrugged, then yawned. "I gotta get my beauty sleep. I'll call to check on you tomorrow, 'kay?"

"What, you don't have anything better to do?" Noel tried to laugh, but just then, a dull ache stabbed through his shin, and his laugh ended in a groan.

Jared chuckled. "Guess not."

At a noise from the door, Noel looked up to see a familiar feminine figure in understated floral scrubs hustle into the room. His stomach clenched and his pulse raced. Of all the people he wouldn't have wanted to see him this way, Stephanie Neufeld was in the top five. And if he could have made a list of ideal situations for their first real interaction in four years, having her tend his wounds wouldn't have been in the top five hundred.

"Ready to get that cast on?" Her professional tone bore a noticeable edge.

Must be a stressful night in the ER.

"I was born ready," he said, trying to elicit a smile, even if the joke was a bit tired.

Her expression didn't change. In fact, she didn't even look at him, which irked him slightly. Her firmly set mouth and brusque movements were all business as she went and retrieved a cart from the wall and rolled it over to a cupboard, then started stocking it with the things she would need.

Jared gave Noel an encouraging grin. "Right. See ya, man."

"Yep," Noel said.

Jared responded with a firm nod and disappeared from view.

After filling a stainless steel basin with water from the small sink along one wall, Stephanie rolled the cart near to the exam table and gently but efficiently began the task of carefully wrapping his injured leg in gauze. He examined her profile as she worked—something he hadn't been able to do since that night at the party. Despite her scrubs, she was just as gorgeous as he remembered, in a classically beautiful sort of way—long lashes framing almond-shaped grey eyes that were arguably her best feature, peaches-and-cream complexion, and long, mahogany hair, which she'd pulled back into a smooth ponytail.

In the flurry of activity when he'd first come in to Emergency, they hadn't had time to exchange any words. Now, he found himself replaying their last evening together, and the familiar yearning filled his chest. He better distract himself before his thoughts started wandering down roads he'd long since decided against travelling.

"Been keeping busy?"

As soon as he said the words, he regretted them. Steph was a full-time ER nurse with a part-time job at her widowed sister's coffee shop. What a lame question.

Her jaw tensed, and she kept her focus on her work. "Yep."

"Good. Good." He fidgeted with his hands, trying to think of something else to say. "Got plans for Christmas?"

She gave him a dry look and said nothing.

He frowned. *So much for polite conversation.*

He decided to stop interrupting her and let her focus. Instead, he lay back and watched as best he could from his position.

The warm repartee they used to have when he'd been a regular at Cool Beans seemed to have evaporated, and he couldn't deny his disappointment. What had happened to the quippy banter they'd enjoyed over the coffee counter, or the lively conversation they'd shared that night at the Christmas party? Sure, he'd only begun talking to her at the party as something to do while his sister was occupied with her friends—another night like so many others before, spent in pleasant company with a woman he had no intention of pursuing beyond that. But that night had been different—*she* had been different—and he'd known it the moment they'd kissed.

Dang. That was a good kiss. His gut warmed, but he ignored the sensation. He'd promised himself he wasn't going there, with Stephanie or anyone, and he didn't intend to change that.

She finished wrapping his leg with deft fingers he wished he could feel—and wished he didn't wish that—and started unwrapping dry plaster strips from their plastic packaging, casting an occasional glance in his direction. As she dunked the strips in the basin, she frowned at him. "What were you doing on that roof, anyway?"

Noel blinked, surprised that she'd spoken. "Fixing the bell. I wanted to make sure the Christmas bells got to ring."

She snorted. "Instead, *your* bell got rung."

He heard the amusement in her tone and smirked. "Guess you could say that."

He felt an inexplicable sensation of relief. The ice between them seemed to be thawing a bit. Maybe he'd been imagining it—she might have just been super focused on her task. He lay back, a little more relaxed, ignoring the occasional tweaks of pain elicited by her manipulations of his leg.

"Steph, I have a question."

"Yes?"

Her voice sounded guarded, and he frowned. Why was she being so aloof?

He soldiered on anyway. "What's the best way to keep my foot warm on the youth group sleigh ride with this thing on?" He pointed at the cast she was applying. His bare toes peeked through the plaster around his foot.

She cast him a quizzical look. "You go to youth group?"

"In a sense. I help Jared Larson run the one at Christian Assembly. I'm organizing the Christmas sleigh ride. And chaperoning." Or he was supposed to be.

"I see." She pursed her lips and bent over his leg again. "When is it?"

"In two weeks."

She straightened and gave him an incredulous look. "And you're worried about keeping your foot warm? You probably shouldn't even go. No telling what could happen that might cause further injury."

"I shouldn't need to skip it altogether, should I?" he said. "That seems like overkill."

She put a hand on her hip and quirked a brow. "You're speaking from your deep well of medical knowledge, are you?"

"I took combat first aid in the army," he offered.

It almost looked like she wanted to laugh at that, and a sense of victory stirred in his chest. Instead, she pursed her lips again.

"Didn't Doctor Ross tell you how long you were supposed to be on bed rest?"

"Yeah, but I just wanted to make sure he wasn't pulling my leg. So to speak." He glared at his injured appendage, which had had the nerve to interfere with his plans. He sighed. "But if you're telling me he wasn't, there's no sense crying about it. I'll just have to find another chaperone."

She smoothed another plaster strip on his calf. "Can't the parents help out?"

"Oh, they will. We have some great parent volunteers. But some of the kids who come are from the group home, and there are a couple who probably won't go if I don't."

Stephanie frowned. He could see the wheels turning in her head.

"There's this one kid, Ryker Dyck," Noel explained. "He could really use some guidance right now. He mostly comes to see his sister, I think. They recently got split up in foster care—the family kept his twin sister, and he got moved to the boys' home. I'd hoped he could make a few friends on this sleigh ride. The kind who will be a positive influence."

After Ryker's foster family had requested he be moved, Noel had seen through the kid's tough act to the devastated boy beneath. He didn't have to imagine how that kind of rejection could affect a teenager—he'd watched his high school buddy Jackson spiral after years in the foster system, falling in with a bad crowd and making choices that had eventually landed him in prison. Noel had heard his childhood friend was doing time somewhere in British Columbia now. He hoped he could prevent Ryker from following the same path—a path the teen might already be considering, if his foster family's accusations were true.

"To be honest," Noel continued, "I think Ryker's struggling in general. Jared tells me he seems calmer when I'm there, but sometimes he'll show up and then leave if he sees that I'm not."

He met Steph's gaze. "Are you sure I need to stay home? I'll basically just be sitting."

She turned to face him with another strip in her hands, tilting her head. "When have you ever been anywhere and 'basically just been sitting'?"

She had a point. He grinned sheepishly. "The down side of having known your nurse since junior high."

"Uh-huh." She arched a brow, then went back to her task.

He brightened. "You should come. You can keep me out of trouble."

She blinked. "Excuse me?" Surprise that bordered on alarm—or was that anger?—flashed in her eyes before she turned away and started smoothing another plaster strip onto his shin, her jaw tight. And were her hands shaking? "I don't think that's a good idea."

What had he said to upset her? Just when he'd broken through her reserve, she'd gone and clammed up again. She hadn't been this distant since high school.

Back then, Stephanie had been Delanie Fletcher's shadow. Since Delanie had been dating Caleb at the time, Noel had seen Stephanie pretty often, but he'd mistaken her quiet reserve for emotional distance. He wasn't the only one. His face flamed as he remembered how he and his friends used to mock her behind her back.

But after he'd come back to town and run into her at Cool Beans, she'd seemed different—warmer, more confident. And that night at the Christmas party, with the music and the lights, she'd come alive, captivating him with her warmth and razor-sharp intelligence—not to mention her flashing grey eyes and those soft, inviting lips that were so often curved in a smirk. He'd loved that version of Stephanie—lively, encouraging, open. But now they were back to square one.

He wished his thoughts weren't so floaty from the painkillers, and that those same flashing grey eyes weren't holding a storm that made him want to find out what other secrets they held. His reasons for keeping his distance in the past still mattered. But not as much as his desire for Stephanie to come on this sleigh ride with him . . . or, rather, the youth group.

"I only meant that it would be great if you could come along and help out," he continued, hoping he sounded nonchalant. "You might even have fun."

She shook her head, her lips pressed together. Finishing with her task, she began cleaning up her mess with jerky movements, throwing wrappers in the trash and rolling her cart over to the sink.

"Was it something I said?" he ventured.

She spun to face him, her eyes shooting daggers. "Something you said. Something you did. It's your whole exasperating self."

Noel blinked at her. "What are you talking about?"

She gaped. "The Christmas party. You know, the one where we talked and danced all night, and . . . did a little more." She looked sideways at the floor, her face flushing.

Noel frowned. "Yeah, I had a great time that night. I thought you did too. So why are you mad at me now?"

Her gaze snapped to his. "Seriously?"

He shook his head, at a loss.

She crossed her arms, glaring at him. "Because, in my world, a night that special is the beginning of something. Some might even call it a *date*, no matter how unplanned it was. But since I haven't heard from you since, apparently it meant nothing to you. And now it's just one more horrible Christmas memory I get to treasure."

Noel frowned. He knew he should say something, but he was so stunned by her revelation, he couldn't think of what.

After a moment, she let out a huff. "Doctor Ross will come check on you. When he has time." Her tone said not to expect that to be soon. With a glare, she shoved the cart against the wall and practically stormed out of the room.

He lay back on the pillow and stared at the ceiling, his gut bubbling with anger and a strange sense of loss. Part of him wanted to call Stephanie back and let her know in no uncertain terms that if he ever took her on a date, she would know it, and she had no right to be angry with him for an expectation he hadn't even known she had.

But he didn't.

Because the truth was, he'd desperately wanted to call Stephanie after that Christmas party. Instead of saying goodnight after a single innocent kiss under the mistletoe, he'd wanted to wrap her in his arms and protect her from all the worries he'd seen lurking at the corners of her mind, the ones she tried to cover with sarcasm and competence. She was a light, and his thoughts couldn't help returning to her warmth.

But after Maddie Kennedy had left his heart and his trust in the trash, he swore he would never let anyone do that to him again. And with all the bad decisions he'd made after that heartbreak, he was lucky he was still alive to talk about it. Not that he blamed Maddie. But he no longer trusted himself.

Which was why, as much as he regretted the hurt he'd caused Steph, and as drawn as he was to her fire and spirit, he had to let this go.

"Just what I needed . . . a broken leg with some complimentary emotional baggage on the side."

As he waited for the doctor, Steph's final words kept circling in his mind. At least he hadn't been the only one who thought they could have been something special . . .

Chapter Five

STEPHANIE MARCHED TO THE nurse's station, her stomach knotted in confusion and anger—mostly at herself—and not a little embarrassment at her outburst of moments before.

You already knew that night didn't mean anything to him. What else did you expect?

Samantha Crawford glanced up from her computer, her face framed by wisps of silver-touched ginger-coloured hair that had escaped her ponytail. "Everything okay?"

"It's fine." Steph flopped into a chair at another station and began entering Noel's chart data.

Samantha shrugged, then turned back to her own work.

If only Steph could shrug off her frustration so easily.

Then again, did she really want to? Without her anger, she might have to admit that the man she'd thought had ghosted her hadn't even known she'd been upset all these years. And she might remember the disappointment on his face when she'd told him she wouldn't go on the sleigh ride because of it, like a little boy who'd been reprimanded for bringing his mother flowers.

That was ridiculous. He had to have known what he was doing all along, and he'd been acting like a selfish blockhead—the same way he'd treated Maddie Kennedy in high school. After he'd come back to town six years ago, she'd thought his time in the army had smartened him up—it certainly hadn't hurt his tattooed physique and the muscles he'd grown on his muscles, which she'd been trying hard to ignore while she'd tended to him. Guess she'd been wrong.

But isn't that partly why you liked him? Because of that edge of danger and mystery?

She frowned, moving her fingers over the keyboard with tightly controlled precision, taking comfort in the loud clacking it created as she typed.

It had been four years since that Christmas party, but somehow, seeing Noel again made it all come rushing back. The years of flirting as she took his coffee order. The growing warmth between them. That special night that had started off with her as Autumn and Denis's third wheel, but which had ended up with her and Noel talking about anything and everything for hours and culminated in one of the most romantic moments of her life—a slow dance and a kiss while being held in his strong arms, surrounded by lights and music and joy.

At the time, she'd thought that night had been truly special—the kind that got written into a pop song about unrequited love finally getting a second chance. It had taken her hours to fall asleep after she'd gotten home, and the subsequent wait for him to call had been agonizing. But as days had stretched into weeks, her phone had been deafeningly silent. He hadn't even texted. And the next time Noel had come into Cool Beans, when he'd acted as though nothing had even happened? She'd finally realized she'd been played. From then on, she'd always beat it to the kitchen anytime she'd seen him coming to the door. Tonight was the first time she'd actually talked to him in years. No wonder she was a little triggered.

Her phone vibrated in her pocket, and she pulled it out. Another text from Eddie.

Call me. It's important.

Steph shook her head and returned her phone to her pocket. She'd learned young not to believe her father's compelling lies. He'd been a bad boy, too, and that's why Angelica had fallen for him—which she'd admitted to her daughters years after she'd remarried to Reuben.

Steph had no intention of treading that treacherous road of charm and bad boys and heartbreak. Yes, she'd had a secret crush on Noel in high school that she'd allowed to blossom to something more years later beneath his flirtatious attentions, and yes, she'd given him more brain space than he deserved since their not-date at the party. But that was a thing of the past. If and when she ever gave dating another try, it would be with someone who took responsibility for how their behaviour affected others. Not someone who flippantly bestowed kisses under the mistletoe.

No matter how memorable and toe-tingling those kisses might have been . . .

"Whoa," came Sam's voice from behind her. "What's gotten into you?"

Stephanie stopped her marathon typing, realizing the intense clacking and mouse-clicking must have caught Sam's attention. A dull pulse had started behind her eyes, and she pinched the bridge of her nose. She needed to get a grip. Their patients depended on her to be in control.

After drawing a long, deep breath to slow her pounding heart, she spun her chair to face Samantha. "Sorry, Sam. I didn't mean to bring my irritation in here."

Sam's face filled with compassion. "It's okay. Want to talk about it?"

Stephanie hesitated for a moment, then shook her head. She'd never felt comfortable discussing her personal life with her colleagues. "No, it's not important. Just some personal stuff."

Samantha raised an eyebrow, her expression compassionate. "You know I'm here if you change your mind."

"I appreciate that." Steph relaxed slightly, her chest warming at Samantha's support, the tension draining from her shoulders. She pushed her hair off her forehead with a long sigh. "Tell me something about you. How's Ainsley doing?"

Samantha sat back in her chair and wobbled her hand back and forth. "Oh, you know. Teen girls. It's all about the drama with them. Pretty sure my mother got her wish that I'd have a daughter just like me." She laughed dryly. "Still, Ainsley has it so much harder than I did. Modern teens have to deal with things I never had to think about. Sometimes, Doug and I wonder if we're paddling this canoe in the right direction—and sometimes, we wonder if we even have a paddle."

Stephanie chuckled. "I can only imagine. But you're doing great. Ainsley is a wonderful kid."

"Thanks. I appreciate you saying that. Speaking of teen girls, though, that reminds me that I have to stop and pick up some marshmallows from Miller's Market after work." Sam pulled a neon pink sticky note from a pad and jotted herself a note, then slipped it into her pocket. "Ainsley's having her new friend from handbell choir over for a sleepover tomorrow, and apparently 'hot cocoa with marshmallows' is a must-have. Ainsley doesn't care so much, but she knows Ryleigh likes them. Which means I'm going shopping."

Steph smiled, but a stab of sadness made it strained. Melody had always loved having marshmallows in her hot chocolate. She would insist on stirring them until they'd melted into gooey foam on top of the cocoa before she'd drink, and then she'd end up with a white moustache when she finally took a sip. Steph hadn't thought about that for years. But, as per usual, this time of year brought memories of her sweet little sister to mind. If only good memories like that weren't so tainted by the accident that had taken her from them so suddenly.

"Ryleigh's lucky to have a friend like Ainsley," Steph said absently.

Sam sighed. "Yeah. The fact the sleepover is even happening is a minor miracle—Ainsley's been asking about it for weeks, but Ryleigh's foster mom was super hesitant until we met and went for coffee."

Steph turned back to the computer and kept entering data while she talked. "A little over-protective, huh?"

Sam's chair squeaked. "I probably would be, too, in her situation. You know, Doug and I were a little hesitant about the sleepover ourselves, but we decided we'd rather be part of the solution than the problem. If parenting is tough with a kid you raised yourself, it's probably even worse when you're trying to raise kids with a background like Ryleigh's. So when her mom finally said yes, we could do no less. Maybe her mom knew Ryleigh needed the night out after she lost her brother recently."

Stephanie blinked and turned to face her co-worker. "You mean he died? How?"

Sam looked startled, then relaxed, giving a sheepish laugh. "Oh, no. Sorry. Her twin brother, Ryker, got moved to the group home a few weeks ago. The foster family kept Ryleigh, though, which is weird. I can only imagine how hard it must be on all of them. I'm just glad we can help out and be there for Ryleigh. It truly does take a village."

"So they say." Stephanie returned to her data entry, thinking. *Ryker.* That was the boy Noel had been talking about. The one he'd been worried wouldn't go on the sleigh ride if Noel didn't. There had to be way more to this story, and her heart broke for the siblings. She knew all too well what it felt like to be abandoned, with only your sibling to watch your back. After Melody died, things at home had gotten a lot worse for a couple of years, and Stephanie and Autumn had had to fend for themselves most of the time.

At least their mom had finally tired of Eddie drinking away every paycheque and eventually divorced him, moving the three of them to Peace Crossing for an extra bit of distance. Things had gotten easier then, but Angelica had been busy working to provide for them, so she still hadn't been around much. Stephanie couldn't imagine how hard her teen years would have been if she hadn't had Autumn. Starting over in a new town with no friends or family nearby, it had been the two of them against the world.

But even they hadn't been completely alone. Their Grandma Jill, Angelica's mother, had frequently called to check on them, and had often driven down from La Crete to visit until she'd died of cancer five years ago. And then there was Mr. O'Connor, Steph's high school biology teacher, who'd always gone out of his way to show her kindness. He'd been the one who'd encouraged her to go into nursing.

Samantha was right—raising kids did take a village. It sounded like Noel was part of the village helping Ryker out, just as Sam was part of Ryleigh's. And as upset as she was at Noel, she had to admit a begrudging respect that he cared enough about kids like Ryker and Ryleigh to want to help them.

"Hey, Sam?"

The other nurse glanced up, a questioning expression on her face.

"You go to Peace Crossing Christian Assembly, right?"

"Sure do."

"Do you know if Ryleigh and Ainsley are planning to go on that youth group sleigh ride in a couple of weeks?"

Sam looked thoughtful and drummed her fingers on the desk. "I haven't heard about it yet, but I'm sure Ainsley will want to go. I don't know about Ryleigh, but if I know Ainsley, she'll want Ryleigh there. Why do you ask?"

Steph gave a small shrug. "Just putting pieces together, that's all."

Sam raised her eyebrows, but before she could dig deeper, a tired-looking middle-aged male patient with dishevelled hair came up to the counter. Sam's mouth twitched at Steph. Then she turned to answer the man's query, taking the papers he'd received at the front desk when he'd checked in.

Steph glanced down the hall toward the casting room where Noel waited. Hurt, anger, and embarrassment still trickled through her, but there was something new there, too—curiosity. Noel was certainly far from being an angel, but he was obviously trying to be a role model to kids like Ryker, and she had to admire that. Maybe he was making up for past mistakes. He certainly had a few to atone for—probably including some she knew nothing about.

Don't we all?

Her phone buzzed in her pocket, reminding her of the text from Eddie she'd ignored. She gave her head a shake and went to call the next patient from the waiting room. Some mistakes could never be atoned for.

But the next time she passed the casting room, she paused. She couldn't see Noel's face from the hall, but she watched his chest rise and fall in the gentle, even rhythm that indicated he'd fallen asleep. Was she being too hard on Noel for *his* mistake?

Maybe.

She blinked in surprise at her own response. She didn't forgive easily. But she'd seen a side of Noel tonight she hadn't seen before—and it was enough to make her realize how little she knew about him. She'd been carrying around her hurt for years, and he hadn't even known he'd offended her.

Should he have? Absolutely.

But did she intend to bear a grudge against him forever for the crime of being clueless?

The memory of their shared kiss caused her stomach to tighten, and she frowned. Nobody was *that* clueless.

And I'd sooner go back to celebrating Christmas than be stupid enough to fall for his false charms again.

Turning away from the door, she hurried to complete her task, strengthening the guard around her heart with every step.

Chapter Six

"Aunty Steph, can I have one? Pweeeease?"

Stephanie glanced away from the vendor's table full of baked treats and smiled at Julien's cherubic face. The table was one of many among a long row of vendors set up in the rec centre gymnasium for the annual Christmas Market. Reuben's promise to watch his grandson that day had been circumvented when the bartender at the Ferryman hadn't shown up for work, so the little boy had joined Stephanie, Autumn, and Angelica at the market after all.

Steph had taken Julien on a walkabout so her mother and Autumn could decide on some Christmas ornaments for the coffee shop at another stall. When Julien had seen the table full of fudge, jams, and cookies, he'd practically dragged her over to it with the surprising strength only a three-year-old on a sugar hunt could possess. Now he clutched the edge of the red checked tablecloth-covered table, which was only a little below his eye level, and peered up at her with every dimple in his arsenal hard at work.

"Honestly, how does your mom ever tell you no for anything? Fine." Steph pulled her wallet out of her purse and handed the grey-haired bespectacled woman behind the table some cash. "Two dozen of the chocolate chip cookies, please. And one of those giant snowman sugar cookies for my nephew."

Julien jumped up and down as he watched the kindly woman bag up the order, his snow boots clacking loudly on the cement floor. Her sister certainly wouldn't be happy that Steph had given Julien the sugar and food dye. But when Steph took the snowman cookie from the paper bag of goodies and handed it to him, he looked as if he'd just been given a pot of gold. He took a bite with relish, his face covered in sheer delight.

"Fanks, aunty," he said through a mouth full of sugar cookie.

Worth it.

She eyed the crumbs hitting the floor with every bite. "Let's go sit at those tables over there until you're finished, okay?" She pointed to the end of the gym where picnic tables had been set up near a fast-food stand.

"'Kay," he said, spluttering even more crumbs with the muffled reply.

She led the way, matching her pace to the little boy's. Julien dawdled, paying more attention to his cookie than the destination, and other shoppers flowed around them. She took the opportunity to glance over the wares of some of the other vendors, admiring stalls displaying handmade willow furniture, stacks of hand-knit blankets and dishcloths and baby sweaters, original art and photography, handmade soaps and bath bombs, local honey, and more. Despite the ubiquitous Christmas motifs and decorations putting a slight damper on her mood, she couldn't help but be amazed at all the local creativity and resourcefulness that had been gathered in one place.

Her gaze moved from a table full of handmade knives with tooled leather sheaths to the man standing in front of it with his back to her. Taking in his cast, crutches, curly-haired black crew cut, and muscular dark brown neck and shoulders beneath the pale blue heavy fleece sweatshirt, her stomach did a little flop, then sank. She had half a mind to go over and chastise Noel for being on his feet so soon, but really, it was none of her business. And instead of correcting him, she'd prefer not to talk to him at all. She glanced over her shoulder at Julien, who had already made the snowman's head and part of his torso disappear.

"Can you walk a little faster, munchkin? You're going to be finished that cookie by the time we get to the tables."

He giggled, deliberately wrinkling his nose. "I know."

She rolled her eyes and held out her free hand to him. "C'mon."

He absently took it, and she started urging him to move a little faster, though his attention was still mostly on the cookie.

"Stephanie?" came Noel's familiar deep baritone from behind her.

Drat.

She stopped, took a breath, put a smile on her face, and turned around, still gripping Julien's small hand. Noel had walked away from the knife vendor and stood in the middle of the aisle, braced on his crutches. For some reason, the stooping posture forced by the crutches accentuated how tall and broad-shouldered he truly was. Stephanie was five foot nine inches barefoot, and even with her heeled winter boots on and him just in a single sneaker on his good foot, he still towered over her like a fortress of invulnerability. Her mouth went dry, and she swallowed to work some moisture back into it.

"Noel. Hi. What are you doing here? Shouldn't you be somewhere with your leg up?" She shot a pointed glance at the cast poking out from beneath his black track pants, which now sported several signatures. "The plaster on that thing is barely dry."

He looked down, then gave an awkward shrug and chuckled. "Can't keep a good man down, I guess. I'm here with a couple of kids from the youth group. Promised them we'd get out and about today, and this seemed as good a place as any to go."

A lanky teenager with a shock of shaggy black hair shuffled up to stand behind Noel, looking at Stephanie with interest before turning to the taller man.

"Noel, what do you think of this?" He extended his arms to display the vintage-looking dark brown leather bomber jacket he was wearing.

Noel glanced over the jacket appreciatively. "That must have cost a fortune."

The kid's pale face flushed. "Nah. There's a guy in the next aisle selling cool stuff like this that he picked up at garage sales. I'm sure he marked it up a lot, but this didn't cost nearly as much as it was worth. I got a great deal." He bit his lip. "It looks just like that one you always wear, don't you think?"

Noel nodded. "Yeah, you're right. Guess we'll match now, huh?"

The young man grinned shyly. "Yeah, I guess."

Stephanie shifted, glancing down at Julien, who now had less than two bites of cookie remaining.

Noel noticed and cleared his throat. "Hey, Stephanie, this is Ryker. He's got better fashion sense than almost anyone I know. Honestly," he said, turning back to the blushing teen, "you're wearing the heck out of that thing. I might have to turn mine in out of embarrassment."

Ryker looked down at his battered Converses, his face redder than before. "Thanks." He shoved his hands in his jeans pockets.

A pang of sympathy stabbed Steph in the heart. She recognized the emotion behind those slumping shoulders, and the shine in Ryker's eyes whenever he looked at Noel. The kid needed a boost of self-confidence, and he was harbouring a serious bro-crush, maybe more. She couldn't blame him—even with his broken leg, Noel was a guy who exuded confidence. And she'd harboured her share of crushes just because someone made her feel safe.

But she wasn't falling for that again.

For Noel again.

"It's nice to meet you, Ryker," she said, dropping Julien's hand for a moment so she could extend her hand to the young man. "I'm Stephanie. And this is Julien, my nephew."

Ryker gave her hand a firm shake, surprising her with his grip strength. "Nice to meet you, too, ma'am. Young sir," he added, touching an imaginary hat brim to the little boy, who giggled before cramming the snowman's last licorice gumdrop button into his mouth.

Steph gave a wry smile and said, "Just Stephanie is fine. And where'd you say you found that?" She pointed at his jacket. "I'd like to check that vendor out." Autumn was a huge fan of vintage stuff, and Steph was always on the lookout for gifts for her sister.

Ryker's eyebrows shot up. "Uh, in that aisle over there," he said, pointing, "about halfway up on the left."

"Thanks." Steph turned to Noel. "Say, did you ever find someone to chaperone that sleigh ride?"

She didn't know why she'd asked, but now that she'd met Ryker, she could see why Noel had a soft spot for him. And after her conversation with Samantha last weekend, she had a bit of a soft spot for Ryker and his sister, too, even though she hadn't met Ryleigh yet. For the life of her, she couldn't see why Ryleigh's foster family would have asked for Ryker to be placed somewhere else. It's not like the kid was covered in tattoos or sporting a Yukon-sized chip on his shoulder. How rebellious could he have been to warrant such treatment?

Noel gave a subtle shake of his head, glancing sideways at Ryker. "I figured I'd just go myself."

Steph frowned. "I told you—"

"Not on the actual sleigh. Probably. Depends how I feel by then." He cut off the next objection on Stephanie's lips with a raised hand. "I can at least go as far as the cabin and help serve cocoa after." He turned to Ryker, whose face had fallen when Noel said he wouldn't be on the sleigh. "I heard your sister's coming, too. Ainsley's mom told me while I was in the hospital. You're still going, right?"

At the mention of Ryker's sister, a flicker of pain Stephanie would have missed if she hadn't been looking right at him crossed Ryker's features. Then he brightened. "Yeah, for sure. Wouldn't miss it. Besides, I've never been on a sleigh ride before."

"Glad to hear it." Noel shared a glance with Stephanie, and she sensed relief beneath his nonchalance.

"Mmmm," Julien interjected loudly. Steph glanced down to see the little boy licking his fingers with exaggerated motions, like a character from one of his cartoon shows. The only remaining traces of his cookie were the crumbs littering the concrete floor and the bright blue and red icing all over his cheeks.

Ryker grinned down at Julien, then looked at Steph. "You should come, Stephanie. I think my sister would like you."

Stephanie swallowed, her gut clenching.

"What a great idea," Noel said deliberately, dry amusement in his voice.

Stephanie fidgeted with the paper cord handle of her shopping bag and bent to scoop up Julien's hand again. "I don't know . . ."

"The invitation's still open, if you want to join," Noel added. "The kids are a real blast to hang out with, promise." He quirked his mouth in a half-grin. "And, uh, I'll do my best to stay out of your way. As I said, I can hunker down in the house. If you want."

Steph swallowed, mesmerized by his warm brown eyes and his vulnerable expression. Despite his offhand declaration that he'd avoid her, she got the sense he wanted her to go for more than just the chaperoning duties. And part of her didn't even mind. Why did this man make it so hard to dislike him?

Julien shifted impatiently. "Aunty, I wanna go find Mommy and Gwandma."

Steph glanced down, hesitating, then looked back at Noel, her chest suddenly tight with foreboding. Sleigh rides didn't result in many injuries, but they weren't unheard of. And the last thing she needed was one more Christmas disaster on her conscience.

"Fine," she said with an exaggerated sigh. "I'll do it. But if you fall and break something else, don't come crying to me."

Noel's mouth twitched, not quite letting a grin escape. "Wouldn't dream of it."

Stephanie rolled her eyes and ignored the flutter in her stomach. Darn that man's charm!

Ryker pointed out the knife stand. Noel said his goodbyes, adjusted his crutches, and swung after the teen to go look at the display again, answering Ryker's shy questions and comments as they went.

Steph turned and walked away, conflicting emotions in her chest. Noel's appeal might be the cause of her current consternation, but he'd obviously used his powers for good to get Ryker to open up and trust him. Maybe he'd never intended to sound flirtatious all those times at the coffee shop. Maybe she'd misjudged the whole thing.

But he *kissed* me, *not the other way around.*

She frowned to herself. It was hard to reframe a kiss as *not flirtatious.*

Get a grip, Stephanie. It was a kiss under the mistletoe, not a declaration of eternal love.

And now she'd agreed to go on the sleigh ride, guaranteeing hours of interaction with Noel, despite his promises to stay out of her way. Her stomach did another flop—but her agitation wasn't just about spending time with Noel Butler. *First, Christmas decorating, then the market, and now this?* She was going as soft as her mother.

"Dere dey are!" Julien exclaimed, pointing ahead.

Autumn and Angelica were walking toward them with their arms laden with several large paper shopping bags each in addition to the bulging cloth totes they'd brought to carry their purchases.

Julien tugged on Stephanie's hand. "Huwwy, aunty!"

Steph chuckled at the irony. *Now he's in a hurry.* "Coming, munchkin."

She happened to catch another glimpse of Noel behind her out of the corner of her eye, and a shiver ran down her spine.

This sleigh ride would be interesting, to say the least.

Chapter Seven

NOEL STOOD NEXT TO a metal shelf full of cardboard boxes and stared up at the damaged section of the extra-high ceiling in the dimly lit back corner of the Cool Beans storage room, keeping himself steady with his crutches and trying to ignore his throbbing leg. A large water stain discoloured several ceiling tiles and trailed down the wall in crusty orange trails. Two tiles had collapsed, leaving a gaping hole. If there'd been a light fixture in any of the tiles, it probably would have crashed to the floor.

Of course, if there'd been a fixture, someone might have spotted the problem in time to do something about it before it got to this point.

In the walkway beside him, Autumn Lambert looked upward with her hands on her hips, her dark brows puckered with anxiety. Derrick stood directly beneath the damaged area, frowning up at it from beneath the brim of his dusty Butler Bros ball cap and making notes on a yellow legal pad with a pencil. The boxes on the shelf beneath the leak had been moved and piled high next to the wall, on spare spaces on other shelves, or out in the hallway. Noel sniffed, trying to ignore the slight mustiness emanating from the hole.

"How bad is it?" Autumn asked.

"Pretty bad," Noel said. "But you already knew that." Seeing her scowl deepen, Noel gave her an encouraging smile. "But, like most things, not so bad it can't be fixed."

She nodded, biting her thumbnail.

Derrick muttered as he jotted notes. "Six damaged tiles . . . at least two sheets of sheetrock . . . paint . . . and you might want to add some lighting back here, eh?"

He glanced at Autumn for confirmation, and she nodded. He jotted another note, then paused and stared upward again, rubbing his neatly trimmed short black beard.

"I'll grab the ladder. Back in a few."

He set his pad and pencil on the empty shelf and strode out the door, his work boots echoing on the tiled floor.

Noel adjusted his crutches to a more comfortable position, already running numbers in his head. Technically, Derrick hadn't needed his help with this quote, but Noel had been desperate for something to do. In the week since he'd been home from the hospital, he'd already caught up on all the invoicing and other paperwork for Butler Bros Construction and binged through three and half seasons of his favourite shows. At least he was out of the house.

Though being at Cool Beans didn't do much to take his mind off a certain fascinating brunette nurse, whose sister stood mere inches away from him.

Stephanie wasn't there. He'd already asked. He wasn't sure if he were more relieved or disappointed by the answer.

Autumn drew a breath and glanced at Noel. "I feel as useful as a snowman on a beach. No sense in me standing here in your way. Can I get you something? A latte? Snacks? Ellie made some amazing ginger snaps this morning."

Noel's stomach rumbled, her description giving names to the delicious aromas permeating the air. He chuckled. "I've been sitting around so much, I should probably say no. But only a monster could turn down fresh ginger snaps. A medium black dark roast would be great, too."

Autumn smiled, looking relieved to have a task. "Okay, I'll be back in a few minutes."

"Nah, I'll come out there. Derrick doesn't really need me for this, and it's not like I can manage food and these things at the same time." Noel angled the end of one of his crutches outward. "You go ahead. I'll follow you."

"Sure. Coffee and a cookie, coming right up."

Autumn slipped out the door, and Noel swung himself after her. He'd just gotten to the narrow hallway that connected the dining room with the washrooms, kitchen, and storage room when Derrick returned, coming in through the back door toting a tall aluminum stepladder.

"Where you going?" Derrick asked.

"To drink coffee and crunch numbers. Join me when you're done."

"Yep." Derrick manoeuvred the ladder past him and through the door. Loud clanks followed Noel down the hall as his brother set up the ladder and quickly climbed it to inspect the damaged ceiling.

When Noel got to the dining room, he settled himself at an empty table in the middle of the brightly lit space and pulled his phone out of his pocket, opening his estimator app and creating a new job. The bell above the door jingled. He glanced up and tensed, gripping his phone tighter.

Maddie Kennedy was approaching the counter, the thick waves of her strawberry blond hair caught up in a ponytail that bounced as she walked. She took off her leather gloves and scanned the chalkboard menu, then the room. Her gaze landed on him, and he stiffened. She gave an almost imperceptible nod of her head, which he returned. Then she went back to looking at the menu and stepped up to the till to place her order. He watched her for a moment more, then went back to his phone, his mouth as dry as cardboard.

Sometimes, he wished he didn't live in such a small town. It meant never escaping his past mistakes.

When Autumn emerged from behind the counter with his order, he looked up and noticed Maddie slipping out the door with a brown paper bag and paper cup in her hands. His shoulders relaxed slightly. At least she wasn't staying. Or rather, she wasn't staying while he was here.

No surprise there.

When Autumn reached his table, she placed a large white stoneware mug filled to the brim with steaming black coffee and a small white plate in front of him. His eyes widened at the size of the thick sugar-encrusted ginger snap. The treat looked like a small molasses-coloured pancake.

Noel raised his brows. "Now *that's* a cookie."

"Right?" Autumn grinned and slipped into the seat across from him, glancing at his phone screen, where he'd started entering what he remembered from Derrick's list. "Any idea how much this is going to cost yet?"

Noel shook his head. "I'm getting there, but we'll need to wait until Derrick brings the full list before I can tell you anything definitive."

Autumn pulled her lips to the side. "Sure."

Noel tapped in another item, then stopped, staring through the screen. He'd been dying to ask Autumn something since he'd gotten here. He drew a breath and decided to go for it.

"Hey, I was wondering something. About Stephanie." He glanced up in time to see Autumn's eyes narrow slightly. So she knew about Stephanie's grudge against him. Good. It meant he had less explaining to do.

"Yeah?"

"Something she said when I saw her in the hospital. I got the impression she doesn't like Christmas much. Is that true?"

Autumn's expression shifted, but it wasn't more at ease—just less guarded. And softer, like he'd touched a nerve. She nodded. "Our little sister, Melody, died in a car accident when we were young, right before Christmas. Stephanie's never really gotten over it."

Noel's throat tightened. "I'm sorry. That must be awful for you."

"Thanks. I'm okay. I was only ten, and kids are so resilient. It's harder losing someone when you're older." A shadow crossed her features, and he wondered if she were thinking about her late husband. Then she shook her head and continued. "But it was pretty hard on Stephanie. She was in the car. Our dad was driving. She's hated Christmas ever since."

So that's what Stephanie had been referring to with her comment about *horrible Christmas memories*.

"How did your parents take it?"

Autumn fidgeted with her nails. "Not great. I guess that's to be expected. Mom withdrew from everything, and Dad disappeared into a bottle, except . . . when he didn't." She paused, clearing her throat. "They split up a couple years later, we moved here, and Dad kind of faded from our lives. Honestly, that was a good thing."

From the heaviness in her voice, Noel knew there was much more to that story, and he could only imagine what Autumn meant about her dad . . . a grieving alcoholic who'd been driving the car when his daughter died in it. If something had happened to Jenny the night he'd driven off the road, he's not sure he could have forgiven himself. Ever. Had Autumn and Stephanie's dad taken his guilt out on his family? From Autumn's tone . . .

"Wait, your dad left? Is Reuben not your father?"

Autumn smiled. "No, Mom married him a few years later, and he adopted us. Marrying him was the smartest thing she ever did, I think."

Noel smiled in relief and nodded. "That's good to hear. I'm a sucker for happy endings."

"Me, too." Autumn's smile faded, and she looked back at her hands, frowning at something.

Noel didn't push. He got the sense there were a lot of unspoken pieces of that story, but he'd poked enough at Autumn's old scars. At least he understood Stephanie a bit better. As the oldest sister, Steph might have even taken the brunt of whatever unhappiness had permeated their household. And with a history like that, no wonder she had taken his perceived rejection at the party so personally.

Now, hearing what she'd gone through growing up, he was glad he hadn't pursued the relationship. Stephanie was the kind of girl you didn't mess around with. You were either there for her, or you didn't bother. Besides, if her father was an alcoholic, how would she feel about his and Jenny's close call on the way home from the party that night—and his pitiful excuse for it?

Still, he'd been doing a lot of thinking about what she'd said at the hospital. And this final piece of the puzzle explained a lot.

"No wonder she hates me so much now," he muttered.

Autumn shifted. "Who? Stephanie?"

Noel nodded morosely.

Autumn sighed. "For what it's worth, I don't think she hates you. You're just not her favourite person in the world. When her trust is broken, it's really difficult to repair it."

"Yeah, well, I'm not sure it's my place to try. She's made it clear she doesn't want me to."

Autumn cocked her head. "Are you saying you don't want to?"

"Probably better if I don't." He took a sip of coffee, letting the bitterness ground him in reality. "Still, it's a shame she's missed out on all the great parts of Christmas all these years. I understand how losing your sister might shade things, but *you* obviously don't blame Christmas for what happened."

He indicated the cheerful decorations around the shop, several of which reminded him of ones he'd seen at the Christmas market the other day. An upbeat carol pumped through the dining room, and a lush fake spruce tree covered with vintage-looking miniature tin coffee pots and decorative teaspoon ornaments tucked between more traditional balls and even some candy canes sparkled near the door.

"No, but that's just how Stephanie has worked out her grief. Still," Autumn said, looking around the shop, "I think she might be softening up. She helped decorate this year, which was a first."

"Yeah?" Noel perked up. "She also went with you to the Christmas market. And she's coming to the youth group sleigh ride this weekend."

"She is?" Autumn smiled. "Maybe there's hope for her yet."

An idea occurred to Noel, and he leaned forward. "Do you think there's enough hope that we could make your sister fall in love with Christmas?"

Autumn blinked at him. "What do you mean, *we*? I thought you were trying to stay out of Stephanie's way."

Noel jerked back. She was right. "I am. I will. As much as is civil, I mean. But that's no reason to let your sister miss out on all the Christmas joy." A rush of excitement filled him as the obstacles became clear. *This* was what he'd been looking for. "But I might need a little help to pull it off."

Autumn looked at him skeptically. "Seems like an awful lot of trouble for someone who doesn't even like you."

Noel grinned. "What can I say? I like a challenge. Besides," he said, tapping the cast beneath his jeans, "what else have I got to do?"

Autumn chuckled. "Well, there is that." She gazed at the glittering tree thoughtfully, then glanced back at him. "What do you have in mind?"

Noel looked out the window. The steam rising from the river had settled over the town, making it look as though the coffee shop were a submarine filled with sparkling lights in an ocean of misty grey cloud.

"Maybe . . . a Christmas party? I bet Delanie and Caleb would come. And then there's you and Julien and your parents. What better way to share the joy of Christmas than with all the people she cares about?"

"And you? Are you going to plan this party and then not go?"

Noel hadn't thought of that. He didn't like the idea of missing it—he loved Christmas parties—but he didn't see much choice. "Yeah, I guess. I'm not much of a party planner anyway. That's why I'll need help."

"Hmm. So your grand idea is to make me do all the work. Kind of like Derrick will be doing for this renovation project. Everyone says you don't know when to quit, but I'm beginning to think you busted that leg on purpose to indulge your inner couch potato. You're a clever man, Noel Butler."

Noel laughed. "You caught me. Nothing like breaking a leg to ensure you have nothing to do but go crazy from having nothing to do."

Autumn tapped her fingernails on the table, thinking, then looked up. "I like your motivation, but not so much your plan of execution. I think I have a better idea."

Noel perked up. "Yeah? Lay it on me."

"Not so fast. You have to agree to do whatever I say first."

Noel's gut tightened. "You want me to agree before I even know what it is?"

Autumn leaned toward him, her gaze intense. "The way I figure it, you owe Stephanie one. A big one. And you seem interested in making it right, which is the only reason I'm helping you. I know my sister better than anyone. So if you want to do this, you're going to have to follow my plan. Agreed?"

Noel took a bite of his cookie to give himself time to think and washed it down with a sip of coffee. "What will it cost me?"

"Mostly time. Plus a little cash, if you're serious about this. Are you?" She narrowed her eyes at him again, her challenge prickling his skin.

Noel scowled. The idea of agreeing to something without knowing the details made his gut twist. But Autumn wasn't the vengeful type, and she'd never do anything to hurt her sister. How bad could it be?

Clanking sounds from the hallway caught his attention, and he looked over to see Derrick propping the ladder against the wall and weaving between the tables toward them.

"Agreed," Noel said to Autumn. "What's your plan?"

"Plan for what?" Derrick asked, plopping himself in the chair next to Autumn.

Autumn looked between them, smiling like she'd just won the lottery. As Noel listened to her ideas, his gut twisted in a combination of glee and guilt. Her plan was good—but it would mean spending more time with Stephanie than he was entirely comfortable with. Part of him clammed up at the thought.

The other part—the part that couldn't get that kiss under the mistletoe out of his mind—couldn't wait to get started.

Chapter Eight

T HE NEXT MORNING, STEPHANIE went to the front picture window of her mobile home to remote start her car so it could warm up before she left for work. It was dark out, but the snow that had been falling when she had finished her shift last night had finally stopped, and moonlight glistened from the fresh blanket of white.

Ugh. I'm going to need to shovel the sidewalk before work, too. I really need to get myself some snow pants.

She leaned forward to look through the window, confirming that the car lights flashed when she pressed the remote starter, and then blinked. The sidewalk in front of her home and beside the driveway leading up to her stoop had been freshly cleared, and her lawn was piled high with shovelfuls of powdery white snow.

Her chest warmed. She glanced across the street at the faded yellow metal siding and brown trim of Mr. Connelly's older-model mobile home. Sure enough, his lights were on, and she could see the elderly gentleman drinking coffee at his dining room table in the depths of the house, hunched over the paper with his back toward her.

"He must have been up with the owls."

She vowed to bring him one of Ellie's fresh-baked apple pies as a thank you as soon as she could. He wouldn't accept cash—she'd tried to pay him for his help before, and he would never hear of it.

When she opened her front door to leave for work, she got another surprise. A large paper shopping bag sat on the welcome mat on the cleared concrete landing. Curious, she brought it in. There was no gift tag and no card. She pulled out a pair of navy snow pants. Holding them up to her hips, she confirmed her suspicion—they should fit perfectly.

No way these were from Mr. Connelly.

"But who . . . ?"

Then the obvious answer came to her. Autumn. After Steph's comment about needing new winter gear the other day, Autumn must have dug these out of her closet for her.

Then Steph noticed the shopping tags, still attached to the pants. Had Autumn bought them for her? Maybe. That would be just like her sister. She'd probably seen a sale and picked them up. Stephanie pulled out her phone and opened her text conversation with her sister.

Thanks for the new pants. You're the best.

The time at the top corner of her screen caught her eye. She had to hurry, or she would be late for work. Draping the snow pants over a kitchen chair, she dropped the phone in her purse and sped out the door.

When she got to the hospital, she noticed Autumn's return text—

???

So it hadn't been her. Huh.

Never mind, she sent back, then hustled into the hospital to begin her shift.

When she got home, she hung the pants in her front closet, no closer to solving the mystery. The feeling was slightly unsettling.

The following day when she got into work, Kate Thomson was getting off night shift.

"There's something for you in the nurse's station," Kate said as she hurried past Steph in the hall, her chestnut curls bouncing.

Stephanie frowned. "You didn't have to get me something for covering your shift," she called after the other nurse.

Kate spun, walking backwards, no doubt in a hurry to get home and relieve her babysitter. "It's not from me."

"Then who's it from?"

Kate shrugged and grinned. "A secret admirer, maybe?" Chuckling, she turned around and disappeared into the staff room.

Confused, Stephanie made her way to the nurse's station. Sure enough, a small gift bag sat there—a nice one, printed with a fancy Christmas scene in reflective metallic foil and stuffed with printed tissue paper. A small tag hanging from the handle read *Stephanie Neufeld* in smooth, graceful cursive. She didn't recognize the handwriting.

Justin Ross, the square-chinned doctor whose rugged, model-like features tended to make her a little breathless, came up to the station while making notes in a chart on a clipboard. He glanced at the bag. "What's that?"

"I don't know yet."

He paused to watch her as she pulled out the tissue paper and withdrew a large stoneware mug. It looked hand cast, with an elegant wide-bottomed shape. Earthy blue paint striped the natural clay beneath the slick-looking glaze. It was gorgeous.

"Wow," she breathed. She'd taken some pottery classes as a teenager and recognized the craftsmanship that had gone into the design.

"Who gave you that?" Justin asked.

Stephanie peered into the bag, but there was no further tag or any indication of who had left her the gift.

"I have no idea."

He grinned. "You must have made quite the impression on someone. None of my patients have ever gotten me a mug."

With a wink, he spun and strode off toward the exam rooms and his next patient. Just then, Kate emerged from the staff room door down the hall and headed in the other direction toward the front doors of the hospital. Justin paused and watched her walk away for a few moments, then shook his head and continued on his route.

Steph repressed a smile. If those two had something going on, she hadn't heard about it—but she doubted Kate would be that foolish. Justin was a doctor—and a looker—but from what she'd seen of him, he seemed to have commitment issues. Not that Steph talked to him much about his personal life, but she'd taken a few phone messages on his behalf, and every few weeks, the name of the girl calling seemed to change. Kate needed someone stable. Someone who would be there for her and Tristan. Not someone who'd treat her like a passing fling.

Too bad things hadn't worked out between Kate and Caleb. Then again, Caleb and Delanie seemed so happy now that Steph could hardly wish it otherwise. Besides, Kate had told Steph after her second and final date with Caleb that he was a little too predictable and boring for her tastes. Delanie didn't seem to mind his steady nature.

But neither Kate's nor Delanie's love lives were Steph's immediate concern. She tucked the heavy artisan mug back in the bag and scooped it up to take to her locker. Unless someone 'fessed up, she had no way of knowing who her admirer might be, if Kate was even right about that. But whoever it was had great taste. And if they didn't want to take credit for the gift, she supposed she could respect that. She didn't much like taking credit for her acts of service either.

But three days later, her collection of anonymous gifts had expanded to include a bag of fresh-baked chocolate chip cookies, a pillar candle that smelled like pine, and a home-burned CD with a computer-printed label that read *Party Mix*. She'd been a little speechless at that. Who had a CD burner anymore? She didn't even have anything to play it on.

When she took the disc to her mother's to borrow a CD player, she discovered it held a mix of classic and modern Christmas songs.

"So someone made you a mix tape?" Angelica grinned, sitting down at her dining room table across from Stephanie with a steaming mug of tea in her hands. "How sweet."

"Yeah. Sweet." Stephanie frowned at the small stereo between them that blasted a pop cover of "Deck the Halls". "Whoever it is doesn't know me very well though, with the whole Christmas theme. I don't know, Mom. I'm getting a little creeped out."

"Oh? Why?" Angelica took a sip, peering at her over the rim of her mug.

Steph leaned back in her chair, warming her hands around the mug of peppermint tea her mother had made for her. She told Angelica about the gifts and other acts of kindness for which no one would take credit. "I've asked everyone, and no one seems to know anything about them. It wasn't even Mr. Connelly who cleared my sidewalk the other day. He says he didn't see who did it."

Though Steph had still given him the pie. It had seemed the neighbourly thing to do, since she'd been standing on his doorstep with it and all.

Angelica looked thoughtful. "Whoever it is obviously doesn't want to be recognized. Maybe someone is trying to make amends for something. Does anyone owe you an apology that you can think of?"

Stephanie started to shake her head, then froze. She looked up at her mother, her heart thumping. "You don't think Eddie . . ."

Angelica frowned like she always did when Stephanie referred to her father by his first name, then shook her head. "No. I doubt that man would go through the effort."

Stephanie swallowed, relieved. No matter how much Autumn insisted that their father had changed, Stephanie's skin crawled every time she thought of the man who'd caused their family so much misery, and who was responsible for Melody's death.

"Do you think I have a stalker?" Steph forced from a dry mouth. The CD player started pumping out a jazzy up-tempo version of "God Rest Ye Merry, Gentlemen."

Angelica cocked her head, looking thoughtful. "I'm no psychiatric professional, but I doubt a stalker would do so many things for you that are just plain nice. Don't they tend to be a bit more obsessive and weird?"

"I suppose so. Although the focus on Christmas does seem a bit obsessive, if you ask me. Almost like they think they can force me to love Christmas just by inundating me with it. As if the rest of the world doesn't already do its darnedest at that every December." Steph took another sip of tea, considering. Who might think something like that was a good idea?

She could see Autumn doing it as a prank. Autumn could be both sweet and annoying that way. But Autumn didn't have time to come and shovel her walk in the dead of night or to make mix tapes. And besides, Steph would have recognized her sister's handwriting on that gift bag.

Maybe Delanie?

Stephanie froze. Delanie was exactly the kind of person who would think she could persuade Steph to love Christmas, and she was also the kind of person who would take the time to do a daily gift drop of some kind. She was busy with that community theatre reality show project for that high-profile producer, but that still left her with plenty of down time.

Steph had already asked Delanie about the snow pants, and her friend had denied knowledge of the gift. But Delanie might fib to play a prank like this. She wasn't dishonest in general, but maybe she'd consider telling a white lie in order to keep up the fun—Steph hadn't become reacquainted enough with her old friend to know. And that handwriting on the gift bag might have been Delanie's . . . Steph hadn't seen Delanie's cursive since high school and couldn't be sure.

Steph frowned at her tea, taking a soothing sip. Maybe Delanie had picked up on Stephanie's reluctance to rekindle their friendship and had decided to up her efforts. If this was Delanie's attempt to break through Stephanie's barriers, Steph had to give her props for the thoughtfulness and energy it required. Her heart softened a little. Maybe she'd been holding back more than she should.

"I think I know who it is," Steph said.

Angelica perked up. "You do?"

"Yeah. Delanie." With a pinch of guilt, Steph remembered that Delanie had been bugging her to come to a board game night with Caleb, Emma, and some of their friends. "And you know, it *is* kind of sweet."

Angelica's eyebrows lifted in agreement and a hint of amusement, and she took another sip of tea.

Steph pulled out her phone and typed a text to Delanie. *I'll be sure to bring the Christmas party mix CD to your next games night. When is it?*

A few moments later, her phone buzzed with Delanie's response.

CD? I'll see if Caleb has a CD player. So excited for games night, though. I'll arrange one when I'm home from Vancouver in a few days. Btw, my friend Marie wants to meet you. Maybe you could come out here with me sometime. How does a dress shopping trip for the wedding sound?

By the time Steph finished reading that message, it had already been followed with another one.

Wait, I forgot to ask. Will u be one of my bridesmaids?

Steph blinked at the phone. She didn't know how long Delanie had been in Vancouver, but she obviously hadn't dropped a CD in the mailbox outside Steph's door a few hours ago.

Another dead end. But that didn't mean Delanie wasn't making an effort.

Steph smiled, despite the ongoing mystery, and texted back, *I would be honoured. Thanks. Dress shopping would be fun. Looking forward to games night.*

She put her phone away, the tension back in her temples. She rubbed them gently as a cover of "Jingle Bell Rock" blasted from the stereo. Annoyed, she hit the player's stop button.

"Not her?" Angelica got up and started clearing the tea things.

"Apparently not."

"Oh, well, I'm sure whoever it is will make themselves known eventually. For now, just enjoy trying to solve the mystery . . . and all the fun little gifts." Angelica came back to the table for Steph's empty mug. "You've got to hand it to whoever it is . . . Whatever their reasons, they sure are displaying the spirit of the season."

Steph nodded grimly. She usually adored mysteries . . . in fiction. But not when it involved her real life. Mysteries were dangerous, because they meant a surprise was coming at any time, and you had no idea how to prepare for it. And, in her experience, most surprises weren't good.

By the time she got home, snow had once again started falling in thick, fluffy flakes. She parked the car and hurried inside her dark trailer, thankful she had the next day off. She wasn't even scheduled to help at the coffee shop or babysit. She could sleep in, relax, and get caught up on *Murdoch Mysteries*—where the mysteries were all solvable in forty-five minutes without any real potential threats.

Then she remembered—tomorrow was the day of the youth group sleigh ride. Her heart sank, and she peered at the near-blizzard outside her window.

"Well, at least they'll have plenty of snow."

Maybe they would cancel. But a quick look at her phone told her that the snow would only continue until sometime in the night. Tomorrow was supposed to be clear and not too cold.

Perfect sleighing weather.

She sighed, then set about heating up some leftover beef stew she'd made earlier in the week. After she settled herself on her sofa in front of the TV to eat, she glanced outside again. The flakes falling in front of the streetlight looked like little balls of orange fire. She'd have to give herself time to shovel the walk in the morning before she left. Those new snow pants would get a lot of use tomorrow.

Unless . . .

Would her mystery benefactor come clear her driveway again?

She couldn't be sure they would, but she was determined to find out. And she knew just how to do it.

When she finally turned in, it wasn't to her bedroom in the back of the house, but to the newly made up sofa bed in the living room. She wasn't the world's lightest sleeper, but she was pretty sure she would hear if someone started scraping snow off her steps when she was on the other side of the door.

Sure enough, in the wee hours of the morning, she awoke to the sound of someone shovelling the walk out front. She crept out of bed and, keeping her head low so she wouldn't be spotted through the picture window, surreptitiously peeked through the glass.

The snow had stopped, leaving a blanket of glistening white lit by pools of orange from the street lamps. Only a few vehicles had broken trail on the street, and a truck Steph didn't recognize was parked next to the curb in front of her house. A man in a dark parka and a fleece cap was industriously shovelling the walk, his back to her. He was tall, that was certain. And those broad shoulders filled out his parka nicely. There was something odd about the way he moved, the way he favoured his one leg. Odd, and familiar.

"Come on, turn around so I can see your face," she muttered, her stomach churning more with each passing second. The list of men who would shovel her walk in the dead of night like this was so short as to be nonexistent. Was this guy trying to make her feel indebted to him? Had she been right about having a stalker?

But would a stalker make her a mix tape of peppy Christmas tunes and take no credit for it? That seemed unlikely. Maybe the gifts were unrelated to this act of service. Because the only guy she could think of who would do something like this was still Eddie Bell—and that was a long shot. It would be totally unlike him to do something nice without making sure she knew about it. And he would *never* pick out a hand-cast mug in her favourite colour.

Just then, the man straightened, rolling his shoulders and lifting his face to the streetlight. The fear fell out of Steph's belly to be replaced by shock, followed by a profound blanket of confusion.

Noel Butler was clearing her sidewalk.

He glanced toward the window and she ducked, letting herself slide to the floor, her thoughts racing.

What is he thinking, clearing snow with a cast on?

But that wasn't the most pressing question. It was only the one she processed first. Then her brain caught up, and she asked no one in particular, "Why in the name of Twelve Foot Davis is Noel Butler shovelling my sidewalk?"

Chapter Nine

NOEL SAT IN THE back seat of the small church bus and peered out the window as Jared eased the vehicle along the narrow country driveway. The dozen teenagers filling the rest of the seats gazed through the windows just as eagerly. Fresh snow sparkled in the midday sun, weighing down the dark green bows of the towering pine trees on either side of the lane.

When they reached the yard, the trees opened up to reveal a large clearing containing a sprawling log house surrounded by fenced-in paddocks and a large red-and-white barn. Noel scanned the yard for Stephanie but didn't see her or her compact silver SUV anywhere. He stifled his disappointment.

She's probably just late, looking for the place.

He'd sent her a map pin, but she still could have misjudged the time. He wondered if he should call her to make sure she wasn't lost, but decided against it. Stephanie was a smart, capable woman who owned a cell phone. If she got lost, she'd call.

And if she'd decided not to come . . . well, he'd know where they stood.

In front of the barn stood a man bundled in dark green insulated coveralls and a red plaid faux fur-lined trapper hat. He was occupied with hitching a team of Belgian draft horses to a long wooden flatbed sled that looked like a wagon whose wheels had been replaced with two sets of red skids. Large golden bells studded the black leather horse harnesses, and the horses nickered and tossed their thick blond manes against their arching bay necks as Paul Anderson worked. Paul looked like a midget next to the horses, barely reaching their withers. But Noel doubted he'd be able to see over those horses' withers either, despite the several inches he knew he had on their host.

"Whoa," Ryker breathed from the seat in front of Noel. "Those horses are *huge!*"

The teenagers started buzzing excitedly about the horses, the sleigh, and the prospects for the day. Noel glanced at Trevor Harris, who sat rigidly next to him. The boy's naturally tan face had gone a little pale. His shaggy black hair poked out from under his blue-and-orange knit Oilers beanie, providing stark contrast to his ashen complexion.

"You alright, man?" Noel asked.

Trevor nodded mutely, still staring at the team of enormous draft horses through the window.

Noel leaned closer. "I know they look big, but my friend Heath is Mr. Anderson's son, and he calls them 'gentle giants.' Give 'em a carrot and they'll love you forever."

"Like Pete's dragon?" Trevor asked, a slight tremble in his voice. He might be fourteen, but his autism meant he came off as a little younger than other boys his age. His unexpected comments often made Noel chuckle. Like now.

"A bit like that, yeah."

Ryker turned around and gave Trevor a nervous smile. "You want to sit next to me on the sleigh? We might even be able to meet the horses together."

Trevor blinked, his eyes wide with interest and alarm. "Really?"

Ryker nodded. "As long as it's okay with Mr. Anderson. I got to work with horses sometimes at one of my foster families. Noel's right. Just because a horse is big doesn't mean it's mean. And horses love treats." He patted his pocket and dropped his voice to a whisper. "Mrs. Wood gave me a few sliced apples to share with them this morning."

Trevor relaxed and brightened. "Mrs. Wood was always my favourite. Okay. Sounds fun." He renewed his staring at the horses, but this time there was more excitement and less fear in his expression.

Noel glanced between the boys. Sometimes he forgot that Trevor and his brothers, Lionel and Byron, had once lived in the same group home Ryker had recently moved into. Seeing how their story had turned out—adopted by the Harrises and thriving, for the most part—gave him hope for Ryker. The kid might have come under some bad influences recently, but Noel was nowhere near ready to give up on him. If all went well, maybe Ryker would even make a new friend or two today.

In his experience, good influences were powerful too. Maybe Lionel and Trevor could become part of Ryker's new tribe. Or Jordan, the pastor's kid. Noel could only hope.

He glanced toward the boys in question. A few seats ahead of them, Lionel stared back over his shoulder at Ryker and Trevor. His meaty hand gripped the bus seat so hard that the upholstery wrinkled. When he saw Noel looking, Lionel quickly turned around. His glance landed on Ryker's sister, Ryleigh, on the way by, and a fleeting look of guilt crossed his face. She didn't notice—she was too busy looking out the window at the horses.

Hmm. Maybe Lionel would need to warm up to Ryker before they became buddies.

Jared parked the bus next to one of the Andersons' vehicles and stood to face the small group of teens. Their chatter hushed to a few whispers as Jared reiterated the rules and etiquette of the outing one last time, then stepped aside so they could file past him and leave the vehicle.

Noel waited until he was the last one on the bus, then heaved himself to his feet, using a combination of his crutches and the back of the seat in front of him. He'd just gotten his cast replaced by the air boot yesterday, when the doctor had been astounded at the progress of his healing. While he was grateful he was now allowed to put some weight on his foot, his muscles already ached from his secret mission to Steph's that morning, and he hoped he hadn't overdone it. At least this time he'd been able to shovel Steph's sidewalk himself instead of conscripting Caleb to do it. He owed his friend big-time for that one, no matter how much Caleb had insisted he was happy to contribute to Noel's efforts.

He hobbled down the steps, and cold air hit his face as he stepped out of the vehicle. He pulled his toque down further on his ears and inhaled deeply. Crisp, evergreen-scented air tingled all the way to his lungs.

"All good?" Jared asked, indicating Noel's crutches with a jerk of his chin as he moved behind Noel to push the bus doors closed. "You're becoming a pro with those things."

"Yep. Every day is arm day. In fact, I think I'll hang onto them for a while. I'm getting my army physique back. On the top half of my body, anyway."

Jared chuckled, then moved away to talk to Paul. Noel kept an eye on the teens—when his gaze wasn't wandering toward the driveway in a far-too-anxious rhythm. He realized what he was doing and snorted at himself.

"Like my dad would say," he told himself under his breath, "a watched beaker never boils." He shook his head, then deliberately turned his back toward the driveway, facing the group instead. If Stephanie did come, he didn't need to be mooning over her arrival like an anxious puppy.

The teens milled around in groups of two or three. Ryker stood with his hands shoved into his pockets next to his sister and her friends. Ryleigh, Ainsley Crawford, and a brown-haired girl whose name Noel couldn't remember teased each other, and Ryker threw in the occasional humorous quip of his own. Ryleigh kept her arm looped around her brother's as though to make sure he didn't walk away and leave her there—or to make sure he felt included.

A short distance away, Trevor Harris hovered near Lionel, Jordan, and a couple other boys. They were talking and laughing loudly about inane topics—but Noel didn't miss the fact that Lionel's antics seemed designed to catch the attention of the girls. He shook his head and chuckled to himself. While he loved working with teenagers, he sure didn't miss the trials and tribulations of being one himself. All the uncertainty, the vying for attention and validation—and, in his case, his rebellious escapades to establish his own identity as separate from his family's upstanding reputation.

If only he hadn't been so determined to shrug off his father's expectations of him and prove himself as his own man, he'd have realized what an idiot he was a lot sooner. Before so many people got hurt. Like Maddie Kennedy.

He shook his head, thinking once more of the moment his relationship with Maddie was truly over. They'd been standing in the middle of the school gymnasium at the Grade Twelve Harvest Dance, her in a fancy dress with an expression of horrified indignation on her face, him with his face burning in humiliation and anger because of what she'd done. Though he hadn't seen it at the time, his relationship with Maddie had been a series of one-ups and look-at-mes that had been anything but healthy. His AA sponsor, Mark, had often reminded him that healthy relationships weren't about overshadowing the other person—they were about lifting each other up.

If only there was a twelve-step program that would help him get rid of the unexpected nerves making his palms sweat.

The sound of a vehicle crunching on the snow and gravel caught his attention, and he turned to see Stephanie parking her little silver crossover next to the bus. His heart leapt. He wished he could have seen her face when she saw that her sidewalk had been cleared again that morning.

But her gaze through the windshield chilled his excitement somewhat—the look she gave him could have frozen fire.

Noel frowned. That wasn't the greeting he expected. Maybe she was thinking about something else—something from work? Hopefully, the fun she was about to have would take her mind off it.

She got out of the car, and he grinned a hello, disappointed that her shapely figure was concealed by the navy snow pants beneath her winter coat—which was silly, since he'd given them to her. At least she was wearing them. Curiosity about how she felt about the gifts he'd been doling out all week burned in his chest. Was she delighted? Excited? Indifferent? He doubted it would be the last one—who wouldn't love receiving gifts from a mysterious Secret Santa? When Autumn had suggested it, he'd gotten excited just to *be* the Secret Santa. Still, he wanted the satisfaction of hearing her reaction. He wondered if he could tease Steph into letting something slip.

But when she walked by, the *hello* she gave him was so formal, and her smile so stiff, he kept his glib remark to himself. Instead, he returned a simple nod and a muttered, "Hey." She barely acknowledged it before she went over to the sleigh to stand near Jared and Paul, pointedly ignoring his curious gaze.

That behaviour seemed prompted by more than an incident at work. Had something happened that morning?

No, you lunkhead. You keep forgetting that she doesn't like you.

After one final long look in her direction, he sighed and turned toward the house, using his crutches to steady him as he made his way toward the wide log steps. He'd promised to stay out of her way if she came, and he intended to honour that promise. Especially since she obviously wanted him to.

He heard another vehicle pull in, and he glanced at the parking area to see Pastor Vic—Jordan's dad—getting out of their family mini-van. Good. There would be plenty of chaperones without him.

"Noel, aren't you coming on the sleigh?" Ryker said from behind him.

Noel spun, noticing Stephanie's attention had been caught by the question too.

"Nah," he said, trying to sound casual. "I'll go inside and help Mrs. Anderson prepare the snacks for after. Looks like we'll need the extra room on the sleigh."

"No need," said Paul with a jovial smile. He gave a final tug on a harness buckle and, with a pat for the animal, walked closer to the group. "Brenda's got everything ready to go except the hot chocolate, which she'll make while we're out. And there's plenty of room on the sleigh."

Noel cast a guilty glance at Stephanie. "Er, I promised my nurse I wouldn't do anything foolish and re-injure my leg."

"Oh," Paul said in surprise, glancing at Stephanie. "Well, I don't have anything to say about that." He cleared his throat, glancing between the two of them.

Ryker seemed to catch the tension too, because after glancing uncomfortably between Noel and Stephanie, he turned to Paul and said, "Mr. Anderson, could you introduce me to the horses? Trevor and I have some treats to give them." He pulled a sealed clear plastic bag of apple wedges from his pocket.

Trevor noticed and perked up, coming over and looking hopefully at Paul. "Can I meet them too?"

"Er, sure," the man said gruffly. With a final glance at Noel and Stephanie, he turned and led the boys toward the horses' heads, explaining how to approach so the animals wouldn't be startled.

Stephanie still stood near the sleigh, but she hadn't looked away from Noel's gaze. Her expression was full of distrust, curiosity, and something he couldn't identify. He gripped his crutch handles a little tighter. He'd love to find out what that mystery emotion was, but if she didn't want him around, he was determined to keep his word to her. He pivoted to start up the steps to the house.

He caught the motion from the corner of his eye—Stephanie stepping toward him. He paused, his shoulders tense, and waited until she stood in front of him. Steam billowed around her face with every breath.

"I see you have an air boot now," she said, indicating his leg.

Noel glanced down. "Yeah. Doc Ross says I should start using the leg more, as long as I'm careful."

"Are you gonna be warm enough in that thing?"

"I've got two layers of wool socks on. I think I'll make it to the house without getting hypothermia."

"But what about on the ride? Won't you get cold?"

He glanced at her in confusion.

A smirk slanted across her face, and she arched her brow in challenge. "Come on, you don't think I believed for a second you came on this outing to sit in the house and serve cookies, do you?"

Noel's shoulders relaxed. "It wasn't my first choice, no. But I promised I'd stay out of your way, so . . ."

Stephanie glanced at the sled, where Pastor Vic and Jared were directing kids to clamber aboard and get settled. The two rows of square hay bales that had been arranged along the rails of the sled to make seats were filling up, but there were still several gaps.

Stephanie turned to face Noel again. "Looks like there's plenty of room on that sleigh, like Paul said. I think we could both fit on there without digging our elbows into each other's ribs."

Warmth tingled in Noel's abdomen, and a spark of attraction prickled his chest. This woman was something else. "Careful, Ms. Neufeld. If I didn't know better, I'd think you were flirting with me."

The smile dropped from her face like an icicle from a roof. "Don't push it. I just didn't want you to miss out on your fun day with the kids for me."

With a parting glare, she marched stiffly toward the front of the sleigh, climbed the ladder, and made her way to the farthest back corner to sit in a space next to Ryleigh and Ainsley.

Noel's jaw tightened. *Smooth move, Ex-lax.* Then he chuckled in satisfaction. There was something about Stephanie Neufeld he found fascinating, and if the only way he could get her attention was to get under her skin, he was okay with that.

Then he realized where that sentiment originated—from the spark he'd felt a few moments ago that had now ignited a flame somewhere in his lower gut—and swallowed. He'd told Stephanie to be careful, but apparently, he was the one who needed the warning.

He made his way up the sled steps and found a seat of his own near the front.

As far from Stephanie as he could get.

Chapter Ten

STEPHANIE WATCHED THE PASSING scenery while listening to the conversation of the teenage girls beside her, trying to ignore the ruggedly good-looking man with the crutches who was sitting in the front of the sleigh. It wasn't easy when she caught a glimpse of Noel's profile every time she glanced sideways. She kept picturing Noel standing in the streetlight on her cleared sidewalk that morning. She desperately wanted to ask him why he would do something like that for her . . . and if he was also the one who'd been leaving her gifts. Like her snow pants.

She glanced down, realizing that if he *had* left her the snow pants, that meant he'd now know she'd accepted them and was making use of them. Part of her wanted to rip them off and throw them away . . . but that would not only be foolish in this freezing weather, it would bring too many questions from the teenagers.

She peeked toward Noel again. He looked so casually strong, as though the crutches he held upright before him were a fashion choice instead of the consequence of a moment of human error. He was carrying on a spirited conversation with Ryker Dyck and Trevor Harris, who sat on either side of him. Victor Olson, who'd been introduced to her as the pastor of Peace Crossing Christian Assembly, sat nearby with his arm propped on the bale behind him, listening in. Noel's deep voice carried back to her in the still air, easily heard over the swish of the runners in the snow and the giggling conversation of the girls. He was telling them a story about one of his friends from the army who'd been dared to streak across the base on a chilly night. He'd taken the dare, but as he was running, he'd forgotten about the security cameras and had been caught. The punishment? He had to do a whole week of night watch, and every hour on the hour, he had to stop and do a hundred jumping jacks.

The boys and Pastor Vic rolled with laughter, and Stephanie couldn't help but chuckle despite herself. She had to admit, Noel had a way with the kids. And his humour was infectious.

She studied him, conflicting emotions in her chest. Ever since he'd so easily dismissed her all those years ago, she'd wanted to hate him. But, she suddenly realized, she didn't . . . and the more she saw what kind of man he'd become, the harder it was to stay angry with him. Gone was the rebellious teenager with green hair and a chip on his shoulder whom she'd found so attractive in high school. By that night at the Christmas party, his youthful defiance had been replaced by a sarcastic cockiness she'd found intriguing, which had since matured into a self-possessed confidence mixed with protective kindness. It was unexpected, but not as unexpected as the way this new version of him made her feel—drawn like a moth to a flame. Like the draft horses who dutifully pulled the sleigh, he exuded power restrained by gentleness. She found it electrifying.

And now, he was clearing her sidewalk in the wee hours of the morning, despite a leg injury. The thought still filled her with anxiety, but also curiosity. Why would he do that? Was he trying to make amends for the past? If so, she had to admit, it was working.

He looked right at her, and she glanced away, her face flushing with heat when she realized she'd been staring at him—but not before noticing how the sunlight filtering through the trees caught flecks of golden amber in his warm brown eyes. Then she realized if she'd seen him looking, he'd seen her looking too, and angled her body determinedly toward the back of the sleigh.

They'd left the expansive farmyard behind and were gliding along some cleared paths through the forest in an area Paul had called the back quarter. The sleigh eased to a stop. Stephanie swivelled toward the front along with her companions in time to see Jared stand up and face the group. He gave a wide grin, his cheeks already rosy despite his neck-warmer and toque. As he spoke, his breath billowed in clouds of steam through the cold air.

"You probably noticed the sleds tied to the back of the sleigh," Jared began. "Mr. Anderson seems to think you guys would enjoy being dragged through the snow. I tried to tell him that none of you would like that sort of thing, but he insisted I ask you about it, so . . ."

He cut off, grinning, as several of the teens shot their hands into the air with cries of *Me first! I want to go. Pick me!* Beside him, Paul leaned a hip against the front of the sleigh, the thick leather reins wrapped around one hand and the ends pooling on the floor as he twisted to look at the kids, grinning beneath his iron-grey moustache. Noel glanced around at the exuberant teenagers, his eyes sparkling.

Stephanie felt his deep chuckle rumble through her ribcage and tried to ignore the thrill she felt in response. She was here for the kids, not for Noel-the-Betrayer Butler. The last thing she needed was to get involved romantically with anyone, and especially him. She wished it wasn't getting harder and harder to remember that.

"Three can go at a time," Jared continued. "Ryker, Ryleigh, and Ainsley, you go first. Next batch will be Lionel, Jordan, and Trevor. Off you go. And be careful."

The kids tumbled off the sleigh and raced through the snow to claim their sleds, leaving space next to Stephanie. She swivelled on her hay bale bench at the back of the sleigh to watch them, smiling with delight. The kids clambering onto the brightly coloured plastic sleds reminded her of when she and her sisters would take their sleds to the hill on the north end of Peace Crossing, where a steep bank of the river valley created a natural but terrifying slope. After Melody died, she and Autumn hadn't gone much anymore. Autumn had wanted to, but Stephanie's heart had no longer been in it. Guilt pinched her—how many wonderful memories had she missed out on with Autumn because she couldn't stop missing little Melody? She determined not to make the same mistake with Julien. Next time she babysat her nephew, she'd take him to the sledding hill.

She was startled to hear Noel call out to the kids from right beside her. She glanced up to see him easing himself down on the vacant spot next to her with the help of his crutches.

"Ryker, you better hold on tight, or you'll be walking back to the barn!" he called as the boy threw himself onto a purple sled.

Ryker laughed, his eyes alight. "Don't worry, Noel, I got this!"

But within minutes, all three teenagers had been left behind in the sleigh's wake and were running to catch up. Stephanie turned to warn Paul to slow down, but the driver was keeping an eye on the kids over his shoulder, his mouth twitching, and she realized it was all part of the fun. Sure enough, the teens soon dove onto the sleds, laughing so hard they could barely latch on.

When Noel's laugh rumbled through her once again, Steph became blindingly aware of how close he was. Not close enough to feel his body heat in this weather, but close enough that his body protected her from the slight breeze. Close enough to occasionally feel the hard muscles of his leg bump her thigh.

She cleared her throat and glanced around her. Jared and the other kids had migrated toward the back to watch the fun, too. Now was definitely not the time to ask Noel about his appearance at her house, nor what he might intend by plying her with Christmas gifts.

Instead, she focused on the kids and their laughing struggles to stay on board their sleds. Before long, she almost forgot about the man beside her who kept tying her stomach in knots.

Almost.

Until Ryleigh's sled hit a bump that sent the girl flying high into the air. She landed flat on her back in the snow with a loud *whump* and lay there, unmoving.

Panic seized Stephanie by the chest. She jumped to her feet, shouting for Paul to stop. The weathered rancher tugged on the reins. The sleigh lurched to a halt, and Stephanie lost her balance, toppling backward toward the front of the sleigh . . . right into Noel's lap.

She glanced up into his surprised face, more than aware of the muscular arms keeping her from falling all the way to the floor.

"You all right?" he asked, his breath cloudy in the cold air.

She nodded, her nerves singing like wind through electrical wires. Then she remembered why she'd landed there and stiffened. "Ryleigh!"

Noel helped push her awkwardly to her feet and she jumped off the sleigh, surprised to find Lionel a few paces ahead of her. Ryker had already run over and was leaning over the inert girl, asking if she was all right with a note of desperation in his voice.

Just like Steph had once done over her little sisters. She fought her way through the deep snow, a surge of adrenaline giving her strength she didn't know she had.

When she got there, she found Ryleigh gasping for breath, but conscious. Lionel and Ainsley stood nearby and watched, giving Stephanie room to examine Ryleigh. Steph did a quick tactile inspection and found no evidence of anything broken. With each passing second, Ryleigh's breath came easier, and she was able to answer Stephanie's questions about pain.

Reassured, Stephanie relaxed. She turned so Jared, Noel, and the other kids could hear her.

"I think she's just winded. She'll be okay in a minute."

"Thank you, Jesus," Ainsley whispered fervently.

Lionel's shoulders relaxed, but he didn't remove his worried gaze from the fallen girl.

Relief flooded Ryker's face, and he turned and grasped his sister's hand in both of his.

"I told you, you're not allowed to leave me," he whispered. "You promised."

She gave her brother a weak smile. "Never," she replied between gasps. "You know that."

Stephanie watched the exchange, her chest tight as she blinked back tears. These two had obviously been through a lot together. The fact that they were foster kids already told her that. But despite their history, or maybe because of it, the bond between them was plain. It wasn't right that they'd now been separated from each other too. She wiped a bead of moisture from her cheek.

"I think I can sit up now," Ryleigh said, her voice steadier.

Stephanie helped her stand, then walked beside her back to the sleigh. Ryker walked on her other side, with Ainsley trailing off to the side and keeping an eye on her friend. Lionel followed close behind Ryleigh, looking ready to help at a moment's notice. Steph suggested Ryleigh sit near the front behind Paul, where the jolts and jars of the sleigh would be less noticeable.

The next group of teens piled off to take their turn on the sleds—except Lionel, who abstained from his turn. Steph noticed he seemed to be keeping subtle tabs on Ryleigh and wondered if he were nursing a crush. Ryker and Ainsley huddled on either side of the girl, but she seemed truly recovered, though a little shaken.

After assuring herself that Ryleigh wasn't in shock, Stephanie took a seat in the long empty space on the bales between Lionel, who sat next to Ainsley, and Noel, who'd remained near the back of the sleigh.

Noel cast a concerned glance at the group of teens at the front, then leaned toward Steph. "Will she be all right?" he asked in a low voice.

Stephanie nodded, a reassuring smile born of long practice coming instinctively to her lips. "She's fine. I'll keep an eye on her, but these things happen." She frowned, thinking of what Samantha had told her about Ryleigh's overprotective foster mother. "I don't know how Mrs. Richardson will react."

Noel grimaced. "I'm wondering about that too. These youth group events are some of the only times Ryleigh and Ryker get to see each other outside of supervised family visits and school. And if Ryleigh's mom starts keeping her home . . ."

He didn't need to finish the thought. Steph already knew it would be one more hardship the twins shouldn't have to endure.

She cleared her throat. "Say, um, you might not be at liberty to talk about it, but do you have any idea why Ryker is at the group home now?"

Noel gave a knowing flick of his eyes and glanced at the teenagers only a few feet away. "You're right, I'm not at liberty to discuss it," he said. "Not here, anyway."

Steph thought she'd kept her voice for Noel's ears only, but Lionel, who sat with his elbows on his knees staring worriedly at the floor between glances at Ryleigh, muttered something under his breath at the same time Noel shook his head.

Steph tilted her head at the boy. "What was that, Lionel?"

He looked up guiltily. "I didn't say nothin'."

Steph hadn't heard *nothing*. In fact, she was sure she'd heard Lionel mutter something about the Richardsons not wanting a druggie in their house. She glanced at Ryker, who still sat close to his sister while he watched Paul handle the team of horses. She didn't see any typical physical signs of drug addiction, but that didn't mean the boy hadn't experimented. Of course, Lionel could just be repeating schoolyard gossip, too, and the rumour mill wasn't always based in facts. She cocked an eyebrow at Noel for confirmation, but either he hadn't heard Lionel, or he was pretending he hadn't. And he was right—now wasn't the time to talk about it. Nor the shovelling-her-sidewalk-at-five-a.m. issue.

When I get you alone, Noel Butler, we'll have a lot to talk about.
She shifted to watch the teenagers having fun behind the sleigh, allowing herself to be distracted by their antics.

An hour later, everyone was tucked safely into the Andersons' rustic log house great room. Groups congregated at the kitchen island to munch on snacks or around the expansive dining room table to play board games. Waves of laughter filled the space. Steph wandered away from the noisy crowd to survey the titles on the book spines of the floor-to-ceiling shelves on one side of the vaulted room. Noel made his way over to her, and she watched his slow progress with his crutches from the corner of her eye. Her questions for him still burned in her gut. Maybe now she'd finally get to ask them.

He stood beside her, keeping his weight off his boot cast. He also appeared interested in the books for a few seconds before breaking the silence. "Nice job handling that emergency."

She turned to face him, looking up and swallowing at the reminder of how very tall he was. There weren't many people, even men, who towered over her by nearly half a foot.

"Thanks."

"I mean, it's not like I didn't think you could or anything," he added. "But . . . I can't tell you how glad I am you came. Put a hammer or a rifle in my hand, and I'll know what to do. But when it comes to medical emergencies, I'm as useless as a bent nail." He chuckled, glancing down at his crutches. "But the Big Guy had matters in hand, as usual. Guess I was worried for nothing."

He frowned, glancing at the group of teens playing UNO around the dining room table, his gaze lingering on the dark-haired twins. Another wave of raucous teenage laughter broke around them.

Steph studied him, intrigued. Worry was her domain. Noel had always struck her as having every situation fully under control. "What were you worried about?"

His frown broke, and the confident smile returned. "Oh, nothing, really. This stupid injury has just reminded me I'm not as invincible as I think."

She arched a brow. She might have let Lionel get away with a non-answer like that back on the sleigh, but she had no intention of being so lenient with the man before her, whom she'd known most of her life.

"So is that why you were shovelling my walk at oh-dark-thirty this morning? To prove to me that you could come out here today and not re-injure yourself? Were you trying to impress me?" Even though she kept her voice low, she could hear the tension in it and cleared her throat, schooling her features to something more playful. Besides, a small part of her kind of hoped he *had* been trying to impress her . . . and another part of her kind of hated herself for it.

Noel's caught-in-the-headlights expression told her exactly what she needed to know—he truly hadn't wanted her to see him, which confused her more. If he'd been trying to get in her good books, hiding the fact that he'd done a random act of kindness for her would be an odd way to go about it.

"I, uh, don't know what you mean," he stammered, fidgeting on his crutches. "Wait, was someone shovelling your walk in the middle of the night? That's weird."

But she was onto him, and he knew it. She may as well go the distance. "That's not the only weird thing that's been happening lately. I've been getting Christmas gifts, like, *every day*. And no one I know will admit to being the gift-giver. Would you know anything about that?"

Noel spluttered and shook his head, exaggerated innocence all over his face. "Me? Nope. Why would I?"

She dropped the teasing act and let the anxiety and uncertainty that had been simmering in her gut all day boil over, smacking him on the arm. "I saw you, Noel. This morning. You scared the living daylights out of me. I didn't know if I had a stalker or what.

And now that I know it was you, I'm still not sure I don't. What's your deal?"

He dropped his innocent act, too. But what she saw looking back at her wasn't a man satisfied at having pulled something over on her, or even upset at having his trick revealed.

Instead, he leaned toward her, and the intensity in his eyes made her heart thump against her ribs and her mouth go dry. His gaze fell toward her mouth, and her heartbeat thundered in her ears like a herd of running horses.

Then he swallowed and glanced away, his knuckles whitening on the handles of his crutches. "UNO."

"Pardon?" she said, trying to gather her scattered thoughts.

He straightened and grinned, jerking his head toward the table where Ainsley was shuffling the deck of cards. "I promised Ryker I'd play a few rounds. Want to join?"

Steph eyed him. She fully intended to get to the bottom of Noel's mysterious behaviour, but now was obviously not the time. When she gave a reluctant nod, he grinned and swung himself toward the table. Begrudgingly, she followed him across the room. Ryleigh offered her a shy smile when Steph sat next to her, and Ainsley gave them a warm welcome and added another two piles of cards to the hand she was dealing.

Noel fell into easy banter with the teens, teasing and making each of them feel important in one way or another. Steph wanted to stay angry with him and keep her distance, but there was something about him that tugged her toward him, like a planet toward the sun. She even found herself laughing at his jokes and falling into their old playful banter.

But once in a while, he'd glance at her and she'd remember they still had something unresolved between them. Something that made her breath a little short whenever he looked at her.

Because when they'd been standing across the room, she could have sworn he wanted to kiss her again. And then something had flashed behind Noel's eyes that she'd never seen on his face, before his expression had closed to its typical invulnerability—fear. But of what? Her?

Looking up from his cards, Noel caught and held her gaze, his warm brown eyes catching glints of firelight from the hearth and swirling with thoughts she couldn't read. Was it warmth or hesitation that lay behind his bottomless gaze? And which one did she want it to be?

The question left her thoughts spinning until well after she'd tucked herself into bed that night.

But when she fell asleep, she was smiling . . .

Chapter Eleven

"**S**O, YOU'VE BEEN PLAYING Secret Santa, have you?" Reuben Neufeld deposited several fresh glasses of drinks onto the large corner booth table, his bulky frame blocking the view of the Ferryman's rustic, festive dining room. He stood above the table with his arms crossed and his face unreadable, glaring down at Noel.

Noel leaned back, his gaze drifting to the antique oar above them, searching for a way to dodge the question. Jared, Caleb, Derrick, and the Anderson brothers—Luke and Heath—stared at him, waiting with varying degrees of amusement and interest.

After months of talking about it, the six of them had finally gotten together for long-overdue drinks . . . though the only one with a brown beer bottle sweating in his hands was Heath, whose visit home to Peace Crossing had been the excuse for the occasion. Most of these guys rarely drank, especially around Noel. Noel had ordered his favourite seasonal beverage—eggnog. *Just* eggnog. He'd been sober for three years, eleven months, and twenty-seven days, and he had no intention of breaking that streak soon. Or ever.

He met Reuben's gaze.

"You heard about that, did you?" Noel said, trying to sound casual.

"*I* haven't," said Heath, a crooked grin that had melted many a lady's heart on his excessively handsome blue-eyed face. "Do tell. Does Noel-the-Stoic Butler have a crush on someone?"

"A crush? What is this, junior high?" Noel scoffed. "Nah, I just needed something to keep me from going crazy while I recover from this stupid broken leg." He tapped his thigh for emphasis. He'd kept the foot with the rigid boot as close to the outer edge of the booth as possible to give it space—but not so close as to risk being kicked by a server. "And trying to soften up a grinchy attitude seemed like just the ticket." He glanced at Reuben. "If Stephanie told you, maybe she's not as upset about it as I thought."

The name drop was met by a round of exchanged glances.

"Stephanie Neufeld?" Luke whispered to Heath, who responded with a shrug, a disbelieving shake of his head, and a surprised chuckle.

Caleb and Jared, who'd been helping Noel, exchanged knowing smiles. Noel's project wasn't news to Derrick, so he only watched his brother's exchange with Reuben with amused interest.

Reuben's face had broken into his typical jovial grin. "Oh, no. Steph's jumping mad. But you're not wrong about her being a bit grinchy." He glanced over his shoulder dramatically to check that no one else was close by, then leaned toward Noel and lowered his voice. "Between you, me, the table, and these fine gentleman here? I think she's not as upset as she's letting on. In fact, I think she's actually pretty flattered."

"Could have fooled me." Noel snorted. "Judging by the wall of glacial silence I've been getting from her, I'd wondered if Santa should hang up his hat and call it a season."

Reuben laughed, and it boomed around the crowded dining room. "Santa's job ain't done until the last gift is delivered, if I'm not mistaken. Keep it up, young man. It's about time someone got through to that girl, and you've got as good a chance as any." He harrumphed. "Now, if you'll excuse me. I'm covering for my normal bartender tonight, so I'll have to take my leave." He scooped up their empties onto a tray and hustled back to the bar.

"Stephanie Neufeld?" Heath asked, echoing Luke's question. His expression was as incredulous as his tone. "The Ice Queen?"

Noel frowned, a twinge of guilt and a protective surge running through him. "Don't call her that. We're not in high school anymore."

"Alright, man. I'm just surprised, that's all." Heath shook his head and took a sip of his beer. "Weren't you the one who gave her that nickname?"

Jared, who'd gone to the other high school and who was several years behind them, looked between them questioningly. "Why did you call her the Ice Queen? She seems nice enough to me."

Heath chuckled. "Because she's been gorgeous since grade school, but nothing could melt that frozen heart—or so these guys used to tell me. I didn't meet her until I moved here in Grade Twelve, but she definitely suited the title."

"You asked her on a date and she turned you down, eh?" Luke said.

Heath shrugged, looking sheepish. "I didn't try hard, or anything."

Luke rolled his eyes. "Not succumbing to your charms doesn't make a girl an Ice Queen, bro. It means she's got some sense in her head."

Heath gave his brother a solid punch in the shoulder, and Luke rubbed the spot, scowling.

"Well, apparently, Noel thinks a few gifts can break the Ice Queen's curse, if I understood correctly." Heath winked at Noel.

"Yeah, yeah, it's no big deal." Noel rolled his eyes, wincing internally at the nickname. He hadn't actually coined it—that credit belonged to Jackson—but he'd certainly helped to spread it around. Knowing what he knew about her now, he couldn't blame her for being reserved in high school. *Kids can be idiots.* And by *kids,* he meant himself. And Jackson. But that was a different kettle of fish.

Besides, he'd since discovered that nothing could be further from the truth. Not only from his time with Steph herself, who had sparkled with warmth and joy on that night that spent more and more time in his brain rent-free these days. But the more he'd learned about her from Autumn while brainstorming appropriate gift ideas, the more he'd realized just how kind, selfless, and generous Steph truly was. Everything she did seemed to be for other people.

"As I said, I needed a project," he continued. "And Stephanie was a 'right time, right place' type of situation. You know how I love a challenge."

"That's the truth," Derrick said, and snorted. "A little too much. Remember the Chili Pepper Incident?"

Noel groaned and made a face. "You had to bring that up."

"The Chili Pepper Incident?" Jared perked up, curiosity in his dark eyes. "Intriguing."

Heath raised his brows. "Was that when you were in the army?"

"High school," Noel said begrudgingly. "Before you moved here. Not one of my brightest moments."

Heath leaned forward with an anticipatory grin. "Do tell."

"No, thanks." Noel looked across the room, his face growing uncharacteristically warm.

Caleb caught his eye, a look of sympathy on his face.

Derrick cocked his head with an amused *hmmph*.

"If you ain't telling it, I am." He glanced around at his rapt audience. "So, back in the day—Noel was in Grade Eleven, I think,"—he glanced at Noel, barely waiting for confirmation before continuing—"the youth pastor at Christian Assembly had this great idea to do a chili cook-off as a fundraiser for something or other."

"New youth room furniture," Caleb supplied with a sideways glance at Noel, then took a sip of his iced tea, his expression studiously blank.

"Yeah, that was it," Derrick said. "The old stuff was pretty trashed. Anyway, there were different categories each chili would be graded on—flavour, texture, visual appeal, spice. You know, the typical stuff."

The guys nodded, listening with rapt attention, but Noel noticed Caleb looking toward the room as though he were uncomfortable. His old friend knew what was coming . . . and Caleb wasn't the type to rub in a painful ending by enjoying an amusing beginning.

Unlike Noel's brother, apparently. Derrick was practically bursting to tell this story. Noel resigned himself to endure it.

Derrick leaned forward. "Noel was dating Madeleine Kennedy at the time—you know her, Jared, she works at Pearl's Petals now—and she decided to enter the chili cook-off in the sweet chili category." Derrick whistled at the memory. "Mm-mm. Now *that* girl can cook."

Luke perked up. "Can she? Huh. Wouldn't have thought that."

The thought of Maddie produced a twinge of irritation, as always, and Noel rolled his eyes. Luke ducked his head and took another sip of his pop, maybe to cover the pink tinge in his cheeks. *Interesting.*

Heath grinned. "Lemme guess—our boy Noel here couldn't let his girlfriend have all the glory."

"You know it," Derrick replied with a tip of his half-empty glass of cola. "Noel wasn't much of a cook, but he wasn't about to let that stop him. He figured the spice category didn't require much talent. It only had to be the spiciest thing there. So he conscripted our dad to help him source the hottest chili peppers he could find. Well, our dad is always happy to experiment for science, so he had a friend who runs an African grocery store in Calgary order and ship up some habanero peppers. The guy sent a pound of 'em."

"A pound?" Heath chortled in delighted anticipation. "A Mexican friend of mine dared me to try one of those once. I took the tiniest nibble, and my mouth was on fire for a week!"

Heath glanced at Noel, who snorted and took another sip of eggnog. He hoped he looked nonchalant.

"A nibble, eh?" Jared said with a wide grin. "I'm guessing Noel used a little more than that."

"Of course he did." Derrick laughed, then raised a sardonic brow at Noel. "Hey, bro, you wanna tell them how many habaneros you threw in your pot of chili?"

"Six," Noel deadpanned.

"*Six?*" Heath guffawed.

Derrick burst out in uncontrolled laughter. Between snorts, he added, "Plus . . . a handful of jalapeños . . . and . . . a metric tonne of Tabasco sauce."

The other guys laughed, glancing back and forth between Derrick and Noel.

Noel shrugged. "What can I say? I like to win." He allowed himself to crack a smile. "Couldn't touch my face for three days after chopping up those peppers for fear of making myself go blind."

Caleb glanced at Heath and Jared, finally chuckling. "I told him he was lucky that chili didn't eat through the pot."

"I'll say," Derrick added. "That chili was the hottest thing I've tasted in my life." He shook his head, trying to get a grip on his mirth and wiping away a few tears that had formed at the corner of his eyes.

"I'll tell Iya-agba you said that," Noel said, thinking of how their Nigerian grandmother—who prided herself on her spicy cooking—would react.

"Your funeral," Derrick replied, still laughing. "Anyway," he said after regaining some control, "Maddie is almost as competitive as Noel, and Noel knew it, so he didn't tell her he was planning to enter the competition. You should have seen her face when Noel showed up the day of the cook-off with his own entry."

Luke smiled and nodded knowingly. "She must've been furious."

Noel glanced at the younger Anderson brother, wondering at the implied familiarity in his comments about Maddie. The Anderson family had moved to Peace Crossing right before Heath's grade twelve year, which was when Heath had become friends with Noel and Caleb. Luke had been in Derrick's grade, a couple years behind them. Since graduating, Luke had been working at the local pulp and paper mill while doing drywall plaster art on the side—Butler Bros had worked with him a few times—and Maddie had gone from helping out at Pearl's Petals to practically running the place. Had Luke and Maddie become friends in the meantime? Or maybe even something more? Could easily be. In a town this small, it was more surprising when people *didn't* know each other.

He wondered if he should give Luke fair warning of the type of person she was. Then he decided he'd be better off keeping his nose in his own business. Despite being laid up most of the time, he had plenty going on with his "Secret Santa project," as Reuben had called it. And the longer the project went on, the more he found himself enjoying it. Even if Stephanie's response when she figured it out yesterday had been less than warm.

His gut tightened. Despite knowing he should stay away from Stephanie and her infuriatingly adorable temper, he was having a harder and harder time finding the willpower to keep his distance. He hadn't yet gotten up the nerve to examine why.

"*Furious* is an understatement," Caleb said, bringing Noel's thoughts back to Derrick's story. "You could almost see steam coming out of Maddie's ears."

"So what happened next?" Jared asked.

Derrick snorted. "Noel's chili won the spice category, and Maddie's—which was amazing, as usual—won the sweet category *and* the entire contest. But that barely mattered. It was Noel's chili everyone kept talking about."

"I think I remember you mentioning this now," Heath said to Noel. "Was that the time you two broke up around spring break and didn't talk to each other for three weeks?"

Noel nodded. "Yep, that's the one." He and Maddie had fought a lot during their turbulent high school relationship, so it was no wonder Heath needed to sort out which break-up this incident had caused. He'd only been witness to the final, most spectacular one—the reason Maddie still glared daggers at Noel whenever they happened to meet. Noel had to admit, his timing could have been better. Like, *not* in the middle of the school gym in front of the whole high school.

Derrick shook his head. "Jenny said you and Maddie were done for sure after that one. But you had one final lap in you yet, hey?"

"For better or for worse," Caleb added with a half-teasing, half-sympathetic grin.

Noel looked up, a smile tugging at the corners of his mouth. "Yeah, well, I never claimed to be the brightest bulb in the box."

The group laughed, but Noel's chest tightened. After the cook-off, Maddie had shouted in his face, dumped her chili in the trash, and stomped off. He'd done the right thing by apologizing to her, but getting back together? That was another story. If he'd just walked away, he could have saved them both a lot of heartache.

Slow learner much? He shook his head, staring at his nearly empty tumbler.

"Are you sorry it turned out the way it did with her?" Derrick asked. His voice had gone from teasing to sympathetic, as though he'd been reading Noel's mind.

"You mean that it ended? Nah," Noel said. "It was probably best for us—and the rest of the world—when we finally broke up for good." He smirked, meeting his brother's gaze. "It was the only way to prevent another world war." Even if a part of his soul still stung because of it.

Heath shook his head and took a swig of beer. "See, this is why it's better not to get so involved with women. Keep it light, keep it fun. Don't let things get too serious, or this is the result."

"Yeah, I tried that for a while too," Noel said, thinking of his years of weekend flings while serving in the army. Those nights flirting with girls at the club and then heading back to base alone had guaranteed he never got his heart broken—but they'd been far from satisfying. "Trust me, brother. It gets old eventually."

Heath's eyes twinkled. "Oh, I doubt spending time with pretty girls is going to get old before I do. If even then," he said. "And there are just so many to spend time with. Like that one." His gaze swivelled to the door, and he gave a low whistle. "Speak of the she-devil. She's grown up fine, hasn't she?"

Noel glanced over his shoulder to see Maddie standing at the door next to a guy he didn't recognize. She was wearing skinny jeans and tall boots beneath her quilted parka and scarf, and it looked like she'd made an extra effort to look nice, with her fiery hair falling down her back in soft curls. No guy with a pulse wouldn't want a woman like that on his arm. She saw him and glanced away, and he turned back to the table.

"Yeah, she has." Noel took another sip of eggnog, hoping he sounded less off-kilter than he felt. It wasn't Maddie he was thinking about now, but a certain grey-eyed brunette with full, smirky lips who'd come to occupy more than her fair share of his waking thoughts. Strictly platonically, of course. For the project.

"Excuse me," Luke said stiffly, his cheeks flushed. "I . . . I think I better get going. There's, uh, something I forgot to do. Glad you could make it up here, bro," he added to Heath. "Should I tell Mom you'll be home for Christmas?"

"Uh, sure," Heath said, looking surprised by his brother's sudden departure. "I'll call her about it."

While Luke made his rushed goodbyes, he kept glancing furtively at Maddie and her date as they were seated, then practically loped toward the restaurant's front door. Noel felt a pang for the guy, certain his hunch about Luke's feelings for Maddie had been correct—though she apparently didn't reciprocate.

Believe me, Luke, it's better this way. Maddie had broken his trust, and his buddy Jackson had gone to jail because of it. He wouldn't wish anyone who would do that on his worst enemy, let alone a decent guy like Luke. He felt sorry for her date.

"I actually better make my exit too," Heath said. "It'll be late by the time I get back to Grande Prairie. But it's been a slice, guys. Glad you could meet me tonight. If you're ever down my way, you'll give me a shout, right?"

"You know it," Noel said.

Heath shrugged into his heavy wool-lined winter jacket. Derrick decided to follow suit, leaving only Noel, Caleb, and Jared at the table.

"How's the Secret Santa thing going, anyway?" Jared asked Noel. "I wondered if you'd keep it up, now that it's not-so-secret and all."

"Yeah, I thought about it," Noel said. "Autumn convinced me otherwise."

Autumn's exact words when he'd talked to her earlier that day were, *You're giving up? I never pegged you for a quitter.*

That had clinched it. He hadn't really wanted to stop anyway, only to not infringe where he wasn't wanted. But Autumn reminded him that he'd promised to do what she'd said, and she wasn't done with Operation Grinchbuster just yet. Now Reuben had encouraged him to continue too. And yesterday at the sleigh ride, Stephanie had been frosty at first, but she'd seemed to warm up to him a bit eventually. She'd even worn the snow pants, despite having guessed they were from him.

The image of her standing in the Andersons' great room, glaring at him with her gorgeous grey eyes afire with indignation, flashed through his mind. She'd been stunning, like a lioness ready to pounce. It had taken all his self-control not to kiss her right then.

Which was the real reason he'd tried to back out of his deal with Autumn. The more time he spent thinking about Stephanie and what he could do to make her fall in love with Christmas, the more he wanted his efforts to be about more than just the holiday.

"You really like her, don't you?" Caleb said with a knowing glance at Jared.

Noel's heart skipped a beat. Caleb had been his best friend since grade school, but right then, Noel wanted to give him a knuckle sandwich. But that's only because Caleb's words had revealed the truth bomb he'd been trying to deny for weeks. Years, really.

The truth was, Noel was in trouble. The kind of trouble he'd been trying to avoid for more than a decade . . . the palm-sweating, heart-palpitating, throw-you-for-a-spin type of trouble. And trouble's name was Stephanie Neufeld.

"Yeah," he said finally. "I guess I do."

Caleb grinned, leaning back against the bench. "Well. It's about time you realized it."

Jared nodded. "We've been wondering when you'd finally admit it to yourself."

Noel drew in a deep breath and ran a hand over his face. Despite all his promises to himself, he'd let himself get tangled up with a girl he'd known deep in his heart he couldn't remain uninterested in. And who seemed to want nothing to do with him, either.

"Oh, boy. I'm in trouble," he admitted aloud, then blew out a long breath. "And I'm committed to this Secret Santa thing. What am I gonna do?"

Jared frowned. "Why wouldn't you just ask her for a date?"

Noel shifted uncomfortably. "We have a, uh, history. More than that, I don't have the best track record. As we already discussed."

Caleb snorted. "High school was a long time ago, Noel. The very fact you're worried about repeating your past mistakes means you probably won't. Weren't you the one encouraging me to take a chance on Delanie not so long ago? And look how that turned out. You don't know how Stephanie will react."

"I'm pretty sure I do," Noel muttered. He explained what happened at the Christmas party and how Stephanie had reacted to him while he was in the hospital. "She hates Christmas, and she hates me."

"But she did kiss you once," Caleb said. "If she didn't care, she wouldn't have been so upset that you ghosted her after that. They say there's a thin line between love and hate."

Noel winced at the reminder of his behaviour.

"And she came on the sleigh ride," Jared pointed out. "Maybe she's not as indifferent as you think, like Reuben said. I still think you should ask her on a date."

Noel thought about it. Then he heard Maddie laugh somewhere behind him, and his gut churned. "I don't know, man. I've been fine on my own up until now. Sometimes I think it would be best if it stays that way."

Jared frowned in confusion.

"Yeah, that's what's going on," Caleb said dryly.

Noel blinked at Caleb. "What are you talking about?"

Caleb kept a hand around his glass, looking as though he were choosing his words carefully. "I don't think you really want to be alone. I think you're afraid."

Noel blinked. "I've never been afraid of anything in my life."

Caleb raised his brows. "If you say so."

A hot ball of rage erupted in Noel's chest, and he straightened, glaring. "What do I have to be afraid of? Answer me that."

Jared sat back, surprised.

Caleb regarded him carefully while sipping his iced tea, then set the glass down. "Letting someone get close to you, maybe? I don't know. But I think *you* do." His brows raised. "Am I wrong?"

"Heck, yeah," Noel growled.

Caleb shrugged. "Okay, then. Sorry. Forget I said anything."

Noel took a steadying breath, clenching his fists beneath the table. He ground his jaw, but then gave Caleb a nod to acknowledge the apology. Caleb didn't have a mean bone in his body. He'd been out of line, but Noel wasn't going to damage a friendship over it.

"We're good, man."

Caleb breathed a sigh, looking relieved. Soon after that, they packed up and went home for the night—Caleb gave Noel a ride, since he lived near Noel's building.

But Caleb's comment wouldn't leave Noel's mind for days, rankling and twisting through the layers of his defences. He finally had to admit that his friend had been right. He *was* afraid—afraid that he'd be the same guy who'd let himself be betrayed by his high school girlfriend. The same young kid who'd sobbed himself to sleep like a baby that night after the dance before swearing never to let himself be vulnerable like that again.

In fact, the more he thought about Caleb's comment, the more Noel realized he was mostly afraid history would repeat itself. Stephanie might be the girl of his dreams, but what if he let her in and she found a way to hurt him, just like Maddie had?

But Stephanie wasn't Maddie. And he wasn't that same stupid kid who'd put his trust in the wrong girl.

He'd show Caleb who was afraid. It was time to stop hiding behind his Santa hat and let Stephanie know how he really felt about her.

Trouble or no, Stephanie Neufeld wouldn't know what hit her.

Chapter Twelve

STEPHANIE PLUNKED HERSELF INTO a plastic chair in the hospital break room, thankful for a few minutes to herself. She'd just cracked open her library book—a cozy mystery she'd had on hold for months—when Kate breezed in, still in her coat and winter accessories, to prepare for her shift.

"Whatcha reading?" Kate tried to catch a glimpse of the cover while she removed her toque, revealing a mess of chestnut curls semi-controlled in a poof at the top of her head. "A mystery? I thought you had enough mystery to keep you busy in real life."

Stephanie blinked at her in confusion. "Pardon?"

"You know," Kate said, "your secret admirer?" She stuffed her toque in her coat sleeve, hung her coat on her locker hook, and draped her scarf over it.

"Oh. That."

Kate made a face. "'Oh, that?' So that's old news now, is it?" She closed her locker and carried her food to the fridge, then slid into the chair across from Stephanie, fluffing the curls in her messy bun to reduce the hat-head flatness. "That must mean you know who it is. So 'fess up. Who's our Prince Charming? Someone tall, dark, and handsome, I hope."

With a sigh, Stephanie closed her novel and set it down. Noel's strong features filled her thoughts—his dark eyes, warm brown skin, and towering muscular frame. *Tall, dark, and handsome doesn't cover the half of it.* Her belly did a little flip, and she pushed the thought aside in annoyance.

"He's not a secret admirer. I think he's just doing it to annoy me, since Christmas isn't really my thing." Noel hadn't exactly made his reasons clear when she'd confronted him, but why else would he persist in his little game? And that had to be what the whole thing was to him—a game. Right?

Kate's eyebrows shot up. "So it *is* a him. Don't leave me in the cold, Steph. I need details! Did you break the poor guy's heart?"

"Hardly." Stephanie rose and pushed in her chair. "I need to get back to the floor. See you down there?" She'd said it to be polite. Her break wasn't over for fifteen more minutes, but she wanted a reason to get out of the conversation.

So when Kate followed her out the door, she kicked herself. Of course. Kate was just starting her shift. Stephanie couldn't even be upset.

"If you don't want to tell me who it is, that's up to you," Kate said, keeping pace with Steph as they made the short trek to the nurse's station. "But I bet I can guess. Is it . . . Jeff?"

Stephanie wrinkled her nose, picturing the raily barista with the coppery man bun and freckles who worked at the coffee shop. "Jeff from Cool Beans? He's, what, six years younger than me?" She couldn't keep a smile from her face at the idea.

Kate laughed. "Well, you're not giving me much to go on. And odder couples have existed."

Stephanie side-stepped to avoid a collision with Justin Ross, who was walking down the hall with his attention on the chart he held.

The doctor glanced up in surprise. "Sorry. Oh, hi, Steph. Kate." He flashed Kate a grin, who gave him an awkward smile back, and then he returned his attention to Stephanie. "There's someone at the desk to see you."

"Thanks," Stephanie murmured, her heart lurching. Was it Noel, making an in-person delivery of today's gift?

Kate must have had the same idea, because she brightened. "Oo, maybe I won't have to keep guessing." She sped her pace to reach the end of the hall—and the view of the nurse's station—faster.

Stephanie's face grew warm. "Wait, Kate," she said, hurrying to catch up. What would she say if Noel was standing there in plain sight? To him, or to Kate?

She hadn't actually seen Noel since the sleigh ride almost a week ago, but he was never far from her thoughts—especially since her collection of gifts kept growing. He still left each package unsigned, but she no longer had any doubt who they were from. And he no longer seemed to be trying to hide it—each accompanying note card was scrawled in his distinctive handwriting. So far, her gifts had included a bestselling mystery novel that looked like it had come from the deals table at Walmart, a box of Christmas tree ornaments shaped like little gnomes in coordinating outfits that she had no idea *what* she was going to do with, a box of her favourite chocolate truffles, and an elegantly painted tin of ginger snaps that she couldn't help but wonder if he'd baked himself.

Almost as diverse as the gift selections were the methods of gift delivery. She'd found them waiting on the hood of her car before work, tucked into her purse after a shift at Cool Beans, and even stashed in her locker in the hospital break room. She never saw him leave the gifts, and she had to admire his resourcefulness—and his strength, given that he was somehow accomplishing all this shopping and delivery with a broken leg.

When she'd confronted Noel at the Andersons', she'd expected the gifts to stop—but she'd underestimated Noel's tenacity. And, in truth, Stephanie had stopped being upset about the gifts days ago. In fact, now that she knew where they were coming from and that the flow seemed unlikely to ebb, she woke up each morning wondering what surprise might come her way today.

I guess I'm learning to enjoy the mystery, she thought, remembering her mother's admonition. Then she blushed harder, her cheeks so warm she thought they must be steaming. Hadn't she told herself there was no way she would fall for Noel Butler?

But when she rounded the corner, hoping to run interference between Kate and Noel, she stopped short, ice slashing through her veins. The barrel-chested older man who stood resting one hand on the tall station countertop, gazing toward the emergency room doors with his back toward her, was definitely not Noel. His thinning hair was more grey than dark brown, and a slight paunch sagged over the waist of his jeans, but he still bore himself like the world had better watch its step if it knew what was good for it. Stephanie hadn't seen him since his disastrous and brief drunken appearance at Autumn's high school graduation, but other than having more wrinkles and less hair, Eddie Bell had hardly changed.

Kate looked uncertainly between the man and Stephanie, a question and a tinge of judgment in her eyes. Steph gave a slight shake of her head, and Kate moved around the desk to a computer station, probably to review patient charts in preparation for her shift—though she kept glancing furtively over her shoulder at Stephanie and her visitor.

Stephanie's heart thundered like a herd of galloping horses, and she drew a long, steadying breath before speaking. "Eddie. What are you doing here?"

Her father glanced up and turned toward her, a guarded expression on his face. "You weren't returning my calls or texts, so I thought I would come by to make sure I had the right number."

"Yes, you had it right." Steph crossed her arms, giving him a cool stare to see whether he understood her implication that she'd been ignoring him.

"Huh."

His return glance was unsurprised, as she suspected it would be. This visit had nothing to do with checking on his information, and everything to do with imposing himself on her, whether she wanted it or not.

The shock of seeing him dissipated in a flash of anger. What right did this man have to come here, to her place of work? To her safe space?

"What do you want, Eddie?" she said in a low voice.

"I want to talk to my daughter," he said stiffly.

Kate glanced up and watched them, looking like she was trying to decide whether she should interfere.

Samantha emerged from one of the curtained examination rooms down the hall and approached the desk, taking in the situation at a glance. "Steph, Room Five needs his vitals checked. Want to take that?"

Eddie's gaze shifted toward the doors. "You're busy, so I'll go. Just call me when you're done work. Since you have the number, apparently. It will only take a few minutes."

His manner was polite, but his imperative tone dripped with the bitter arrogance of the man she remembered. And suddenly, Stephanie was tired of avoiding him. She was tired of wondering when the shoe would drop, tired of scanning for his face, however subconsciously, whenever she went out in public. Whatever Eddie wanted to discuss with her, she wanted to get it over with. And what could he do to her here, really?

"Actually, I have a few minutes left in my break," she said, with a sideways glance at Samantha and Kate. "I'm going outside to talk to my father. Be back in a few minutes." To Eddie, she said, "I just have to get my coat and boots."

The painted wooden picnic table on the hospital lawn was used by staff as often as patients. It sat several paces away from the long, wide, cleared sidewalk between the Emergency Room entrance and the parking lot. In the summer, this table was one of

Stephanie's favourite places to eat lunch. Now, a sheen of frost glittered on its surface, impervious to the midday Peace Country sun that hung low in the pale blue sky. Fortunately, the clumpy ridge of cleared snow lining the sidewalk wasn't that tall, and since the snow on the grass was only a few inches deep, the table seemed the best place to pull her father aside for a few minutes. No way was she going to get into a vehicle with the man, no matter how chilly it was. And the sun's thin rays definitely didn't have enough warmth behind them to thaw the anxiety frosting her heart.

She followed Eddie to the picnic table, picking up each foot and placing it carefully down on the crusty snow. Eddie turned and sat on the edge of the tabletop, which unleashed a creak of protest. The slight difference in his altitude meant she was looking him in the eye.

Steph stopped and stood in the snow a few feet away, glaring at the man she wished she could forget. "So, you've got me here. What's so important?"

Eddie met her gaze with grey eyes that matched the winter sky—eyes much like the ones she saw in her mirror each morning.

"I'm sober now," he said without preamble. "I thought you should know. Just got my eighteen month chip." He pulled a small red plastic disc from his pocket, fingered it for a moment in his palm, then tucked it away again.

Steph nodded, not sure what to say. "Good for you," she ventured at last. *Better late than never, I guess.* "Is that it? You just wanted to tell me you're finally getting your act together?"

He frowned, swiping his hand over his mouth, then drew a breath. "I want to get to know you and Autumn again. To be part of my grandson's life."

Stephanie clenched her gloved fists. "You stay away from Julien," she said, surprising herself with her own vehemence.

"You already ruined our childhoods. You don't have a right to ruin his."

Hurt flashed across Eddie's face, but then his eyes narrowed. "I messed up, Stephanie. But I'm trying to change. To be better. I can't change the past, as much as I wish I could. I want to make amends, to move forward."

"Eighteen months of sobriety can't erase years of pain," Stephanie said, crossing her arms. "And a sobriety chip won't bring Melody back. I'm serious. Leave Autumn, and Julien, and *me* alone. We're doing just fine without you."

Eddie clenched his jaw. "I'm not asking for your forgiveness right now," Eddie said, a hint of desperation in his voice. "But I miss my daughters. I want . . . I want to be part of your lives again."

Stephanie studied him. Could he actually be sincere? Even if he were, did she want him to be part of her life again? Maybe. Probably not. She didn't know. But part of her was annoyed that he didn't bother asking.

Still, the fact that he was here even making an effort was more than she'd ever expected to see in her lifetime. She had to give him credit for that much.

"You can't just waltz in and expect everything to be okay," she said stiffly. "Trust takes time to rebuild."

"I know," he said, glancing away. "I know."

He looked past her, gazing toward the cars driving by on the highway beyond the open, snowy field next to the hospital complex. He looked older than he had moments ago. Smaller, as though some of the vitality that used to infuse his every movement had leaked out of him. Maybe the years had taken more out of Eddie than Stephanie had realized.

"I brought something for you." Reaching into the inside pocket of his jacket, Eddie withdrew a small jewellery box and held it out to her.

She frowned at the oblong forest green box. It wasn't new—the edges were slightly worn, and the jeweller's logo looked vintage. There was something familiar about it. "I don't want anything from you."

"Melody would have wanted you to have it," he said, his hand still outstretched. "I should have given it to you years ago, but I couldn't bear to part with it. Just take it. Please." His voice cracked on the last word, and he swiped at the corner of his eye with his thumb.

Stephanie blinked, taken aback. She'd never seen Eddie like this—never seen beneath the tough facade he'd always worn like armour. Slowly, she took the box from him, curiosity getting the better of her. When she opened it, she found a child's silver nameplate bracelet engraved with Melody's name in a fancy script.

That's why the box was familiar. She had a bracelet just like this in her jewellery box at home with her own name on it, and she was sure Autumn had kept hers.

She remembered receiving these, two years before Melody died. Eddie hadn't been good at gift wrapping, and when he'd pulled out the plain green jewellery boxes without any bows or wrapping that Christmas morning, even Angelica had looked confused. He'd sheepishly explained they were a last-minute addition to the Christmas gifts, and then told the girls to wait to open them at the same time before handing one to each of them. When they'd seen the bracelets, Autumn and Melody had been exuberant in their thanks. Melody had gleefully thrown her arms around Eddie's neck and run to their mother for help putting hers on, while Autumn had jumped up and down in excitement. But Stephanie had gazed in wonder at the little silver bracelet with her name on it—an indication that her father had been thinking of her. That he loved her.

She'd eventually outgrown her bracelet, but hadn't ever gotten rid of it. She'd always assumed Melody had been wearing hers when she was buried. Seeing her youngest sister's dainty bracelet sitting on the white satin before her, Stephanie's chest constricted, and her knees started shaking.

"Th . . . thanks," she said. She glanced up at Eddie, unable to say more.

He gave her a long stare, then, with a single nod, he pushed himself off the table, moved around her, and shambled toward his rusting pickup in the parking lot.

On the way, he passed another tall figure, whom Stephanie barely noticed through her blurred vision. She turned and sank onto the picnic tabletop while staring at the bracelet, listening to the pickup's engine roar to life and pull away.

"Stephanie? Are you okay?" came Noel's voice.

She jumped to her feet, ripping her gaze from the bracelet to look up into Noel's concerned face. He stood on the sidewalk, surveying the crest of piled snow and looking like he was about to tackle it, despite his crutches and air boot. A cloud of steamy air surrounded him with every breath.

"Don't come over here," she said with a shaky voice.

He took a step into the drift anyway, and she gave a snort of frustration. Closing the box, she shoved it into her coat pocket and stomped toward the sidewalk.

"Noel Butler, will you just do what's good for you for once?" She grabbed his arm and nudged him backward. He gave her a surprised look, then stepped back onto the cleared sidewalk, and she stepped over the piled snow at the edge of the snowdrift. "Are you trying to break your other leg?"

"Well, at least I'd be in the right place," he said, indicating the hospital with a jerk of his head, but his typical humorous tone was subdued. He searched her face. "Who was that guy?"

At the reminder, the brief surge of energy produced by her annoyance at Noel evaporated, and she started shaking violently. "It was no one," she said, or tried. What came out was more like a squeak, before tears started streaming down her cheeks.

"Hey, it's okay," Noel said. He put both crutches in one hand, balancing his weight gingerly between his two feet. "Do you want a hug?"

She wanted to say no, to flee to the washroom and hide while she cried. Instead, she turned into his open arm and let him press her against his strong shoulder, her tears flowing into the black polyester of the quilted parka he wore. Her traitorous knees wanted to collapse beneath her, and she wrapped her arms around his waist to steady herself with his warmth. She drew several long, deep breaths to slow her racing heart, and the scent of his musky aftershave mixed with the exhaust from the idling vehicles in the parking lot filled her lungs.

After the worst of her emotion passed and she stopped shaking, she pulled back, self-consciously dabbing at her face with her glove to remove any smeared mascara. "Sorry you had to see that."

"I'm not," he said quietly. He reached up and touched her hand to stop her swiping, then pulled off his lined leather work glove and dabbed at her cheeks with his bare thumb. His touch left trails of warmth tingling across her skin. "There. No one will even know."

The unexpectedly tender gesture brought a lump to her throat. She stared up into his warm brown eyes, her heart pounding in her ears. He stared back, a slight smile quirking his lips. Lips she happened to know were particularly good at kissing . . .

"I have to get back to work," she said, hoping she didn't sound as breathless as she felt. She straightened, tugging on her jacket and clearing the lump from her throat. "Are you here for a check-up or something?"

The moment broken, he stepped back. "Actually, I came to see you."

She remembered her earlier conversation with Kate, and her face warmed again. "Oh?" was all she managed.

"Yeah." He grinned down at her. "I came to ask you on a date. But maybe now's not the best time. I can come back later—"

"Yes," she said, then blinked at herself. She never made rash decisions. What had come over her? But she'd committed now—she could ponder the reasons for her quick response later. Still, she didn't need to sound like some desperate schoolgirl. "I mean, sure. That sounds delightful."

Delightful? Yeah, that's loads better. But the gaze he gave her made her knees shake again, and she swallowed the pesky lump that kept trying to resurface.

"Great," he said. "I'd offer to pick you up, but I'm not allowed to drive. Want to pick me up instead? Say, around eight?"

"Tonight?" she squeaked, then cleared her throat. "Um, yes. I can do that."

"Alright, then. Dress warm." He gave her one more lingering look, then turned back toward the parking lot, where she finally noticed the waiting cab.

He took a cab here to ask me on a date?

Then her stomach flip-flopped.

I'm going on a date with Noel!

After watching him all the way to the cab to make sure he didn't slip, she turned and slowly made her way up the sidewalk to the doors. The look on her face as she passed the nurse's station must have been enough to deter any questions, because she didn't get any comments about her unexpected visitors for the rest of the afternoon—except a reassuring squeeze on the arm from Samantha and a single comment from Kate.

"Noel Butler, huh? Could do a lot worse," Kate said before breezing away, smirking.

Apparently, Steph hadn't had as much privacy at the picnic table as she'd thought. And despite her longstanding grudge against the man, she had to agree.

The more she got to know Noel, the more she thought she may have misjudged him. But on the other hand, how could she trust that he wouldn't do what he'd done before and work her emotions up before feeding her heart through the garbage disposal?

But Noel wasn't the only concern badgering her. Every time she thought about her father's sudden reappearance and the box she'd left in her coat pocket, her chest constricted, and she pushed the thought away. Pondering what Eddie's true intentions might be would only work her into a spiral that she couldn't afford while on shift. She would call Autumn to talk about it later, and the two of them could come up with a plan.

Except later, she would be on a date with Noel. The thought made her heart race all over again. She'd never met another man who made her feel so safe and scared at the same time.

Still, why couldn't she get over the feeling that agreeing to this date was the stupidest thing she'd ever done?

Chapter Thirteen

Stephanie eased her CR-V up to the curb in front of Noel's apartment building and put it into park. She was just about to text him that she was there when he swung himself out of the front door and down the freshly cleared sidewalk toward her. Her throat constricted. Part of her still couldn't believe she was going on a date with Noel, of all people. The other part couldn't wait to see what might come of it.

She hopped out and rushed around to the passenger side of the compact SUV, opening it just in time for Noel to reach her.

"Hey, Steph." He surveyed the open door. "I'm pretty sure I should be opening doors for you."

"Yeah, well, chivalry gets a bit wonky for the injured." She stepped out of the way, took his crutches and tucked them into the second row while he manoeuvred himself into the passenger seat. By the time she'd finished, he'd already closed his door and was putting on his seat belt, so she wasted no time getting herself back behind the wheel.

She fastened her own seat belt and turned to her passenger. "So, before we get going, I need to get one thing straight."

"What's that?"

"This *is* an official date, right?"

He gave her a concerned, quizzical look, but when she smirked, he chuckled.

"Let me get *this* straight—when I take a girl on a date, I make sure she's not confused about my intentions. But I'll let you decide. At the end of the night, you can tell me if I've gone to enough trouble for this to be considered date-worthy. I'm sure I've got a comment card here somewhere."

He smacked at his pockets as though looking for the alleged card, but there was an intensity in his teasing gaze that made her cheeks warm. She laughed nervously and glanced away.

What does *he have planned? Darn my moment of weakness earlier!* That afternoon, she'd almost texted him to cancel half a dozen times. While she'd been getting ready for the date, she'd called Autumn in a panic, hoping her sister could talk some sense into her so she could get the nerve to send that cancellation text. Instead, Autumn had encouraged her to take the chance.

If you wanted to cancel, you would have done it by now. And you wouldn't have said yes if some part of you wasn't curious, she'd said with infuriating logic. *If you go and it bombs, at least you'll know.*

Now, Steph cleared the lump of nerves and anticipation that had climbed into her throat and placed her hands on the wheel. "So, where to?"

Noel turned to face her, a mischievous smile on his face. "In an effort to maintain some of the mystery and surprise of this date, I'm going to give you directions instead of destinations. I hope you're cool with that."

Stephanie's gut tensed a little, but she took a deep breath and intentionally relaxed. If she didn't trust him, she wouldn't have come. The realization that she *did* trust him—to a certain extent—startled her a little. "O-kaaay. Which direction, then?"

He gave her general instructions that would take them through the neighbourhood he lived in toward River Road, and she nodded and pulled away from the curb.

The neighbourhood had been built in the sixties and seventies, before cookie-cutter developments became the norm, so each house reflected both the era and the unique aesthetic of the original owners and builders. Many of the houses had been renovated or refinished to reflect more modern tastes over time, but the neighbourhood, like several others in Peace Crossing, was a diverse array of squat bungalows finished in everything from wood to vinyl to rock-and-plaster siding. Many of the houses boasted strings of colourful lights that had been mounted along the eaves troughs or wrapped around the mature spruce trees in their front yards. A few of the yards even had displays that would rival the Griswolds', complete with lights pulsing to the rhythm of jaunty electronically produced carols. In years past, such gaudiness would have made her roll her eyes, but she found herself enjoying the pretty lights and even smiling at some of the more comical decorations.

"I see Gary Harris has his decorations out already," Noel said, pointing out one house with a life-size nativity set up in the front yard. "Bet Trevor's excited about that."

Steph thought of the sweet-natured teenager she'd met on the sleigh ride and smiled. The boy's enthusiasm for Christmas had almost made her envious. She shook her head before her thoughts wandered along the familiar dark road of her grief. *Not tonight.* "I bet you're right. In fact, I remember he said he'd helped his dad set it up a couple weeks ago already."

Noel grinned. "That tracks. And check out that little dog statue—that's all Trevor, that one. Turn left here."

Steph gave him side-eye. It was the third time they'd turned onto River Road on what had already been a fairly circuitous route. "Are you sure you know where we're going?"

He gave her a reproachful look. "You don't trust me?"

She hesitated, then shook her head. "Okay," she said, relenting and turning the vehicle. Instead of being anxious, though, she found herself relaxing into the drive. This man was full of surprises. He must have a reason for this drawn-out and convoluted journey.

Before long, they'd travelled through the entire north end of town, and he was directing her across the bridge toward the west side.

"I see you brought your snow pants." He gestured toward the back seat, where his crutches lay atop the quilted pants.

"You said dress warm."

He chuckled again. "Yes, I did. You never know, you might be glad you've got 'em. Turn left at the lights."

She frowned. The only restaurant on that side of the highway was a motel diner. There was also an industrial park and several other large neighbourhoods, but they were soon running out of town to travel through, and, with it, possible restaurant-like destinations. Where were they going? Her stomach rumbled, but not loudly enough to drown the anticipation in her chest. After the significant effort and creativity Noel had gone to in his Secret Santa efforts, what had he devised for their first official date?

Noel directed her along another meandering route that took them the long way through one of the newer, fancier neighbourhoods. These homes also boasted impressive holiday light displays—many of them even brighter and fuller than the ones they'd seen on the other side of the river.

Her gut grumbled again. Loudly.

He glanced over. "Is your stomach not enjoying the Christmas light grand tour?"

"Is that what this is?" She frowned. "Here I thought this was some mystery route toward supper, just to make this very small town seem more exciting."

"Who says it's not? It can be both-and. I thought you might enjoy a little trek to admire the beautiful lights before dinner. Something tells me you don't do this much on your own."

She glanced at him, surprised. She *had* been enjoying the displays, though not as vocally as Noel had. But the fact he'd planned this for her to give her a few minutes of joy made her throat tighten.

"You really love Christmas, don't you?" she observed more than asked.

He laughed. "You could say that. December twenty-fifth is also my birthday, so I have a lot of fun memories around this time of year."

She blinked. She should have realized about the birth-day-slash-Christmas connection, with his name being Noel and all. It seemed too specific of a name choice to be insignificant. "You didn't feel like your special day got a little lost in the Christmas festivities?"

Noel shrugged. "Yeah, sure, maybe once in a while. But my parents always went the extra mile to make sure I felt celebrated, giving me a separate birthday party sometime that week. And, hey, Jesus is my birthday buddy. How cool is that?"

She smiled wanly. "You know they say he wasn't born on December twenty-fifth, right?"

"Yeah, I know." He waved a dismissive hand. "But I wasn't born on December twenty-sixth, and that's usually when my party was. The important thing is remembering to celebrate, not the actual day. Don't you think?"

Stephanie squirmed. She wanted to tell him that she hadn't celebrated Christmas at all for almost sixteen years, but she didn't want to get into the reasons why when they'd barely broken the ice. Besides, if she told him that, he may feel bad for all the Christmas-related efforts he'd been making. She wasn't prepared to send the evening off to such a rocky start.

Instead, she cleared the lump of emotion from her throat. "Well, thank you for the thoughtful, and economical, pre-dinner entertainment. You went all out on that one, hey? She said, making notes on the comment card . . ."

He laughed, but his attention was focused down the street a short ways. "Okay, you can park in front of that place." He pointed at a large family dwelling that was still under construction. The house looked like it had reached lock-up, but plastic sheets covered the outer walls, the yard was a lumpy mess of snow-covered clay, and the windows were completely dark.

"Here? Why?"

"My brother forgot something here today, and he wanted me to pick it up for him."

"Derrick sent his gimpy brother to a job site to run an errand for him?" She couldn't keep the annoyance out of her voice. Peace Crossing wasn't that big. It would have been much smarter for Derrick to run this errand himself than to risk his brother breaking his other leg on an uneven construction site just to pick up a forgotten item.

"Yeah, but it's no problem." Noel had already removed his seat belt and was getting out of the vehicle. "Don't suppose you'd mind coming in? Just in case."

Stephanie narrowed her eyes. Something about this felt off, but she couldn't put her finger on it. This was the guy who'd been at a Christmas market only a week after breaking his leg, and on a sleigh ride a week after that. While she had definite opinions about the precautions he ought to have been taking all along, the truth was, Noel probably didn't know what a precaution was. What was he up to?

"Okay," she said slowly, prickles of nerves dancing along her collarbones.

She got out of the vehicle and waited next to the curb while he retrieved his crutches from the back seat. The neighbourhood was quiet. Several other largish new houses towered along the street, like lit guardians hunkering between the empty lots. There was another house under construction at the far end of the cul-de-sac. In the distance, a generator hummed.

Steph eyed the front of the house. While most buildings she'd seen at this stage were still being accessed by stepladders, this one had what looked like a temporary wooden stoop beneath the front door. It included a rail made of two-by-fours and several low, broad steps. And she'd been wrong about the house being completely dark—somewhere deep in its heart, a small yellow light glowed.

Noel joined her. She cast a doubtful glance toward his crutches, but bit her tongue on the comment she wanted to make, covering her misgiving by turning and pointing her car remote at the vehicle while she locked it.

"Ready?" He grinned at her.

"I expect so. Unless we're attacked by feral reindeer. I left my pepper spray in my other coat."

He chuckled. "I'd hate to see the feral reindeer who'd dare cross you."

He gave her a flirtatious grin, but she remembered the telling-off she'd given him at the hospital and her cheeks flushed with warmth. Pushing her hair out of her eyes to cover her discomfort, she gestured toward the house. "I'll follow behind to keep an eye on you."

Noel picked his way along a fairly well-trodden path through the yard toward the stoop, and Steph followed along, keeping an eye on his progress as well as her own. *Thank goodness I'm not in heels.*

Noel unlocked the door and let them in, and she followed him into the dimly lit interior. As her eyes adjusted, she picked out the angles of a large entrance. Tall empty nooks that would eventually be closets ran along one wall. Another wall featured a door she presumed led to the garage. Between the two doors, several low steps led into the main part of the house. It was warmer than she would have expected for a work site in mid-December.

"Don't worry about your boots," Noel said.

She glanced at him in confusion, trying to read his expression in the low light. "Why would I? You're only grabbing something and we're leaving, right? I'll just wait here."

"Oh. Um, well . . ."

Steph caught movement beyond the archway at the top of the stairs and froze, her heart rate spiking. She caught Noel's arm and whispered, "Is anyone else here right now?"

Noel saw her expression and followed her gaze. When nothing else moved, he said, "Wait here," and swung himself toward the stairs.

Steph wondered what he could do if there actually *was* an intruder in the house. Then again, she didn't think most guys would want to tussle with Noel even now, when he had his leg in an air boot and was using crutches. The man emanated strength as though it were part of his DNA. Her heart stuttered at the memory of his arm around her shoulder that afternoon, and she swallowed, glad he couldn't see her blush this time.

Noel got to the top of the stairs and peered around a corner, then relaxed.

"It's fine," he said to her. "You can—"

A knock on the door behind her cut him off. Steph nearly jumped to the vaulted ceiling.

" . . . get the door, if you don't mind," Noel finished, as though that's what he'd meant to say all along.

"Excuse me?" Steph said, trying to calm her racing pulse.

"The door. That would be our supper." Noel jerked his chin in the direction of the entrance.

She blinked at him, then turned and slowly opened the door. Sure enough, a young guy with shaggy hair and acne patterning his face stood there with a delivery service bag in his arms. When he saw her, he asked, "Delivery for Noel?"

Recovering herself, she nodded. "Uh, yeah. I'll take that."

He reached in his thermal pack and fished out several white plastic bags holding stacked cardboard food containers, handing them to her one at a time. The tantalizing smell of Chinese takeout met her nose.

"I don't have a tip," she said, feeling awkward.

"Already got it, thanks. Prepaid." The driver held up his smartphone by way of explanation. "Have a nice night," he said before walking away.

Steph turned to face Noel, still holding the bags by the tied handles, and nudged the door closed with her foot.

"So that's what you meant about the boots, huh," she said, realization dawning. "We're eating here." She couldn't keep the skepticism from her voice.

He chuckled. "Don't rate the date just yet, m'lady. Won't you join me in the dining room?"

Curious, she made her way up the short run of steps. Noel flipped a switch on the wall beside him.

When she reached the top stair, she gasped. She'd been inside houses under construction before. Never in a million years would she have expected this.

The house had an open floor plan, with a vaulted post-and-beam ceiling and big windows and patio doors in the far wall overlooking a large back yard. The top rung of a ladder that had been set up outside could be seen through one glass door. A small, snowy meadow lay beyond the unfenced yard, and beyond that, stands of barren poplar trees stood vigil like dark sentinels in the moonlight as they climbed the rolling hills of the Peace River Valley.

But it was the view inside the house that stunned her. The walls had been covered by drywall, but were otherwise unfinished. Despite the rustic setting, the room glowed with light and elegance—something that had obviously taken someone a great deal of effort.

In the centre of the plywood floor where the dining area would eventually be sat a small square collapsible table that had been covered with a white linen tablecloth, with two folding chairs on either side. In front of the chairs lay two understated place settings. A lovely Christmas-themed centrepiece of a large glass canister filled with twinkle lights, evergreen twigs, and glittery golden baubles sat between the plates.

Above the table hung an enormous golden paper pompom that had been filled with more lights to create a diffuse glow, and strings of white lights draped from the room's centre above the table to the outer edges in a sparkling canopy. In a puddle of white tulle along the back wall sat a small white artificial Christmas tree. It had been strung with more lights and gold ribbon and hung with burgundy ornaments. A glowing white star on top finished the look. Just then, soft Christmas pop songs began to play, and Steph turned in time to see Noel leave his phone—the source of the music—on the unfinished plywood top of a kitchen island.

"You . . . you did all of this in an afternoon? By yourself?"

Noel guffawed. "I'd like to say I did, but no. Santa's got helpers, and so do I." He raised his voice and called down the hallway. "You guys can come out."

Stephanie spun to see Delanie, Autumn, and little Emma creep out of the dark hallway next to some stairs. Emma was grinning so wide, it looked like her face might break, and she bounced on her toes in barely contained excitement. The other two wore equally pleased expressions, if not quite as exuberant. Derrick followed behind, his hands on his hips, looking embarrassed and a little pleased. A hammer and a tape measure hung from his leather work belt, and bits of sawdust stuck to his dense black curls.

"Hi, Steph," Delanie said with a wave. Her grin was almost as big as her soon-to-be step-daughter's.

"Hi." Steph took in the people, the decorations, the place settings, the tree, her chest light. "Wow. You guys outdid yourselves."

"Barely got that stoop done in time," Derrick muttered. "You owe me big time, bro."

"Yeah, yeah. Add it to my tab," Noel said.

In retrospect, Stephanie had noticed the distinct smell of fresh-cut lumber out on the temporary stoop, and the wood had seemed remarkably pristine for a job site. Now she knew why.

"Um, do you need anything else, Noel?" Autumn asked.

He glanced around, then at the bags Steph still held. "Nope, I think we can take it from here. Thanks so much, ladies. And Derrick. I'll leave five stars on Yelp later."

"You're all about the reviews tonight, aren't you?" Steph said.

He rolled his eyes and grinned sheepishly.

Emma giggled as the helpers made their way to the back patio doors and put on their shoes, which had been tucked behind the tulle swathing the base of the tree. Autumn grinned surreptitiously, and Steph pinned her sister with a glare that promised they would be discussing this later. *No wonder she wanted me to come.*

"We can take the front door now, right?" Delanie asked Derrick. "Not that that skyscraper of a ladder out back wasn't fun, but . . ." She gave a dramatic grimace that revealed her opinion of climbing down that way.

Derrick responded in the affirmative, and the four of them moved past Steph and Noel toward the stairs. They were out the door almost before Steph could blink.

Steph placed the takeout bags on the island and turned to face her date, her hands on her hips.

"I'll give you this . . . You certainly know how to make a girl speechless."

Noel smiled, and she couldn't look away from his mesmerizing eyes.

"Give me time. I'm just getting started."

His gaze fell to her lips for a long moment before he turned toward the island to unpack their food. When he looked away, she felt like she'd just remembered how to breathe.

They piled their plates with Chinese food and fell into easy banter reminiscent of the old days at Cool Beans, but she could barely eat because of the hoard of butterflies that had flared to life in her stomach. Noel had been right—when he planned a date, he went all-out. She felt moved, and amazed, and flattered, and cautious, all at once. And, for the first time, she could hardly wait to see what else this man had in store.

Chapter Fourteen

Noel leaned back in the padded folding chair, his belly satisfied, his curiosity anything but. He felt as though he could spend a lifetime unwrapping the mysteries of the woman across the table from him and still have more to discover. As they'd chatted and ate, he'd sensed her reserve melting, revealing more and more of the thoughtful, clever, and warm woman he'd been drawn to all those years ago—but a chilly veneer remained like a film of ice on a pond in spring, and he could hardly blame her. There was an elephant in this room, and he knew he'd have to address it before they could move past it, where he hoped it would stay.

He was about to open his mouth to bring up that fateful night when she spoke first.

"So who owns this place?" Stephanie asked, looking around the unfinished room.

"It's a spec house we're building." Noel peered up at the wood-finished ceiling that hinted at the splendour to come. "We're creating it to showcase ideas to potential clients."

"*We* meaning 'Butler Brothers Construction', I assume. Does that mean you own it?" Steph asked.

"I guess it does, in a way." Noel glanced around at the beautiful floor plan he'd hashed out with Derrick and Heath Anderson. Heath's brother, Luke, was slated to come in to work his plaster art magic on the walls and ceiling the following week. But to Noel, what made the house special were the details that most people wouldn't even notice. Like the discreetly placed outlets that would be hidden when the room was in use, or the many cubbies and closets that had been inspired by childhood memories of his mother's endless woes trying to find storage space. Touches like these would create an effortlessly uncluttered, cozy home. Eventually. "It'll look a lot better when it's finished, of course."

She dabbed her mouth with a paper napkin, then took a sip of sparkling water from her plastic tumbler as she looked around. "I'm sure it will be gorgeous. The bones are already here. I love how the living spaces flow together so intuitively. And . . . is that a storage nook hidden in that end wall? Wow, that's so clever. No one will even know it's there."

He snorted, both surprised and pleased. "You've got a good eye."

"Observing things is a major part of my job." She smiled, and her eyes sparkled in the gentle glow of the Christmas lights as she looked around the room. "This is really beautiful," she said. "I can't believe you went to so much trouble just for a first date."

"Well, I may have felt I had a bit of ground to make up," Noel said, his chest tightening as he saw his opportunity. "The truth is . . ." His throat closed on the words he wanted to admit.

Stephanie straightened, watching him with interest. "Yes?" she prompted.

The memory of her in his arms beneath the mistletoe hung between them. He knew he owed her an apology for the unintentional hurt he'd caused, but he still debated how much he was ready to share. The longer he hesitated, the darker her expression got.

Say something, man. Nothing risked, nothing gained.

"You know it's been exactly four years today since the night we last, er, danced?" he blurted.

Stephanie blinked. "No, that hadn't occurred to me. I can't believe you know the exact date."

He always knew exactly how many days it had been since that night. The chip in his pocket kept him honest that way. "The truth is," he said again, "there's been hardly a day in the past four years I haven't thought of you."

Her eyes widened. "You had an interesting way of showing it."

He leaned forward, taking her smooth hand in his calloused one.

"I know. I . . . had my reasons for keeping my distance. But as I've been getting to know you better these past few weeks—even if you didn't know it was me until recently—I've realized that those reasons weren't as important as I'd believed. I decided it was worth the risk to see if there could be something between us." He stroked her knuckles with his thumb. "I did feel something under the mistletoe that night. I thought you should know."

She searched his face. "What reasons?"

He glanced down at their clasped hands, revelling in the warmth of her fingers between his. She hadn't taken her hand away, and that had to mean something. He drew a breath.

"Before I tell you, I think you should know that Autumn told me about what happened to your sister Melody. And about your dad."

She blinked and glanced away.

"That was him at the hospital this afternoon, wasn't it?" Noel asked.

Steph hesitated, then nodded.

"I thought so," Noel said. "I could see the resemblance."

Her fingers stiffened, and he increased his pressure on her hand in a silent request for her not to pull away.

"I'm sorry," he added. "For your sister, and for bringing that up. But I didn't want to feel I had an advantage you didn't know about. The last time I got serious about a girl, there were far too many secrets between us. It was our secrets that destroyed us in the end."

Her hand relaxed in his again. "How long ago was that?"

"About eleven years."

She straightened, but there was a steady reassurance in her touch. "Madeleine Kennedy was your last serious relationship?"

He nodded. "After how that ended, I didn't think I'd ever trust a girl again. I never let anyone get too close, but it stoked my ego to think that they wanted to. When I was in the army, I'd go to the club on the weekend and dance the night away with the prettiest girls in the room, then go back to base and never speak to them again." He swallowed. "Sound familiar?"

"Unfortunately," she said. Then she frowned. "But didn't *you* break up with Maddie? At the Grade Twelve Harvest Dance?"

Noel's shoulders tightened at the memory, and his jaw worked. "Technically, yes. And I know she bad-mouthed me to everyone about it. But trust me, things weren't what she made them out to be."

Steph's eyes filled with questions, but she didn't press. Instead, her gaze fell to the sparkling centrepiece and landed on their joined hands. "You're quite the mystery, Noel. You were a rebel in high school, a heart-breaker in the army, and since you've returned to Peace Crossing, you've been the town's Most Eligible Bachelor, and seemingly oblivious to the fact. So, what changed?" She met his gaze. "Why did you come home, start a business, and stop tromping on all the girls' hearts?"

Other than yours, you mean? But Noel didn't need to add that part. He could see it in her tight lips, in the challenge of her arched brow.

His heart raced, and he stared into her captivating grey eyes, sparkling with reflected glints of light. He hadn't been this close to any woman since that night at the party all those years ago, and he wanted to protect this moment, to protect her. Could he tell her all of it? How he'd been thunderstruck by her that night in a way he'd never felt before, not even with Maddie? That landing upside-down in a ditch with his sister in the passenger seat later that same night had shown him he needed to clean himself up before he'd ever be able to be with anyone? That her kiss had set something alive in him he hadn't been able to smother, not in four years of trying?

Her kiss . . .

He leaned in, finally succumbing to the pull that had been drawing him toward her all night, then hesitated, close enough to feel her breath on his face. He'd been the one to initiate their last kiss, and she'd been hurt by it. He didn't want to make that mistake again.

But she closed the connection, and they shared breath and space in a circle of light for several moments. The spark between them was every bit as electrifying as he remembered, maybe more. He wanted to make this moment last, to draw her closer . . .

She pulled back and looked away, covering her lips. Noel frowned, his gut pinching with disappointment.

"Too soon?"

She shook her head, still avoiding his gaze. "I'm just . . . I don't know what to make of you. And you didn't answer my question." She met his gaze now, her eyes guarded, and pulled her hand from his.

"Fair." Noel watched her fidget with her cutlery while he mulled over how to answer her—how to tell her what had changed without scaring her away. "When I came home from the army, I was tired. Tired of the partying, tired of the endless flirtations that left me feeling empty. I realized I didn't want that bachelor lifestyle anymore." He met her gaze again. "I wanted something real. Something that mattered. So I came back here to start fresh, to build a life I could be proud of."

He leaned forward, willing her to understand. "And then at the party, when we got caught under the mistletoe . . . I felt a spark with you that I haven't felt in a very long time. It scared me, to be honest. But it also woke me up. Made me realize I didn't want to keep wasting time on meaningless flings."

"So that's what I was supposed to be? A meaningless fling?" She crossed her arms, glaring at him.

"At the time, yes. But I'm not that guy anymore," Noel said.

She let her arms drop, the tension draining from her face to be replaced by puzzlement. "I can see that. Now you're the guy who volunteers to lead the youth group, takes troubled teens under his wing, and spends exorbitant amounts of energy playing Secret Santa for the girl he once ghosted while he's recovering from a broken leg. When you have a moment of repentance, you go all in, don't you?"

He smirked. "I guess I do. But you know, part of me has always wanted to be this guy. I just lost my way. After Maddie, and Jackson . . ."

"Jackson?"

"Hmm. Yeah." He thought of why Jackson ended up mouldering in jail and decided he wasn't ready to share that story yet. "Let's just say he's the reason I have a soft spot for kids like Ryker." He leaned back in his chair and sighed, glad for an excuse to change the subject. "Speaking of Ryker, I wish I could do more for him. That kid is in a tough spot right now, but I think he's got a real shot, you know? He just made a mistake."

"Oh?" Steph raised a brow, inviting an explanation. "The kind of mistake that his foster family didn't abide, I take it."

"You could say that. They don't allow illicit substances in their house, understandably. And Ryker broke the rules."

"Hmm. I have a similar rule in my house. No drinking, period."

Noel's shoulders tensed. That explained why she hadn't complained about the lack of wine. Should make it easy to avoid temptation around her, though. "Good to know."

"So what happened with Ryker?" she prompted.

"His foster family found some vaping supplies in his stuff. They gave him another chance, but the next time, it was drugs of some kind. Jared couldn't give me many details. I only know Ryker and his sister have been through a lot." He hesitated. "I, uh, understand the temptation to numb pain with substances. But I also know that the right person intervening at the right moment can totally change someone's life."

Her expression was soft, inviting. "And you think you can do that for Ryker?"

Noel thought about it, about how unlikely someone with his own chequered history could fill that role. "I don't think I should aspire to changing his life. I'd settle for helping him connect with the people who can. Like Jared. The kid has no idea how lucky he is to have a guy like that in his life."

"I'd say Jared was a good start," Steph agreed, "but you're no slouch, yourself." Her expression grew thoughtful. "Ryker seems to appreciate cool clothes and crafty things. Is he into any hobbies?"

"Not that I know of," Noel said, searching his memory. "His sister is in my mom's hand bell choir, but I've never seen Ryker excited about much except vintage fashion and spending time with his friends. Somewhat typical teenager stuff." Then he remembered something. "Wait. Ryleigh once mentioned a birthday party Ryker planned for them when they were fourteen, while they were still living with their mom's ex."

Noel ground his teeth, remembering the reason the twins were no longer with the boyfriend who'd taken over their care after the overdose that killed their mom. Fortunately, Ryker had had enough gumption to report his abuse to the police. It's also what landed the Dyck twins in the foster care system.

"Ryker planned their own birthday party?"

"Their guardian was a real piece of work. I doubt he went out of his way to do anything special for those kids, ever. But you've seen Ryker with his sister. He probably did it to make her feel special and loved."

Stephanie nodded in understanding, a shadow flitting across her eyes.

"Anyway, according to Ryleigh, Ryker went all out. Made decorations and cake and even got one of their neighbours to pick up some balloons and streamers and host them in their back yard."

"Sounds like Ryker has a flair for party planning and making things with his hands."

"And for getting on people's good sides." Noel chuckled. "Now, if only we could find a way to funnel all those talents into something that helps him feel accepted by kids who won't pressure him to make bad life choices. Any ideas?"

She thought about it. "Not yet. But I'll let you know if I come up with one. You're not the only one who would really love to see Ryker and Ryleigh get a better deal than the one they were handed. We all need a little help sometimes, and they could use a *lot*."

"Thanks. I appreciate that." His heart warmed that she'd taken an interest in the same teens he'd been trying to help. Like they were on the same team. It was a nice feeling.

She looked at him for a long moment, her expression unreadable, but something about it pulled at his gut. Then she stood and walked over to the window, gazing out at the moonlit landscape beyond.

"Is something bothering you?" he asked.

She turned to face him, nervously pushing her hair off her forehead. "I was just wondering something, but I'm not sure . . ."

"It's okay," he said calmly. "You can ask me anything."

She looked as though she were thinking that over. Finally, she nodded. "It's been four years since that Christmas party," she said hesitantly. "Why did you keep your distance so long?"

Noel couldn't help notice the way the moonlight hit her dark curls and limned her face in light—a face whose guarded expression didn't quite hide the plaintive vulnerability behind it. The more he learned about this woman, the more he wanted to protect that vulnerability that she so rarely allowed anyone to see.

He picked up his crutches from the floor behind him and heaved himself to his feet, then advanced toward her, never releasing her gaze. The closer he got, the wider her eyes became, and he saw both fear and anticipation on her face—the same emotions coursing through his veins.

When he stood only inches away, he leaned his crutches against the wall, balancing on his good leg with a little support from the air boot. Then he clasped her hands in his and held them against his chest. Their faces were inches apart.

"Because I knew that once I got close to you, I'd never want to let you go again."

"Like now?" she said, her voice breathy, her eyes glistening.

He smiled, certain she could hear his thundering heart.

"Exactly like now." He looked in her eyes for a long moment. "Stephanie, can you forgive me for hurting you the way I did?"

She searched his gaze, and he held his breath. What if, despite the progress they'd been making, she said no?

Then her face broke into a smile. "I thought you'd never ask."

She tilted her chin up to his, her invitation clear, and their lips met—but, once again, she broke the kiss after a few seconds, and his heart stuttered.

"I just thought of something." Her broad smile allayed his concern.

"What's that?" he said, her hands still clasped in his.

"When I was in high school, my biology teacher suggested I get involved with the candy striping program at the hospital. It was incredibly rewarding to volunteer there, and that's why I eventually chose to get into nursing. What if you were able to help Ryker find something like that? A way of giving back and helping others to help him feel valuable *and* keep him out of trouble?"

"Great idea. But I have a request."

"What's that?"

"Can we talk about it later?" He grinned.

She smiled. "Absolutely."

This time when their lips met, she didn't pull away. And even with his eyes closed, Noel saw only light. Stephanie's light.

This time, he was done keeping his distance from Stephanie Neufeld. No matter what.

Chapter Fifteen

S TEPHANIE STOOD IN FRONT of the coffee counter at Cool Beans, waiting for Jeff to finish making her drink. Her phone buzzed in her pocket. She pulled it out and glanced at the text from Noel—a reply to the question she'd sent earlier that day about whether he'd figured out what to do about Ryker. The GIF of a sleuth being sneaky and waggling his eyebrows made her giggle.

I might have something up my sleeve. You like surprises, right?

Steph snorted, then replied, *Not as much as you seem to think I do.*

A grinning emoji was his only response. She rolled her eyes.

"Large cinnamon-spice latte?"

Jeff placed a bowl-shaped white porcelain mug on the counter that was full to the brim with froth. A white leaf pattern had been created in the darker coffee foam, and the entire surface had been dusted with cinnamon. Steph had to admire Jeff's artistry.

She returned her phone to her jeans pocket and smiled at the freckled barista. "Thanks, Jeff."

"And here's Autumn's hot chocolate." He put a matching mug on the counter next to hers, this one nearly overflowing with whipped cream dusted with chocolate shavings.

She picked up the mugs and made her way to a table for four near the windows, where Delanie already sat waiting with her own tall steaming mug. For once, Steph would be spending time on the customer side of the counter. Autumn had insisted on this visit after Steph's epic date with Noel, and, since Delanie had also been involved in setting it up and wanted to get together, it made sense to talk to both at once. Maybe talking about what had happened with Noel the other night would help her make sense of how she felt about it.

On the other hand, Stephanie wasn't sure how much she wanted to share. Even though she couldn't hide that she'd been out with Noel, it was all still so new and fresh and sweet that she wanted to keep it between the two of them as much as possible.

Still, she loved that her friend and sister were both so excited for her.

And maybe she'd also have a chance to finish the conversation she and Autumn had started about Eddie yesterday. Would it be asking too much to get her sister to understand what a danger he posed?

Steph sighed. She hoped not.

Autumn had popped into the kitchen for a few minutes, so Stephanie set her sister's mug in front of an empty chair, then placed hers across from Delanie and sat down. Her friend tossed her long blond hair out of the way over her shoulder and gave Steph a broad smile.

"I'm so glad we finally get to have a visit," Delanie said. "It feels like it's been ages!"

The comment felt pointed. Steph repressed a scowl. Delanie had been the one to let their relationship go dark while she'd been in Vancouver trying to establish herself as an actor. Since they reconnected a month and a half ago, Delanie seemed to be trying to make up for lost time, but that didn't mean her previous neglect didn't still sting a little.

"Yes, well, I suppose we've both been busy," Steph said. "How are things going with your theatre kids gig?"

For the past month, Delanie had been working with high-pro-file movie director Tessa Montague on a reality TV show project that would spotlight and benefit community theatre groups across the country. The new job meant Delanie now travelled a lot, but she got to spend the rest of her time at home in Peace Crossing with Caleb and Emma instead of having to return to Vancouver to find work.

"Really well," Delanie replied. "I've got three different communities lined up to participate in our first season, and we're going to start filming in the New Year. It's meant some rejigging of their typical show schedules for these groups, but they were excited for the opportunity."

"Really? Where will you be filming?"

Delanie blew air through her bangs, a beleaguered expression on her face. "That's the interesting part. One community is in Manitoba, another's in northern BC, and the third is in this little town on the east coast, in New Brunswick. And they're all filming concurrently. I'm about to get a whole lotta frequent flyer points."

"Whoa. No kidding." Part of Steph was a little jealous that her friend would be getting so many new experiences soon, but mostly, she shuddered at the thought of having to travel that much. She liked her comfy little home and her routine.

The door chimed, and, over Delanie's shoulder, Steph spied Maddie Kennedy come into the shop and make her way to the counter. Her shoulders tensed. Ever since Noel had claimed that his breakup with Maddie hadn't been what it had appeared to be, she'd been dying to ask him what he meant, but she'd gotten the sense he didn't want to talk about it. She'd heard Maddie's side of the story—everyone in Peace Crossing High had, since the two of them had ended things so publicly at the Harvest Dance. Whenever Stephanie heard the sweet and dreamy love song that had been playing at the time come up on the radio, it triggered the memory of Noel and Maddie's final epic shouting match. Maddie had called him *spineless* and some other names that hadn't seemed like him at all, and he'd said if she felt that way, they should break up. And they did.

Later, Steph had heard rumours that Noel had cheated on Maddie—though Maddie never named a girl he'd supposedly been unfaithful with. She *had* claimed that Noel was a liar and a coward, and she would have broken up with him if he hadn't done it first.

Neither of those labels fit what Stephanie knew of Noel, not even back then, when he'd gone around in leather jackets and green hair with funky designs shaved into the sides. He'd already admitted to his flirtations after that, as well as his reasons for keeping his distance from her for the past several years, and she'd believed him. She'd also believed him that Maddie had embellished the truth—Maddie had definitely been known to colour facts to fit the version of events she'd prefer. But now Stephanie couldn't get the question of what really *had* happened out of her mind.

Steph tore her gaze from Maddie and glanced at Delanie. "Excuse me. I forgot to grab sugar. You need anything?"

Delanie shook her head, and Steph wove through the tables to the coffee counter to collect her fixings, arriving just as Maddie finished placing her order at the till. The other woman then wandered nearer while she waited for Jeff to make it.

Steph caught Maddie's eye and gave her a nod. Maddie gave a half-hearted smile back, but it was enough.

"Hi, Maddie," Steph said cheerfully, then scrambled for something to say next. Spotting one of the cute little coffee tin ornaments Autumn had added to the Christmas tree, she blurted, "These Christmas decorations you brought in for Autumn look great. What a find."

Maddie smiled. "Thanks."

Steph swallowed. Now what? "Getting lots of Christmas orders at the shop?"

Maddie shrugged. "A little more than usual, I suppose. It's been a bit crazy because our delivery guy's been sick. Do you know of anyone looking for a part-time, or, hmm, temporary full-time delivery job?"

Steph shook her head. "I'll keep an ear out and send them your way if I do." She pretended to be absorbed in choosing which sugar she wanted from the little wooden containers. She wanted to come out and ask Maddie what Noel had meant, but what would she say? *Say, remember when you dated Noel Butler all those years ago? Were you lying about him being a liar and a coward to cover your own issues? And did he ever cheat on you?* Ha! That wasn't going to happen.

Besides, she was being silly. After what had happened the other night, she should just ask Noel.

At the reminder of the super-romantic date Noel had created for her and the sweet kisses they'd shared at the end of it, her heartbeat clattered in her ears like reindeer hooves on a tin roof. She snatched up three packages of brown sugar and a wooden stir stick, flashed a quick smile and mumbled "Merry Christmas," at Maddie, then retreated to her seat across from Delanie.

Delanie leaned close. "What was that about?" She indicated Maddie with a subtle twitch of her head.

Steph gave an equally subtle shake of her own head in return just as Autumn slid into her seat.

"So," Autumn said to Delanie, her eyes glittering, "how are the wedding plans coming?"

Delanie's face lit up in obvious delight at being asked. "Good, I think? We've decided on a fall wedding, so I hope the weather'll be nice. But I haven't managed to do much planning. I've got so much going on, it's tough to keep everything straight. At least I have my bridesmaid and my maid of honour on board." She flashed a broad smile at Steph.

"Steph, obviously," Autumn said. "But who's the other one?"

"My roommate, Marie," Delanie said. "Well, former roommate now, I guess. But she's never been a bridesmaid before, and she has *ideas* for the dress style. I'm kind of surprised she hasn't decided to make them herself, but she's pretty busy with making period outfits for her current job. Anyway," she said, turning to Steph, "I was thinking we should plan our dress-shopping trip for January. Get out of the snow for a bit. Marie's game. But then, she's always up for looking at interesting clothes. You should see how excited she is about this dress-shopping trip. Well, as excited as Marie gets for anything." She sighed. "Assuming I can find a weekend to spare. And time to plan it."

Delanie was plainly overwhelmed, and with good reason. She'd recently taken on a lot. Steph vaguely remembered Delanie mentioning Marie-the-costume-designer and felt a little intimidated at the idea of going clothes shopping with her. Still, it was more than time for her to reciprocate the efforts Delanie had been making to rejuvenate their relationship. And this was something she could easily help with.

"I can plan it," Steph said. "Why don't you send me Marie's contact information and let me know which weekend you can do it, and she and I can work out the details?"

Delanie brightened. "You would do that? Thank you so much!" She picked up her phone from the table and, after a few quick thumb motions, Stephanie's phone vibrated in her pocket. "Done. You're a real blessing, you know that?"

Steph smiled, her chest warming. This was the Delanie she'd missed in the decade of her friend's absence. She'd always loved Delanie's energy and enthusiasm for tackling her dreams and many projects . . . even if doing so often left her stretched thin. It occurred to her that Autumn had been on to something a few weeks ago—maybe Delanie's neglect had been less a matter of intention and more that her focus had simply been elsewhere. Steph certainly hadn't sensed that her friend felt any less warm toward her since her return than she had in high school.

Huh.

A donkey bray sounded faintly from somewhere nearby, and Steph recognized Autumn's message notification sound. Steph rolled her eyes, as she often did when she heard it. The donkey bray perfectly represented Autumn's quirky sense of humour.

Autumn fished her phone from her back pocket and checked the message. Her brows lifted, and she looked like she was considering something.

"What is it?" Steph asked, curious.

Autumn shook her head and tucked the phone away again. "Oh. Nothing, really. Noel was texting me about the reno. I'll get back to him later."

She avoided Steph's gaze, and Steph narrowed her eyes, thinking of Noel's comment about surprises.

"The reno, huh? I thought Derrick was handling that. You sure it was just the reno?" She pinned her sister with a good-natured accusatory gaze. She was pretty sure Saturday night hadn't been Autumn's first time abetting Noel's recent Secret Santa campaign. "You two have been talking an awful lot about an awful lot, haven't you?"

Autumn gave Steph a too-innocent look over the top of her mug. When she finished her sip, her top lip was covered in whipped cream, and she was grinning.

"Not nearly so often as *you* and Noel have." Delanie waggled her eyebrows at Steph. "I've been dying to ask how your date went. Now that Autumn's here, it's time to spill the beans."

The heat returned to Steph's face, and she sat back in her chair, momentarily lost in a fairyland of Christmas lights as Noel's strong arms held her tight.

"It was . . . nice."

"*Nice?* That's the best you've got?" Delanie rolled her eyes. "You're more tight-lipped than he is."

"What do you mean?"

Delanie chuckled. "You think Autumn and I didn't grill him already when we went to collect our Christmas decorations? And he didn't say a peep."

A feeling of safety and security wrapped around Stephanie like a warm hug. Somehow, knowing Noel wanted to keep their special moments just between the two of them made her appreciate him even more. He might be a man of mystery, but at least he knew how to keep a secret.

"Thanks for your part in making that night special," Steph said, looking between them. "That house was truly beautiful. I'll never forget what you did."

"It wasn't too 'Christmasy' for you?" Autumn made air quotes as she spoke, her expression sly.

Steph wanted to scowl, but gave her sister a begrudging smile instead. "Actually, it was pretty with all the lights and things. I survived somehow."

"You know," Delanie said, "I think it's *pretty* great that Noel wanted to help you make some new Christmas memories after all these years. No wonder he grew on you." She grinned. "I think that's pretty great, too."

Steph blinked at Delanie. Is that what Noel had been trying to do? Instead of inundating her with Christmas-themed gifts to bully her into liking Christmas by force of will, he'd been deliberately trying to give her a different experience of the season? The thought that his Secret Santa endeavours might have been more of an invitation than a misplaced good intention had never occurred to her.

"You know," Steph said, giving both her sister and her friend side-eye, "I can't help but think the date the other night wasn't the first time he's had help in all this. The guy's been pulling off some miraculous things for someone with a broken leg—even taking his innate stubbornness into account."

Autumn arched a brow. "I'll never tell."

"Won't you? Hmm. Remember that babysitting you wanted me to do, ever again?"

Autumn laughed. "Nice try. Like you'd ever say no to Julien. About *anything*." She gave a dose of side-eye back.

"You got me there," Steph said with a chuckle, then frowned. "Still, I'm not sure how to feel about you telling Noel some really personal stuff about us without checking with me first."

"Melody was my sister too, you know. It's not just your story to tell."

Steph met her sister's level gaze, her throat tight. "You're right," she said finally. "I just felt taken off-guard when Noel told me you'd talked to him about it."

Autumn nodded. "That's understandable. But I know what's *not* my story to tell, and I told him as much. Still," she said, "my Secret Santa idea seemed to work out okay."

"*Your* idea?" Stephanie boggled, her mind racing to recast her recent history in light of this new information. "You were the one who instigated this whole thing?"

"Not instigated. Just guided, so to speak. Noel was the one who wanted to give you a different kind of Christmas this year. I just struck an elf's bargain with him to, you know, help him along."

Steph frowned, the pieces falling into place. "No wonder he knew so many of my preferences. The mug. The mystery novel. The snow pants." Steph put her hand to her head and looked skyward in mock dismay. "I feel so betrayed."

Autumn giggled. "Well, I'll take credit for the mug and snow pants, at least. It's not like the guy doesn't have ideas of his own."

Steph blinked. "You didn't choose the novel?"

Autumn gave a small shrug.

Steph looked at Delanie questioningly, but her friend shook her head.

"I think that one was all him," Autumn said. "What did he pick?"

"A Miss Marple book."

"Good taste," Delanie said. "You love those."

"I know." *But how did he?* Had Noel remembered that she enjoyed reading Agatha Christie novels from high school? Her chest warmed at the thought. But she still had a point to make.

"I have to admit," Steph continued, arching her eyebrow, "I didn't think my own sister would deliberately cause me so much consternation. You know I thought I had a stalker, right?"

Autumn rolled her eyes. "Yeah, Mom told me. If you hadn't figured out who it was when you did, I would have told Noel to come clean."

Steph crossed her arms and glared at her sister, her anger only half-put on. "Sometimes your sense of humour is less quirky and more terrifying."

Delanie had watched the exchange with an amused twinkle in her eyes, her hands wrapped around her mug as she sipped. "C'mon, Steph, you gotta admit that it was at least a little fun getting all those gifts. A Christmas mix CD? Can you imagine the effort that took?"

"You *did* know about that!" Steph turned her incensed glare to Delanie now, but couldn't keep the amusement from creeping into her voice.

Delanie laughed. "Of course I did. Noel borrowed my parents' CD burner. Good thing my Dad likes to keep old tech like that around."

"Speaking of dads . . ." Autumn said, growing serious.

One look at Autumn, and Steph shook her head. "I know what you're going to say next, and no, I haven't changed my mind. I don't want to see Eddie again. Once a decade was more than enough."

Despite the excitement caused by her and Noel's date, Steph had mentioned Eddie's appearance at the hospital to her sister the following day, including the part where she'd told their father in no uncertain terms what she thought of his desire to become involved in their lives again. Autumn had thought Steph was being too harsh and had reminded her that she wasn't the one who got to decide for Julien, or for Autumn. They hadn't been able to finish the conversation because of time constraints, and the tension had been bubbling beneath the surface ever since.

Steph continued, "But you were right yesterday. You get to make your own choices. I just don't want to see you or Julien get hurt."

Her childhood had been shaped by her father's erratic anger. He hadn't been the easiest person to be around even before Melody had died. If she could shelter Julien from the kind of pain Eddie could inflict the way she'd always tried to do for Autumn, she would. Steph fought back the sudden sting of tears.

Autumn gave her a look of understanding. "I get where you're coming from, Steph. But think about this—it wasn't so long ago that you thought Noel was the worst, and now you're so twitterpated, you're outshining the Christmas lights on the mantle."

Delanie giggled, and Steph's cheeks warmed.

"That's different. Noel made *a* mistake with me. One. And I may have made some assumptions and blown it out of proportion a bit. That's water under the bridge now. But it's nowhere near what Eddie did to us, or what he's likely to do again if he gets the chance. I've seen where his good intentions have ended up before, and it's not worth the heartache."

"So you're saying you don't think people can change?" Delanie asked quietly.

No, not him. Not ever! Steph wanted to shout, but she choked on the words. Instead, she gripped her mug handle so hard that her knuckles turned white. "He could change every day of the week, but it won't bring Melody back."

Both Delanie and Autumn said nothing, and all Steph could hear was the gentle murmur of the other patrons, the whir of the espresso machine, faint clanking from the kitchen, and a soul-stirring jazz rendition of "Silent Night" playing over the sound system.

Autumn placed a gentle hand on her arm, and Steph looked up and met her sister's gaze. "I'm not going to try and change your mind. But if there's a chance that Julien could get to know his grandfather, even a little, I want to let him. Dad's not a monster. Yes, he made a lot of mistakes, including one big one . . . which I'm sure he wishes every day that he could take back. We only get one shot at this life, Stephanie, and so does Dad. I choose to forgive him and move forward. And I hope you can do that someday too."

Steph studied her sister's earnest dark brown eyes. "I hope you don't regret it."

"I'll be careful." Autumn squeezed Steph's arm, then leaned back. "Julien and I are meeting Dad at Memorial Park for a play date tomorrow at two. If you change your mind, you're welcome to join us."

Steph's mouth went dry. Her desire to protect her sister and Julien warred with her aversion to her father and her complete mistrust that he would be able to follow through on his intentions of staying clean and doing better. She thought of the little silver nameplate bracelet with Melody's name engraved on it that nestled in the box on her dresser and once more fought back tears. She could admit that she'd been too hard on Noel, and even Delanie for her unintentional neglect. But Eddie Bell had earned every precaution she'd put in place against him over the years. And she had no intention of tearing down those walls anytime soon.

Which was why she couldn't help but feel that sweet, trusting Autumn was tearing down her walls too quickly.

"Fine, I'll be there."

Delanie gave her a sympathetic nod, and Autumn's lips curved in a grateful smile. But all Steph felt was a steely determination to protect her sister from the danger Autumn didn't know their father to be.

Just as she'd always done.

Chapter Sixteen

NOEL TAPPED THE TIP of his pen on the notebook before him, listening to the discussion around his small dining room table. Ryker, Autumn, and Jared had all been on board with his idea of a Christmas Eve party at Cool Beans and had come to his apartment for the evening to make plans. So far, they had helped him sort out the guest list, the entertainment—live music from a local bluegrass band Autumn knew Steph adored—and how they were going to get the word out while doing their best to keep the whole thing a surprise for Steph. Now Autumn and Ryker were hashing out the menu, deliberating between traditional snacks like deli meat platters, cheese balls, cookie trays, and mincemeat tarts—Autumn's suggestion—or the more modern, pun-based snacks that Ryker was advocating for.

Even though Noel had proposed the party, he didn't have any skin in this particular match. He liked eating food, but he certainly wasn't an expert at preparing it. Not unless you counted crock-pot chili, which he'd honed to a fine art since his first high school adventure. Chinese take-out was more his speed. So he watched, jotting notes when something pertinent was suggested. However, he could imagine how much extra work it would be to hand-make pretzels in the shape of reindeer antlers with red gumdrop noses for Ryker's *Rudolph the Salty Reindeer* suggestion.

"I like me a good pun," Autumn said, "but we're already going to be pulling off a minor miracle to make this happen in a week as it is. We should keep it simple."

"You mean boring?" Ryker said, groaning. "Parties are supposed to be *fun*. Keeping it simple is no excuse for mid snacks."

Noel chuckled. When Jared had brought Ryker over earlier, the teen had been reserved around Autumn. His reticence had thawed significantly since they'd gotten into the planning.

"Why not combine the two?" Jared suggested.

"How?" Autumn asked.

Noel understood Jared's idea immediately and smiled. Trust Jared to help them find a middle ground.

"You can make the menu you're suggesting," Noel said to Autumn, "and the rest of us can put our heads together to think of punny names for them. Then you can just make the presentation match."

Autumn frowned uncertainly, but Ryker's face lit up.

"Yes!" he said, nodding enthusiastically. "We could totally do that. Think about it. It's not just chips and guacamole, it's"—he paused dramatically and held up his hands as though presenting a billboard—"*Guacin' Around the Christmas Tree*."

Autumn grinned and gave an appreciative nod.

Noel leaned forward. "Instead of a regular brie-and-cranberry cheese ball, you could make a cheese ball snowman decorated with cranberries and pretzel sticks and call it Frosty the Cheeseman."

Jared grinned. "And you could keep your mincemeat pies. Just put a little sign next to them that says *Good King Minceslas Pies*."

"And no Christmas meal is complete without *Saint Nick's Cinnamon Swirls*—also known as cinnamon buns," Noel added, his mouth watering at the idea of having the signature Cool Beans treat at the party.

"Cinnamon buns! Now you're being demanding." Autumn giggled. "Fine, I get your point. Okay, I can work with that. I'll organize the menu items and send you guys a list."

"Perfect," Noel said, making a note. "Ryker, are you sure you've got time to make the signs and extra decorations you want *and* to plan all the party games?"

Ryker nodded. "Shouldn't be a problem. School's kind of a joke the last week before Christmas." At Noel's expression, he amended, "I mean, I can work on them during my spares."

Noel turned to Jared. "And you'll talk to your buddy Doug Crawford about his band joining us?"

"On it," Jared replied.

"And everyone knows who they're responsible for inviting?"

The question was met with a round of nods and affirmatives.

"Just make sure they all know—*Steph can't know.*" Noel glanced at Ryker, who was now staring through the table. "Right, Ryker?"

Ryker's head snapped up. "Yeah, got it."

Steph had been on the right track with her ideas for engaging Ryker—when Noel had asked him to help plan this event, he'd agreed without hesitation. But even though he'd seemed excited at the time, tonight, Ryker seemed distracted. Noel had had to pull the teen back into the conversation more than once. Mindful of Ryker's recent struggles, Noel had been watching for signs that Ryker might be high and, to his relief, hadn't noticed any. But the kid obviously had something on his mind.

"What will you be doing?" Autumn arched a brow at Noel. "Pulling a classic Noel Butler get-everyone-else-to-do-the-work-for-my-idea manoeuvre?"

Noel shook his head, laughing. "I'm not sure where you get this image of me," he said with mock innocence. "And planning *is* work, you know."

"Uh-huh." Autumn gave him stink-eye.

"Well, my nurse has been pretty adamant that I give my leg time to heal, so I'm trying to heed her warnings. Especially since she's now making regular house calls to check up on me."

Autumn laughed and rolled her eyes, and Ryker blushed with an awkward smile.

Jared shook his head in amusement. "I'm just thrilled you and Steph finally figured out how great you are together."

"Well, it's early days. There's a lot of figuring left to be done. But that's part of the fun, isn't it?" But Noel's gut tensed as he said it. He pushed the feeling aside. Of course they would get a chance to work out their differences long-term. He was determined this would *not* be a repeat of the Maddie situation. As long as their relationship train stayed on their current track, they'd be fine.

Besides, Noel actually had quite a lot to keep him busy for the next week besides the party. Ever since Steph had told him about the bracelet Eddie had given her at the hospital and the story behind it, he'd been working on a special project he hoped would help her find the beauty in all of her bittersweet memories . . . and maybe help her feel the joy of Christmas at last. The supplies were currently tucked into a box beneath his living room side table. Since he could work on it with his foot up, for the most part, he wasn't defying Stephanie's plea that he allow himself the time to heal, but he'd need to put in long hours if he wanted to finish it in time. He didn't feel like explaining all that to everyone, though.

"Besides," Noel continued, "Ryker's got the party games handled, and I'm not good for much of anything else. Unless you want a pot of chili everyone'll talk about for the next decade added to the menu."

Jared snorted with laughter.

Autumn chuckled. "Pretty sure we're not done talking about the last one. Let's not."

"Oh, I don't know. Might be time to refresh my rep with a new generation. What do you think, Ryker? Ryker?"

Ryker brought his gaze back to Noel from somewhere in the vicinity of the Peace River. "Pardon?"

Noel cocked his head. "Something on your mind? You don't seem to be all here tonight."

Ryker glanced around the table, shifting uncomfortably. "It's nothing. Sorry."

It didn't sound like *nothing*.

"Is it because Ryleigh's mom wouldn't let her come tonight?" Noel ventured cautiously.

Noel had been more than a little disappointed when Mrs. Richardson had declined allowing Ryleigh to join in the party planning. Noel had tried to convince her that it would be a good opportunity for the twins to spend time together in a supervised setting, but she had politely and firmly declined. He could have forced the issue by talking to Ryleigh's social worker, but he didn't think that was the best way to resolve the problem, or to get in the Richardsons' good graces.

Ryker glanced at the other adults, especially Autumn, then dropped his gaze. "No. I got to hang with Ry at lunch today. And I get why her mom didn't want her to come. It's fine."

"You do?" Jared blinked at Ryker, then Noel.

Ryker glanced between them. "Sure. Mrs. Richardson has rules, and she thinks I . . . I mean, she's got little Micah and her daughters to think about. I guess I can see why she's being so careful. As for Ry, she's happy with the Richardsons, for the most part, so I'm happy for her. They're decent people." He faded off again, his gaze wandering back toward the front window.

Noel frowned at the boy, surprised and confused by the magnanimous attitude Ryker was displaying toward the family who had rejected him. But there was obviously *something* going on. Noel exchanged meaningful glances with the other adults at the table, especially Autumn. Ryker might have relaxed around her, but that didn't mean he'd bare his soul to a near stranger.

Autumn picked up on the subtle cue. "Well, this was fun, but I better head out. I need to pick up Julien from my mom's before it gets too late. Thanks for the eggnog, Noel. I'll text the menu to you guys later tonight."

"Thanks for making time at the last minute," Noel said.

Autumn snorted in amusement and stood. "After this month, you're going to owe so many favours, you'll be repaying them for the rest of your life."

"I'm pretty sure that's just the economy of being a good neighbour." Noel gave her a half-cocked grin. "And I'm here for it."

After a round of goodbyes, Autumn quickly gathered her things and headed out the door, leaving Noel and Jared alone with Ryker. Noel offered his guests more to drink. Jared declined, but Ryker didn't seem to have heard him.

Noel half-hobbled, half-hopped to the cupboard, grabbed a tumbler, poured a glass of water from the cooler, and placed it in front of the boy, then took his empty 'nog glass to the counter. Ryker focused on the glass. After a small smile of thanks at Noel, he took a sip.

Noel eased himself back into the chair across from him. "Now, what's really going on?"

Ryker blinked at him, wide-eyed as a rabbit caught in a flashlight beam.

Noel leaned back, being sure to keep from crossing his arms—he wanted to invite ease, not close himself off. Instead, he folded his hands across his belly and surveyed Ryker kindly. "You're in a safe space here, Ryker. If you need to talk to someone about something, it won't go further than these four walls."

Ryker's dark eyes met his, and he seemed to be weighing Noel's words. Finally, he said, "It *is* about Ryleigh. Kind of."

He frowned uncertainly, looking between the two men. "You *promise* not to talk to anyone about this?"

Noel realized he might be getting into dicey legal and ethical territory if he agreed *carte blanche* and gave Jared a questioning look.

Jared turned to Ryker. "As long as keeping the secret wouldn't put anyone in danger, neither of us will say anything." He paused, then asked, "Would it?"

Ryker gave his head a small shake.

"Then your secret is safe with us," Noel said.

Seemingly satisfied, Ryker drew a breath, but fidgeted with his glass for several seconds before speaking. "You guys know Lionel, right?"

Noel and Jared affirmed they did. Lionel Harris and his brothers had been regulars at the youth group since Gary and Lou had adopted them several years ago, long before the Dyck twins had started attending at the Richardsons' behest.

Ryker sighed. "Lionel has a huge crush on Ryleigh, and I wasn't worried about it until today. But now, I think Ryleigh might be starting to like him back."

"Why would you be worried about that?" Jared asked. "Lionel's a good kid."

Noel glanced at Jared. In the past, Lionel had been a bit of a bully, but Noel had to admit that the teen had matured a lot in the past year. Still, Lionel's beefy physique could be intimidating on its own, even if he wasn't trying to be imposing. But even though it had been a long while since Noel had seen or heard evidence that Lionel was using his size to get his way, Noel wasn't sure he'd be willing to go so far as endorsing his character the way Jared just had.

Ryker ran his hand through his shaggy hair and bit his lip. "Because Lionel hates me. And I'm worried that if he and Ryleigh start dating, he won't let her spend time with me anymore."

Noel and Jared exchanged surprised looks. There was a lot to unpack in Ryker's last few sentences.

"*Let* her?" Jared repeated.

Noel's mind raced to what he knew of Ryker and Ryleigh's past. Their mom had never been married, and Noel wouldn't be surprised if she and the man she'd been living with—who'd assumed guardianship of the twins after she died until Ryker had turned him in for some truly horrific acts—hadn't been the best role models for what a healthy relationship should be. Abuse was all about control. No wonder Ryker was afraid his sister would be giving hers up by dating someone—anyone, from the sounds of it, let alone someone he thought had it in for him.

But looking at the anguish playing on Ryker's face, Noel knew that the first item to tackle in that complex revelation was Ryker's very real fear of losing his sister—his one ride-or-die.

"Hey," Noel said, "Do you really think Ryleigh would let a boyfriend come between you two? After all you've been through together?"

Moisture glimmered in Ryker's eyes, but he scowled at the table and took deep breaths, blinking it away. Finally, he shook his head as though it had been forced out of him.

"I don't either," Noel said. With a sideways glance at Jared, he added, "And while I don't know Lionel as well as Mr. Larson does, I'm pretty sure he's not the type to try to come between the two of you. What makes you think he doesn't like you?"

"Trust me," Ryker said, still staring at the table in misery. "He doesn't."

He didn't volunteer more, and Noel glanced at Jared in frustration.

"Have you talked to Ryleigh about your concerns?" Jared asked, his voice calm and gentle.

"Yeah, but she thinks I'm being stupid."

That sounded like a typical teenage reaction if Noel had ever heard it.

"You're not being stupid," Noel said. "You're being a good, protective brother, and that's not a bad thing. I intervened a time or two more in my little sister Jenny's life than she would have liked. We still manage to get along."

Ryker gave a tight-lipped smile. "Thanks."

When he said nothing more, Noel tried another tack. He'd been wanting to find a way to connect Ryker with other kids at the youth group, and now seemed like the perfect opportunity to open doors.

"Hey, I saw you and Jordan Olson talking a bit after the sleigh ride. Are you two becoming friends?"

Noel didn't know what reaction he was expecting to that question, but it definitely wasn't the one he got. Ryker's naturally pale face went ghostly white, and he stared at Noel like that rabbit in a flashlight, except one that had now been pinned down.

"Um, yeah. I mean, no. No, we're not friends. It was nothing. Just something lame."

Noel shook his head in confusion. Ryker's tone implied he'd prefer not to be associated with Jordan.

"Do you have a problem with Jordan too? He's such a nice kid." Noel tried to keep his disappointment out of his voice. Go figure that Ryker would dislike the one boy Noel hoped might become his ally and friend.

Ryker shook his head, swallowing. "Um, no, Jordan's fine. We just haven't clicked, you know?" Ryker glanced toward the door. "Uh, I gotta go. I just remembered I have some homework I need to do tonight. Thanks so much for having me over, Noel."

He stood, and Jared stood, too, a surprised expression on his face.

"Don't worry about driving me, Mr. Larson," Ryker said, waving his hand for Jared to sit down. "I'll walk home. It's not that cold tonight."

Jared frowned, then shrugged and nodded, sinking back into his seat. The group home was only a few blocks away, so the walk wasn't an issue. But Ryker's sudden shift in energy hadn't been lost on Noel.

"I'll text Mrs. Wood and tell her you're on your way," Jared said.

"Thanks." Ryker had already pulled on his vintage leather bomber jacket, which he left hanging open, and a black knit toque emblazoned with some logo Noel didn't recognize.

At least he's wearing a toque. Noel couldn't believe how many of the youth group kids seemed to think being cold was better than being uncool.

"I'll talk to you soon, okay?" Ryker added to Noel, his hand on the doorknob.

"Yep. S'later."

Then Ryker closed the door behind him.

Jared pulled out his phone to send the text. Noel hobbled to the front window, watching until he saw Ryker emerge from the building's entrance below and head toward the street in the direction of the group home.

"Is it just me, or was Ryker not being entirely truthful about his relationship with Jordan Olson?" Noel mused.

"Nope. Not just you. I caught that too." Jared laid his phone on the table, frowning thoughtfully.

"And I had no idea Lionel had a problem with Ryker," Noel continued, hobbling back toward the dining nook. "We should talk to the boys about it. Or maybe to Gary and Vic."

"Hmm. Maybe," Jared said absently. "But I'm not sure the issue is drastic enough for us to interfere with. Sometimes teenagers need to figure this stuff out on their own."

"Sometimes."

Thinking back to the way things had worked out between him and Maddie and Jackson, Noel didn't know if he agreed that this was one of those times—but he kept that to himself.

Lowering himself into his chair once more, he used his hands to prop his aching leg on the chair Ryker had just vacated. The molded plastic of his air boot clacked loudly when he rested it on the wooden seat.

"By the way," Noel said, "in case you're thinking of breaking a leg—zero stars. Do not recommend."

Jared chuckled, eyeing Noel's booted foot. "I'll keep that in mind." He took a sip of his tea—Jared was one of the few guys Noel ever served tea to—then set it down and surveyed Noel with a mischievous look in his eye. "So?"

Noel stared at him in confusion. "*So*, what?"

"*So*, how are things going with Steph?"

"Oh. *So*, that." The question was innocent enough, but it dug at the feeling Noel had pushed aside earlier, and Noel didn't like it. He paused to adjust his leg a bit and then took a long draught of his eggnog. When he returned the glass to the table, he stared at it as if it would be able to answer for him. Finally, he admitted, "I guess I keep waiting for the shoe to drop."

Jared shifted in his seat. "What do you mean by that?"

Noel met his gaze. "I mean, it's going so well right now that I'm afraid it can't last. It seems too good. And that's not how my close relationships usually work out."

Jared tilted his head, eyebrow raised. "We've been friends for a while now. And here *we* still are. And there's Caleb."

"True. But there's not much chance the three of us are gonna pick out drapes together, either." Noel chuckled and polished off the last of his eggnog. As he set the glass down, he sighed. "The whole thing with Maddie messed me up real good. And I know Steph isn't her, but there's some part of me that feels it's only a matter of time before everything falls apart."

Jared nodded. "I guess I get that. I haven't exactly dated a ton of women, but I know it's not easy to get over being burned." He paused. "If you don't mind me asking, what *did* happen with Maddie?"

Noel pondered. A little truth between friends wouldn't hurt.

"I trusted her with a secret. She proved unworthy of my trust. And someone I cared about got hurt."

"Ah."

They sat in silence for a few moments—long enough for Noel to remember sharing his secret struggles with Maddie, hoping for understanding, comfort, and advice, and instead, having her betray his confidence—a betrayal that had ended with Jackson facing charges for drug trafficking and distribution resulting in harm to a minor. That was only the first step in a long list of encounters with the law for Jackson, a slide into alcohol abuse for Noel, and the beginning of the end for his and Jackson's friendship. If it weren't for Maddie, would he and Jackson still be friends? Would Jackson have taken the route he did? Or would Noel have found a better way to handle his dilemma so both he and Jackson could have lived a better life?

Noel would never know now. But he'd learned his lesson. And as amazing as Steph was, he didn't know if he could trust even her with the whole truth of his past. How would she react? With acceptance and support, or outrage and disgust? She'd already made it clear to him how she felt about drinking. If she knew about his past history with alcohol and the near misses he'd had because of it, that alone could be the end of their budding romance.

Jared broke the silence. "I forgot to tell you—I got offered a permanent position at PCCA as the youth pastor."

Noel blinked, then smiled. "I can't think of anyone better for the job." And he meant it. Despite his faults, Jared was exactly the kind of guy who would excel at handling the responsibilities of the role long-term. "Are you going to take it?"

Jared smiled, too, looking relieved. "I was worried you wanted the job."

"Me? Nah. I get too impatient. The only reason I haven't lost it on some poor hyper kid is because you're there to keep my head on my shoulders."

"I know you're kidding, but thank you. I appreciate it. And yes, I've decided to take the job."

"Well, congrats. I'm thrilled for you."

"You'll still be around to help, right?"

"Of course! You're not getting rid of me that easily."

"Good. You're doing a good thing with these kids, Noel. Ryker really looks up to you, and so do several of the other boys. You're making a real difference."

Noel felt an unexpected prick in his sinuses at the heartfelt compliment and blinked it away. "Uh, thank you," he said. "That means a lot."

Those words warmed him long after Jared had left. No, he'd never know what could have been different with Jackson. But maybe he could make sure kids like Ryker didn't suffer the same fate. And despite what Jared had said earlier, Noel didn't want to leave it up to chance that Ryker would find a way to work out whatever issue was going on behind the scenes.

He'd definitely be talking to Pastor Vic and Gary Harris about their sons at the earliest opportunity.

Chapter Seventeen

S TEPHANIE STEPPED BACK FROM the Christmas tree standing in the front window of Noel's apartment and turned to the man lounging on the couch behind her.

"Better?"

Noel surveyed her work, his healing leg propped on the coffee table. "A little higher and to the left."

Dutifully, she unhooked the silver angel ornament and moved it to the spot he'd indicated. "Now?"

"Yep, that'll work."

Steph had to agree. Noel had a great eye for these sorts of things. Though, lately, she'd been getting an awful lot of practice, herself.

The last time she was at Noel's place, she'd observed that, for a guy who loved Christmas as much as he did, she was surprised he didn't have a Christmas tree. He'd dismissed her concerns by mentioning that he'd been spending all his Christmas energy on some Secret Santa project and, with his broken leg and lack of ability to drive, hadn't been able to fetch himself a tree and hadn't rounded up anyone else to do it for him.

When Stephanie had shown up with Caleb and Derrick this afternoon—with the two men hauling a live bundled fir tree that Steph had purchased from the local tree stand on their shoulders—Noel had been speechless. After getting the tree set up in Noel's living room, the guys had only stayed long enough for a short cup of coffee, but Stephanie had stuck around to decorate. She wasn't leaving Noel to his own devices—he'd stress his healing leg, for sure. Besides, it was a good opportunity to spend time with him.

And she was surprised by how very much she had come to enjoy doing just that.

"So," Steph said, fetching another few angel ornaments from the box, "how did your talk with your pastor go? About Ryker?"

"Pretty good, I think," Noel said. "Pastor Vic said he wasn't aware of any problem between the boys, but he'd ask Jordan about it. Gary Harris said pretty much the same thing about Lionel." Noel frowned. "I have to admit, one of those two fathers was much more willing to admit their kid might be less than perfect than the other."

"Hmm, let me guess which one. The ex-foster kid's dad?"

"Yeah. How did you know?" Noel said dryly. "How about the date with your dad? How did that go?"

Steph's chest tightened. "It didn't."

"It didn't?"

The image of her nephew's disappointed little face when he'd found out his Papa wasn't coming to the park flashed through her mind, and Steph's jaw clenched. She hung another ornament, then wandered around the tree looking for another spot. "He didn't show up. Autumn and I had a good chat, though. And after it became clear Eddie wasn't coming, we took the play date to the sledding hill. Julien had a blast. My new snow pants came in handy, too." She smiled at him. "Did I ever thank you for those?"

"You have now," he said. He watched her for a moment in silence, then said, "How are you doing with that whole thing?"

"What whole thing? The stalker-slash-Secret Santa debacle? I've mostly come to terms with it." She chose a bough with nothing on it yet, placed the angel, then went back to survey the decorations on the coffee table. Moving the empty angel ornament box aside, she asked, "So, which ones next?"

"Wait . . . stalker?" Noel shook his head, an askance expression on his face. "You really thought you had a stalker? I thought you were joking about that."

Steph met his troubled gaze, surprised at his hurt tone. "For a little while. I mean, all the gifts were so specific and personal, and no one who knew me that well seemed to know anything about them." She rolled her eyes. "Bunch of liars," she added, but her smile belied her annoyance. "I believed them, though, because everyone who knows me that well also knows how much I hate Christmas—" She froze, realizing what she'd said, and glanced sideways at Noel. " Cookies," she finished, thinking of one of his earlier gifts. She actually adored Christmas cookies—the piped shortbread cookies that came nestled in fluted paper holders in blue tins were one of the few things she looked forward to about this season.

"Now who's the liar?" Noel leaned back and levelled his nice-try gaze on her.

She looked at him, her cheeks growing warm and her heart thudding in her chest. "What do you mean?"

Noel crossed his arms. "You love Christmas cookies. Your mom told me."

My mom? Now there was one person Steph hadn't expected to be in on Noel's scheme. *One more person who's going to find coal in their stocking in a couple days*, she grouched to herself.

"But you don't love Christmas," Noel added. "Like, at all."

Steph's breath caught. She sank into the overstuffed chair beside her. "You knew all along?"

Noel chuckled. "You think your family and friends would supply me with a list of all your favourite things without warning me about the possible consequences? They're better people than that. Besides, you pretty much said so yourself when I was in the hospital. It wasn't much of a leap."

Stephanie swallowed. "So . . . why did you go to all this trouble then? It seems like a funny way to go about getting someone to date you."

"It worked though, right?" Noel grinned at her expression. "I'm kidding. Would you believe I didn't start out trying to woo you?"

"No."

His brows arched as though he didn't believe her response.

"Well, why did you do it, then?" She sounded snappier than she'd intended. Looking away, she drew a long breath, trying to calm her racing heart. Why was she suddenly feeling so irritable?

He regarded her for a long moment, then swung his legs off the couch and patted the cushion beside him. "Come here."

She hesitated, then went and sat next to him, nestling her shoulder under the arm he wrapped around her. He took her hand in his on his lap, twining his fingers through hers. It felt . . . nice. Right. Like he would never let anything happen to her.

Steph thought of Maddie and wondered if her feelings on the matter could be trusted. She'd gotten up the nerve to ask Noel about his history with Maddie in a sideways way a few days ago, but he'd cleverly deflected the question. It wasn't until she was home watching her show that she'd realized he'd done it. Having him know about her past and her not knowing about his was a little unsettling. She tried to calm her underlying current of anxiety with reminders that he would tell her when he was ready.

She just hoped that wasn't when their relationship was imploding.

"I did it because Christmas isn't about trees and ornaments and carols." His deep voice vibrated through her in a comforting resonant hum. "It's not about Santa and gifts and turkey. It's not even about family." He squeezed her hand. "Christmas is about peace, and joy, and love. Mostly love."

As he spoke, a surge of emotion welled in Stephanie's chest, and tears pricked her sinuses. She swallowed, trying to keep the impending flood at bay, but moisture trickled down her cheeks despite her efforts. Christmas had been a source of pain for so long, but hearing Noel gently assert that the holiday was about love made her desperately want it to be true. She was tired of the pain. She was tired of the grief. Of associating the season with a time in her life she'd rather forget. Of only feeling heartache when she thought of her sweet little sister.

"I know that that's not what Christmas has meant to you for a long time," Noel continued. "And I know some of the why. But I wanted to rewrite your story of Christmas. I wanted you to find the healing that this season can offer, if you could only hear the message behind all the traditions and rituals."

He extricated his hand from hers and wiped the tears from her face, then leaned forward and kissed the cheek closest to him. Pulling away, he gently tugged her chin so she was looking into his eyes, which shone with intense earnestness.

"Your history doesn't have to be your future, Steph. I know you and your dad have some things to work out, but even if you never do, you can still find healing. That's the promise of Christmas. That's why Jesus came. Not so we could decorate trees and stuff ourselves silly. He came to heal and redeem the broken people of the world. You, me, everyone. He came to show us what love is supposed to look like."

"Hmm." She frowned, something inside rebelling at his words. Their family had gone to church on occasion over the years and she believed in God, but she and the Almighty had always had a pretty distant relationship. She couldn't say that she'd ever felt particularly loved by a higher power of any kind. "It's a nice sentiment, but Jesus came two thousand years ago, and the world is more messed up than ever. So how's that working out?"

Noel gave her a thoughtful look. "I'm healing, by the grace of God. And that's thanks in no small part to you. I'm pretty sure that night at the Christmas party was what I've heard referred to as a 'divine appointment'. God brought you into my life for a reason, Stephanie. And I couldn't be more glad." He planted a kiss on her temple. "He knew I'd need you to help me heal in more ways than one." He tapped his casted leg for emphasis.

She gave a snort of laughter. She wanted to throw back a snarky comment about how ridiculous all his sentiment about Christmas was . . . but the truth was that he *had* been rewriting her story. She hadn't felt this peaceful at the end of December for a very long time. With a jolt, she remembered that the next day was the anniversary of Melody's passing. She hadn't thought about it in days.

And, she realized as she snuggled against him, she hadn't felt this safe and secure with anyone in a long time. Not even Autumn.

"Well," she said, somewhat begrudgingly, "I think you're helping me heal too."

He smiled at her, holding her gaze for a long moment. Long enough for her to appreciate the flecks of gold accenting his warm brown irises and the reflections from the Christmas tree lights twinkling in his eyes. Then he swung his arm off her shoulders and leaned away from her, fetching a box from beneath the side table on the far end of the couch. When he straightened, he handed it to her.

"I haven't given you your gift for today yet. I was going to wait until Christmas for this one, but I want you to have it now. I hope you'll forgive me that I didn't have time to wrap it."

She looked down at the loosely folded corrugated cardboard flaps in curiosity. Despite the fact that this gift had been delivered with the least amount of pomp and circumstance of any he'd given her that month, she got the impression that it was the most special one of all. Carefully, she pulled the flaps apart and glanced inside.

She noticed the tangy smell of freshly sanded wood first, then the carved wooden surface. She reached into the cardboard box and pulled out the gift—a delicately carved jewellery box. The red-grained wood was still unfinished, and bits of dust clung to the surface. The sides were covered in floral garland patterns. The centrepiece in the lid was a carved tiara with empty holes where gems should be.

"A crown?" she asked.

"And garlands. Like the meaning of your name, Stephanie."

Stephanie's throat closed. It was the most touching thing anyone had ever done for her.

"It's not finished," Noel said apologetically. "I'd just got done with the sanding when you buzzed my apartment. I barely had time to stow it away before you and Caleb and Derrick got up the stairs. I still need to stain it and set the crystals into the tiara, but—"

"It's beautiful." Stephanie moved some ornament storage boxes aside to make room on the coffee table and carefully placed the box beside them. Then she turned and gave Noel a heartfelt kiss. "Thank you. I . . . I don't know what to say."

Noel smoothed some of her hair behind her ear. "I wanted you to know how much I treasure you, Stephanie. And I hope it will be a place to keep your own lovely treasures . . . like Melody's bracelet."

She swallowed, trying to contain her emotion. "That's really thoughtful. Thank you." She drew a breath. "The anniversary is tomorrow. Of her death. So the timing couldn't be more perfect."

He pulled her against his chest again. "I figured it had to be soon. And I'm sorry things are still so hard with your dad. Maybe tomorrow, you and I can go do something fun together. Can I take you out for dinner?"

Steph sat up. Tomorrow was Christmas Eve. And during her talk with Autumn, her sister had accidentally let Noel's party plans slip—or rather, Julien had mentioned that his mommy said they were "busy" on Christmas Eve, and Steph had pestered the reason out of her sister. So she recognized Noel's ploy to get her to the party for what it was. Steph had no intention of ruining his fun . . . but that didn't mean she was going to make it easy for him.

"I don't know. I'm babysitting Julien until five. How about I just grab takeout and bring it over after and we'll eat here?"

Noel appeared to think about it. "Dang. I guess I'll have to cancel those reservations."

She glared. "Someone was being a little overly confident, weren't they? And won't everything be closed? How on earth did you manage to get reservations on Christmas Eve in Peace Crossing?"

"With great difficulty," he deadpanned.

She chuckled, and then made a show of sighing and giving in. "Fine. But this better not be another one of your big surprises, Noel Butler."

He shook his head innocently. "Me? Surprise you? Where would you get such a notion?"

He leaned in and gave her a long, lingering kiss that tasted of candy canes and hot chocolate and winter nights by the fire. Steph wrapped her arms around his neck and melted into him. She could get used to this.

Her phone buzzed in her purse—her reminder notification. With regret, she broke their connection and glanced at the clock on Noel's dining nook wall.

"Shoot. I have to go to work. Sorry." She stood and surveyed the mess of boxes and other decorations. "I can help you finish tomorrow, um, after our date."

He laughed and shook his head. "Don't bother," he said. Then, to her surprise, he rose to his feet with only the help of the couch armrest and not his crutches. "I'd be happy to watch you decorate my tree anytime, or do just about anything else, for that matter. But, given the time crunch, I can manage the rest on my own. The doc says I'm supposed to start putting weight on my foot sometimes. This would be a perfect opportunity."

The twinkle in his eye told her all she needed to know—that he'd chosen to lounge to humour her, and to enjoy the show.

She gave him a playful slap on the arm. "You're a real piece of work."

He grinned. "And I ain't even finished yet." He glanced at the jewellery box. "Like that box. Leave it with me, though, and I'll take care of that issue shortly."

She tilted her head, examining it. "I don't know. I kind of like it like this. The raw beauty of the wood is sort of appealing. A reminder that beauty is often a work in progress."

"Yeah?" Noel gave the box another look. "I can see your point. But at least let me add the jewels. It looks weird with those empty holes, and I ordered some crystals in special."

"Okay." She wrapped her arms around his waist and stretched to give him another kiss. "I gotta go. See you tomorrow."

Noel's phone buzzed on the coffee table. As Steph gathered her coat from the front closet and put it on, Noel picked up the phone and read it. His smile faded to a frown.

Steph's stomach clenched. Something was wrong. "What is it?"

"It's Ryker," Noel said, re-reading the text. "He got beat up pretty bad, and Jared's taking him to Emerg." Noel glanced up at her. "Can I hitch a ride to the hospital with you?"

Chapter Eighteen

Steph sat in the nurse's station and glared at her phone, but the last message in her text conversation with Eddie was still her own. She'd sent it two days ago, giving him a lashing about how disappointed Julien had been when he hadn't shown up and warning him that this was exactly why he shouldn't have interfered with their lives in the first place. She didn't know what she'd expected. An apology? An explanation? At least an excuse? Apologizing and taking some responsibility would have been ideal, but even an acknowledgement that she'd communicated with him would have been better than nothing at all. Still, she should have expected this. Why did she keep hoping for more?

Noel and his pragmatic optimism are getting to me.

"Worried?" came Samantha's voice from the other computer in the nurse's station.

Steph swivelled her chair to face her colleague. Sam jerked her head toward the short hall of open-ended examination rooms, where Ryker sat with Noel and Jared behind a closed privacy curtain while they waited for the doctor.

"About Ryker? Yeah, there's a bit of that."

Ever since she'd heard that Ryker had been in a fist fight, her mind had been racing through what might have gotten him into one and how serious the repercussions might be for all involved. She'd love to know who'd laid into him hard enough that he required stitches so she could give them a piece of her mind. But her righteous indignation was shared between Ryker's bully and her father. Her suggestion to Autumn to spend the afternoon sledding had been as much a chance to make good on her promise to herself to create some fun winter memories with her nephew and sister as it had been a timely distraction from being ghosted again—for Julien, Autumn, and herself.

"Only a bit?" Sam arched a brow.

Steph realized she'd pretty much left an open door for Sam to ask about her personal life. Still, if there was anyone at work she could trust with this stuff, it was probably Sam. Taking a breath, she said, "And some family stuff."

"I see." The phrase was more of a question than a statement. Sam tilted her head and raised her eyebrows, inviting further comment.

Steph decided that was as personal as she wanted to get. Bad enough that Noel knew all about her ugly past. She didn't need her colleagues knowing too. She deflected any further questions about her statement by focusing on their patient. "Do you know if Ryleigh knows about her brother?"

Sam didn't press. Instead, she nodded. "The twins' social worker called—Meera Patel. You know her, right? Yeah, so anyway, Meera said she would let Ryleigh know. She also said that the Richardsons might bring Ryleigh by if Ryker will be in overnight. I don't think he will, though—a few stitches, and he'll be on his way."

As she spoke, Dr. Carina du Plessis came by the desk. The short, sturdy woman retrieved Ryker's chart from the designated slot in the acrylic wall rack and walked briskly to Ryker's exam room with her typical indefatigable energy.

Noting the doctor's progress, Steph said, "You're probably right. Unless there's more to the situation than it looked like."

When Noel and Stephanie had arrived at the hospital, Steph had gone in to check on Ryker and found him sitting on the exam room bed, holding an ice pack wrapped in a white cloth tinged with flecks of dark red blood to the back of his head. Jared had been sitting in the metal-framed moulded plastic chair next to the small counter. Ryker's hair beneath the compress was matted with blood, but not fresh blood—scalp wounds like that didn't bleed much, and the gash wasn't more than an inch long. Besides the cut on his scalp, an interesting bruise had been forming on Ryker's cheek. But other than looking a little paler than usual, he seemed otherwise uninjured.

Noel's first question had been who had done this to him, but Ryker hadn't given an answer. Then Noel asked if Ryker had started it, and the reply to that had been a small shake of the head. Jared had responded with a slight shrug, indicating that Ryker hadn't told him what had happened either. When Noel had given Steph a pointed glance, she'd gotten the hint that Ryker might be more talkative if she wasn't there and left to start her shift. Noel had a way of getting people to open up, but she could understand Ryker not wanting to talk with a near-stranger in the room.

She only hoped Ryker would relax enough to trust Noel and Jared with his troubles. It could be so hard to get kids to understand that they didn't have to face all their problems on their own. Especially if they were used to no one looking out for them.

Steph knew too well what that was like. She had become the adult in her family far too young. Angelica had hardly been around—a single mom trying to keep the bills paid—and had been too trapped in grief and anger to do anything about their problems even when she was. Steph had been the only one there for Autumn. But, other than her grandmother, there had been no one Steph herself could turn to. And Grandma Jill's distance from Peace Crossing meant she wasn't often there when Steph needed someone the most. Thank God for Delanie, or Steph may not have survived her torturous high school years.

Thinking of how her high school friend had been there for her, something softened in Stephanie's chest, flooding her with a surge of gratitude—and a wash of shame for how she'd been acting recently. She made a note to herself to reach out to Delanie for another coffee soon.

Doctor du Plessis came back, scribbled some notes, and returned the clipboard holding Ryker's chart to the wall rack. "Please take Ryker to the treatment room and prepare him for local anaesthesia," she said in her melodious South African accent. "I'll complete his stitches after I speak with the next patient."

"You bet," Stephanie said. "Mrs. Wilson in six is next. Possible UTI."

"Wonderful. Thanks." Doctor du Plessis selected Mrs. Wilson's clipboard from the slot for exam room six and spun back the way she'd come, reviewing the information as she went.

Stephanie retrieved Ryker's chart from the rack and hurried to do as she'd been instructed. Ryker accepted the move wordlessly, but there was a tense set to his shoulders she hadn't noticed before, a jumpiness in his movements. Jared joined Ryker in the treatment room, which was only slightly more spacious than the exam rooms. Noel stood just inside the door as she prepared the anaesthetic for Doctor du Plessis to administer. Leaning against the door frame and resting his crossed arms on his crutches in front of him, he looked like he was guarding it.

"The doctor will be with you in a minute," Steph said to Ryker when she'd finished.

He nodded almost imperceptibly.

She turned to leave, smiling up at Noel as she made to move around him. Somehow, she'd managed to stay focused on her task, despite his distracting bulk near the door that reminded her of a protective spirit. His returning look made her pulse speed up. She was on the brink of not caring how hard she fell for Noel Butler. The thought startled her, and she swallowed.

"Hey," Noel said to Ryker. "I'll be in the waiting room. Three's a crowd in here. Mr. Larson's got you."

Ryker nodded. Noel adjusted his crutches and followed Stephanie out of the room. However, once she'd closed the heavy wooden door, he followed her toward the nurse's station.

"Did he tell you what happened?" Steph asked quietly when they were far enough away that sound likely wouldn't penetrate the thick door.

"Not exactly, but I'm pretty sure Lionel was involved somehow." Noel looked troubled. "I'm going to call Gary and see what he knows."

Steph nodded. She hoped Noel could get to the bottom of whatever was going on with Ryker. The kid deserved a break.

"Keep me posted."

"Will do. And, hey . . . it'll be okay." He bent a little closer and whispered in her ear, "I'd kiss away that worried frown, but I don't want to embarrass you. Just know I'll be thinking about that kiss until I get the chance to give it to you for real."

Steph's neck and face grew warm as Noel turned on his crutches and swung himself down the hallway toward the hospital lobby. When she glanced at Sam, who was sitting at her station a few feet away, the other nurse was watching her with wide eyes filled with amusement. At Steph's annoyed glare, Sam turned her attention toward a new chart a patient had just put in the basket on the counter. Picking it up, she started processing it for intake—but she had a knowing grin on her face.

Steph tried to swallow her discomfiture. "I'm going to go sanitize." She grabbed the spray bottle and cloth from behind the counter and hurried toward the recently vacated exam room to prep it for the next patient.

Steph had spent her life preparing for the worst. But even though her thoughts still raced with the possible disaster scenarios Ryker might have become embroiled in, when Noel said it was going to be okay, part of her had actually believed him. With a jolt, she realized that despite the embarrassment he'd still managed to cause, her chest was warm, and she was very much looking forward to that promised kiss—but, more than that, to days upon weeks upon months of kisses to follow.

And, instead of terror, she couldn't wait to see what surprises Noel might have in store next.

Was this what love felt like? She didn't know. But by the time she put the cleaner and cloth away, she was humming to herself.

Noel ended the call with Gary Harris and leaned back against the hard plastic chair, staring across the vaulted, airy hospital lobby without really seeing anything. He was still mentally processing what he'd learned in his conversation with both Gary and Lionel. His gut instinct had been right—Lionel *had* been involved in the situation that had landed Ryker here, but not as the aggressor. He'd been intervening between Ryker and his attacker—who was, of all people, Jordan Olson.

Over the course of the conversation, the truth had come out—Lionel's observations of the difference in Jordan's two-faced behaviour when dealing with adults or his fellow students, for a start. According to Lionel, not only was the pastor's kid adept at manipulating his image with the adults in his life, he was also the source of the drugs Ryker had been caught with. Lionel said that's why he'd distrusted Ryker—he'd seen him associating with Jordan and wanted nothing to do with either of them, especially after Ryker had been caught red-handed. He'd even warned Ryker to stay away from Trevor when he'd caught Ryker talking to his younger brother at youth group, thinking Ryker was bad news. But still, when Lionel had come across Jordan and a couple of his cronies laying into Ryker behind the school, he'd felt compelled to intervene—for Ryleigh's sake, Noel suspected, if Ryker's belief in the other boy's crush was founded. And, given Lionel's height and naturally beefy frame, he was one of the few teenagers who could have done so single-handedly.

It wasn't often Noel felt unsure of his next steps, but this was one of those times. He had no reason to doubt Lionel's veracity—other than not wanting to admit he'd been a victim of Jordan's manipulations too. Dang, the kid was good. But as betrayed as Noel felt, Jordan's parents would be devastated. And Noel thought he understood why Ryker hadn't told them what had happened—even without knowing Ryker's side of the story, he could see how complicated the situation was for him. Admit he'd been beat up while trying to get more drugs? That would go over well with everyone. Noel wasn't sure how his social worker or the group home manager would react, but he thought Ryker could face legal consequences the next time he was caught in possession, and he might get cut off from seeing his sister completely.

His heart broke for the boy. Noel knew how tough addiction was to beat, but if Ryker had a shot at doing it, he needed to know he wasn't alone. That people cared about whether he got better or not. That Noel cared.

By the time Noel returned to Emergency, Ryker had been moved back to an exam room for observation. Samantha Crawford, whom he knew from when she'd painted the sets he'd made for the kids' play in the fall, directed him to Ryker's new room, and Noel slipped behind the privacy curtain. He found Ryker laying on the exam room table, his knees in the air and his socked feet flat on the extendable end. A neat bandage that was partially concealed by the teen's shaggy black curls covered a shaved area around the wound. After turning his head to show Noel the damage, Ryker resumed staring at the ceiling. Since Jared had once again taken up residence on the chair, Noel settled himself on the small metal stool that remained.

"I just had a good chat with Lionel," Noel said. May as well not beat around the bush.

Jared turned to him with interest. Ryker jerked upright, or at least tried. After an initial jump, he slowed his ascent, looking dizzy. Blinking, he pushed himself up to sitting.

Finally, he said, "What did Lionel say?" He sounded like he was trying to be nonchalant . . . but he failed miserably.

Noel had pushed aside the curtain covering the open end of the exam room with his elbow when he'd come in. He indicated with a gesture that Jared should close it, and the other man reached up and tugged the heavy fabric to oblige. The clear language drifting their way from other rooms told Noel how effective the barrier would be at actually concealing their conversation, but at least it gave the illusion of privacy.

"What do you think he said?" Noel was genuinely curious. He now knew why Lionel distrusted Ryker. But what did Ryker think of Lionel?

Ryker shrugged and frowned at the floor. "Whatever he said, it probably wasn't true."

"Really? Even the part about him saving you from a whoopin' by the pastor's kid?"

Ryker's gaze snapped up. He looked surprised for a moment, then scowled. "He didn't save me. I had it handled."

Noel crossed his arms and looked at him askance. "Like you have that addiction you swore you didn't have 'handled'?"

Ryker's scowl deepened, and his shoulders hunched. "Things aren't always how they look," he muttered.

Noel exchanged glances with Jared, then looked back at Ryker. "Why don't you tell us your version, then? Mrs. Crawford said we've got some time before they send you home."

Ryker didn't look up, and his unruly mop obscured his eyes so all Noel saw was his jaw working. A moment later, a droplet of moisture fell to the tile floor, and Noel blinked in surprise.

Ryker was crying.

"It's all stupid Jordan's stupid fault," Ryker said at last, his voice cracking in anguish. "I kept trying to do what he wanted, but he kept changing the rules. And now, he's going to make it so I don't see Ryleigh anymore, either."

He swiped at his face, wiping away tears.

Noel pushed himself to his feet, steadying himself with a little weight on his air boot, and hobbled nearer the boy. "Hey," he said gently.

Ryker looked up, his eyes streaming.

"Is it okay if I give you a hug?"

Noel honestly didn't know what Ryker would say to that, but Ryker only hesitated a moment before nodding. Noel wrapped him in a bear hug around his shoulders, and Ryker squeezed him around the waist, his body heaving with sobs. Jared came and stood beside them, laying a comforting hand on Ryker's shoulder. When Ryker started sniffling, Jared retrieved a box of tissues from the counter and placed it next to Ryker on the exam table.

After a few minutes, Ryker pulled away and used the tissues to clean his face. Noel and Jared sat down again and waited.

Ryker looked as though he was struggling to find words and coming up empty.

"Take your time," Jared said.

Noel nodded his agreement and leaned his elbows on his knees, not wanting to rush the boy.

After a few moments more, Ryker drew a long breath. "It started not long after the Richardsons made us start going to youth group."

In fits and spurts, he shared his side of the story—how Ryleigh had soon made friends at youth group, but how the only kid who'd talked to him had been Jordan. How his one attempt to talk to Trevor had been shut down by an angry Lionel. How Jordan had approached him to offer him drugs after youth group one night.

"Like I'd take that stuff after what it did to my mom. No, thanks." Ryker snorted.

When Ryker refused, Jordan had planted some drugs on him, ratted him out, and then threatened Ryker not to tell anyone he was involved, promising him no one would believe the foster kid over the pastor's kid anyway.

"Jordan musta thought I looked like easy prey, I guess. I wasn't, but he didn't know that. So he set me up and blackmailed me. And the worst part was, he was right. People didn't believe me."

"You told the Richardsons that Jordan set you up?" Noel asked.

"No. But I told them the drugs weren't mine. I didn't know what Jordan would do if I pointed the finger at him, so I just said I didn't know how they got into my bag. They let the first time slide with a warning, but I could tell they didn't really believe me. And I think one of them musta talked to the pastor or something, or maybe one of the kids said something, because Jordan came after me anyway, saying he heard that I kept saying the drugs weren't mine. He threatened me again not to tell anyone about him, and gave me reason enough to believe he'd follow through that I swore I wouldn't."

Noel got a sinking feeling in his stomach. Not only had he misjudged Jordan, he'd misjudged Ryker, too. The teen hadn't been on drugs—he'd been being manipulated. Had Jordan been listening in when Noel had called Vic about Ryker and Lionel the other day? Or maybe Vic simply asking Jordan about Ryker had prompted this attack. Noel caught himself clenching his fists. Deliberately, he relaxed them, letting out a long breath. He didn't need Ryker thinking Noel was mad at him and clamming up.

"And I didn't tell a soul. But Ryleigh kinda guessed," Ryker continued. "She told Mrs. Patel, the social worker, but when Mrs. Patel made me tell her who the dealer was who was setting me up, I don't think *she* believed us, either." Ryker faded off, betrayal in his voice. If anyone was supposed to believe a foster kid, it was their social worker.

Jared made a noise in his throat, and Noel met his gaze. Meera Patel and her family went to Peace Crossing Christian Assembly, and they were friends with the Olsons. Jordan had probably had her fooled, too, along with everyone else.

"Anyway, I don't know how Jordan found out I told, but that's when he set me up again, and this time, he said if I didn't admit it was me that he'd hurt Ryleigh." He swallowed. "He said I couldn't tell her. I couldn't tell anyone, or he said . . . he said he'd make sure I went to jail so she'd be on her own. And he'd hurt her. So, that time, I said the drugs were mine, and that I'd been lying before. It broke Ryleigh's heart, I could tell. And, of course, the Richardsons kicked me out." His voice cracked again. "Do you guys know if she's okay?"

"Yeah, she's okay," Jared said. "She's with the Richardsons now. Do you have your phone? She probably texted you."

Ryker shook his head. "My battery's dead."

"You want to send her an update on mine?" Jared handed his phone to Ryker with the screen unlocked. "I'm sure she's worried sick."

Ryker sniffled and nodded, accepting the phone.

As Ryker tapped out his message, Noel fought a seething rage. This kid had been dealing with things beyond his years for his entire life. And the people who were supposed to be advocating for him hadn't been. Noel didn't blame them exactly, but he wanted *someone* to blame. It was so easy for kids like Ryker to get lost in the cracks. And here he'd been thinking he was helping, when he'd been as blind as everyone else to the real situation.

"Do you know why Jordan was threatening you again to-day?" Noel asked.

Ryker shrugged. "'Cause he can, probably."

Noel clenched his fists again. Part of him wanted to track down Jordan Olson and show the kid what a real punch was like . . . but he knew that wouldn't help anything except to release his own anger. He'd hurt enough people by losing control of his temper. Jordan and his friends would be dealt with—the right way.

"Hey, Ryker?" Jared said.

Ryker focused on the youth pastor.

"Uh, I know you're tired and you probably just want to go home, but we need to talk to the police after this. You need to tell them what happened."

Ryker hesitated. "Will they be able to keep me and Ryleigh safe from Jordan?"

"They've kept you safe from Joe, right?"

Noel guessed *Joe* was the name of their late mom's abusive boyfriend.

Ryker nodded. "Okay."

Noel had to give it to the kid, he had guts. If Noel had been as smart at his age, his own story—and Jackson's, and Maddie's—might have gone differently.

Or maybe not. Years and time had allowed him to see that Jackson and Maddie had both made their own choices, and he'd had far less to do with them than he'd thought when he was younger. Besides, being with Stephanie was so much easier than being with Maddie had ever been.

As though the thought had summoned her, Steph swept aside the curtain with a blood pressure machine in tow.

Noel gave her a big grin. "I was just thinking about you."

She blushed in that adorable way of hers, then turned to Ryker. "Okay, I just need to check your vitals, and you should be good to go."

She glanced around at all of them, obviously assessing the situation. Ryker's eyes were still puffy and red, but his posture was straighter and he looked less defeated than he had a minute ago.

Steph gave the teen a kind smile. "Are you getting things sorted out with these two?"

Ryker managed a smile too. "Yeah." He gave Jared and Noel grateful looks. "Thanks, guys."

As Noel watched Steph work on Ryker with practised, gentle movements, he realized, for the first time, that he was ready to let the sting of Maddie's betrayal go. He wondered if she felt the same. Would she be ready to clear the air if he asked her?

He hoped so. Because he intended to, as soon as possible. He didn't want his past coming between him and Stephanie for one more second.

Chapter Nineteen

STEPHANIE STOOD IN PEARL'S Petals and frowned at the mug in her hand, trying to decide if Noel would like it. It featured two cute illustrated cats in Santa hats with a caption that read *Meow-y Christmas!* Strong scents of pine, eucalyptus, floral-scented candles, essential oils, and potpourri permeated the air, fogging her thoughts and drowning out the lighter scents of the fresh cut flowers in the back and the trailing live plants near the big front windows. The mug was funny, but Noel wasn't really a cat person. Frustrated, she set it back on the glass display shelf and looked around for other gift ideas.

She'd come to the shop on a last-minute whim. During her shift last night, she'd realized that, after all the gifts Noel had given her this month, she hadn't purchased a single one for him—not even a birthday present. And there was only one more day until his birthday-slash-Christmas.

She'd already been wandering through the dozens of small nooks in the crowded shop for ten minutes without any luck, her panic increasing by the second. What if, after a month of Noel proving he was the most thoughtful man alive, she failed to find even a single gift that would show him how much he'd come to mean to her? How could she have left this until the very last second? She needed help, but she had yet to see an employee. They were probably caught up doing something in the back.

She had just decided to track someone down when the bell above the front door chimed.

"Be with you in a minute," called a woman's voice from somewhere in the back, followed by the approaching quick steps of the salesperson.

Instead of stepping into the narrow aisle and blocking the woman's way, Steph waited inside the little nook of mugs. Moments later, Maddie swept past to greet the new customer, her slim figure clad in a blue florist's apron and her gingery ponytail bouncing with her determined step. Steph stopped short. She'd known it was possible that Maddie would be here, but she hadn't really counted on needing to ask her for help to shop for a gift for Noel. How awkward would that be? She didn't really have anything against Maddie, or she wouldn't have come in here, but still . . .

She glanced over her shoulder at the mugs, weighing her options. Maybe she could keep wandering on her own for a bit longer. If she got *really* desperate, then she would ask. Or just leave and go shopping online. The gift would be late, but at least it would be a good fit, and she could tell Noel it was on the way. She repressed a sigh. It was her own fault for not thinking of this until Christmas Eve.

Steph was just about to emerge from the mug alcove when a deep male voice made her stop in her tracks.

"Hi, Maddie," he said.

It was Noel.

Steph froze, holding her breath, and stepped back into the alcove. Why was Noel talking to Maddie as though they were on comfortable, familiar terms?

"Hello, Noel," Maddie said stiffly.

Okay, maybe not so comfortable. Maybe Noel was here to buy Steph a gift. Pearl's Petals was a gift shop and florist's, after all, and after a month of daily gifts, he had to be scraping the bottom of the barrel of what Peace Crossing had to offer. Could she blame him, when she was struggling to find only one?

That meant if she stepped out now, she would ruin the surprise. But what if they started meandering around and found her here?

Unsure of what to do, Steph stood in place and listened.

"Can I help you with something?" Maddie said.

"It's surprisingly quiet in here for Christmas Eve," Noel observed.

"It's the snow. We had quite a few last-minute folks earlier, though. Besides, we close in fifteen minutes, and most folks are done shopping." That remark sounded pointed, and Steph squirmed.

"I see."

Noel paused. Steph tried not to move. Catching herself holding her breath, she let it out slowly and quietly.

"Listen," Noel said, "We need to talk. Do you have a minute?"

Steph's throat closed. Why would Noel want to talk to Maddie?

"About what?" Maddie said, sounding truly perplexed.

"You know what. The reason why we avoid each other in public, that's what."

"I don't know what you're referring to."

Steph crept closer to the edge of the shelf and peeked around it toward the front. Maddie's expression was pleasant enough, but she had picked up a cloth and was wiping down the counter beside the till as though it had offended her. Steph could just see Noel, leaning on his crutches and looking at Maddie. Neither of them had noticed Steph.

"That night? At the party? With Jackson?" he said.

Steph cocked her ears. Noel had mentioned a fallout with his school friend Jackson Cardinal once before, though he hadn't given any details. Steph remembered that Jackson had been arrested for drug dealing when they were all in twelfth grade. Did that have something to do with Noel? Or maybe Maddie? Curious, she strained to hear what came next, a sense of impending doom clutching her innards. Whatever this was about, Noel hadn't wanted to tell her. She wasn't sure she wanted to know why.

Maddie stopped wiping and gave Noel a cool look. "And why would I want to talk about that?"

Noel frowned. "You probably don't. But I need to." He let out a frustrated sigh, glancing toward the front window, then back at Maddie. "Look, I'm just going to say something to you, and then you can keep hating me if you want. I get why you did what you did, and I'm sorry for not listening to you when you said not to go to that party. But that's not even the real issue. Maddie, I made a mistake, but so did you. I thought we might be able to be adults and move past it now. Forgive and forget."

"Just like that?" Maddie stiffened, glaring. "As though—poof!—the whole thing never happened? That your buddy Jackson didn't almost get my friend killed? That you didn't try to protect him instead of coming forward with the truth?"

"What happened with Jackson was a mess. I made a bad call, and I regret it. But I came to you first for advice, remember? And you turned around and . . ." Noel stopped and rubbed his hand over his mouth. "You know what? Never mind. This was a bad idea. At least I can say I tried."

"You *tried*?" Maddie stepped out from behind the counter and advanced on Noel. He stood his ground, even when she pointed her finger in his face. "*Trying* would be taking responsibility for your actual mistake. Ignoring my request that you not attend some stupid high school party instead of my basketball game? Yeah, you could have been more considerate, I guess, because I really would have liked you at my game. But that's not the real problem, is it? The problem is, your actions jeopardized someone I care about, and then you lied about it and tried to cover it up. And look where that got you. Jackson went to jail anyway, and you and I broke up. Hope it was worth it."

"I never meant for Sarah to get hurt," Noel said calmly. "What happened to her hit me hard, too. But I was trying to do the right thing. If our positions had been reversed, would you have turned your friend in without a second thought?"

"I wouldn't have been hanging out with a drug dealer in the first place! You put yourself in that bad position, Noel. And what happened to Jackson was on him."

"Yes, it was. But you were the one who betrayed my trust. Instead of letting me work things out my own way, you took matters into your own hands. Things could have gone differently for Jackson, and they could have gone differently for us. Don't you think you could have handled the situation better?"

"Definitely. I could have smartened up two years earlier and stayed broken up with you the first time. And warned Sarah to stay away from you and your friends."

Noel sighed. Steph couldn't see his face, but in her mind's eye, she imagined that frown he wore when he was trying to make a point.

"Look, I understand why you're angry, Maddie. I would be too. But yelling isn't going to solve anything. We can't change the past, and I'm tired of letting it define us. We don't have to be friends, but I was hoping we could clear the air and move on."

"Yeah?" Maddie's voice seethed with hostility. "Well, I'm afraid I'm not ready to sweep this under a rug to assuage your feelings. I'm sorry if that offends you. But since you've been trying to solve your problems at the bottom of a bottle since high school, I think it's for the best we finally broke up when we did, or it could have been me upside down in a ditch one night instead of Jenny."

Steph suppressed a squeak. Bottom of a bottle? Noel didn't drink, did he? And what was Maddie referring to with the ditch and Noel's sister? The claws of doom around her stomach expanded their death grip to her heart. Steph carefully picked up a mug that was blocking her view, clutching it against her belly as she peeked between the shelves.

Noel had gone as stiff and straight as his crutches. "How did you even hear about that?" he said in a low voice.

Maddie arched a brow. "You grew up in this town, and you need to ask that?" Then she snorted. "I was dating the son of the guy who owned the wrecking yard at the time. He said you and your sister were lucky you walked away from that car. It was in rough shape." Maddie crossed her arms. "You always thought you were in control of everything. 'The Man with the Plan.' Isn't that what you told me when I said you should tell the police about Jackson? 'Trust me, Maddie, I know what I'm doing.' But you didn't, did you? And your sister almost died, too. I bet you never planned on that, did you?"

Another few seconds passed as Noel's jaw worked. Blood whooshed through Stephanie's ears. The room felt about ten degrees warmer than when she'd walked in here, and she didn't think she could move if she tried.

Finally, Noel breathed out. "If you ever change your mind, you know how to find me. Please wish your mom a Merry Christmas from me."

Then he clumped to the door. The chiming bell punctuated his departure.

Maddie's posture slumped, and she leaned against the counter as though she'd just been granted reprieve from a boxing match.

Steph's thoughts spun. She'd wondered for so long what had happened between Noel and Maddie, and it couldn't be clearer that this was it—whatever *this* was. She'd heard enough to know Noel had been keeping secrets from her, but not enough to truly understand what they were. Besides some shady business with Jackson that Noel and Maddie had broken up over, it sounded like Maddie thought Noel had caused an accident because he'd been drinking—an accident that had nearly killed him and his sister.

Without warning, Steph was twelve years old and back in the passenger seat of her father's car, her heart rattling and her throat raw as she screamed a warning about the oncoming vehicle. Eddie had drifted into the wrong lane, but when he wrenched the wheel to prevent a collision, their car had spun on some black ice. The side hit the snow piled in the ditch, and the vehicle tumbled over and over again. Unlike Jenny, Melody hadn't walked away from the wreckage.

The mug Steph was holding slipped through her slick hands and clattered to the hardwood floor, bringing her back to the present with a jump. She scrambled after it, horrified. Fortunately, it hadn't broken. However, when she scooped the mug up and straightened, Maddie was standing there, looking at her. Steph's throat went dry, and she tried to gather thoughts that still skittered like anxious mice.

"You heard that, didn't you?" Maddie said.

Steph nodded, not trusting her voice.

"Sorry about that." Maddie smoothed her apron. When she straightened, she had a customer service smile on her face. "Can I help you with something?"

Steph's knees wobbled, and she must have looked a fright. "Did Noel ever cheat on you?" she blurted.

Maddie blinked, frowning as she looked Stephanie over. "In high school? No. Why do you ask?"

"At the dance, when you two broke up, you called him a liar. Why did you say that?"

Maddie frowned, taking Steph's measure. "Are you interested in him?"

Steph shrugged, but it must not have been as noncommittal as she'd hoped, because Maddie pursed her lips.

"Then you should ask him about what happened. If he really wants to clear the air from the past like he says, he'll tell you. And if not . . . you're probably better off without him."

Steph swallowed, feeling a desperate urge to get out of the shop and think. Realizing she was still holding the mug, she shoved it at Maddie, mumbled a thank you, and rushed out the door, breathing hard.

She'd been asking Noel for a peek into his past for weeks. He hadn't exactly lied to her, but he certainly hadn't told her the truth—not about the parts he'd come to discuss with Maddie, anyway. There were obviously a lot of things about Noel Butler that she didn't know, and the weight of them threatened to crush her into the icy sidewalk as she hurried to her little SUV. Her fingers were shaking so badly that she could barely press the button on her fob to unlock her car. How could she have been so careless with her heart? She'd trusted Noel. She'd thought he was different—nothing like the man who'd abdicated his role as a father to a bottle, leaving their family in ruins and her sister dead. But now, it looked like Noel Butler and Eddie Bell might not be so different after all.

She collapsed into the driver's seat, laid her head on her hands on the steering wheel, and flooded them with tears as cold as her fears.

Chapter Twenty

N OEL SHIFTED HIS WEIGHT on his crutches, staring at the bottles of warm brown liquid behind the dark bar. His gut still churned from his encounter with Maddie, and his parched throat begged for the comforting burn of liquor—and the numb peace he knew would follow. Someone else came through the door of the Trading Post in a flurry of cold air. The bartender, a pretty young woman in a body-conscious black button-down shirt, gave the newcomer a nod, but Noel couldn't look away from the alcoholic potions calling his name. The bartender caught his eye, set the glass she'd been drying on a shelf behind her, turned, and placed both hands on the bar, looking right at him.

"Did you decide?" she asked.

"Uh . . ." He knew what he wanted. But he hadn't given up wrestling with his better judgment just yet.

"Two coffees. Dark roast. Black," came a man's deep, familiar voice at his elbow.

Guiltily, Noel turned to face the speaker. Carl Butler's dark toque was dusted with fresh snow, and the warm parka he wore did little to disguise a tall frame that was still pretty lean for a guy in his fifties, thanks to a regular running routine.

"Dad." Noel didn't know what else to say.

"Son." The word was a chastisement and an embrace at the same time. Carl's dark eyes met Noel's. "Join me for coffee?"

"Sure."

He didn't care for coffee much, and he might regret having it this late at night—but not nearly as much as what he'd almost done. With a nod toward the bartender to confirm his choice, Noel followed his father to a booth along the wall. The bar was mostly empty except for a few die-hards, and when the bartender brought their coffees over, she reminded them the place was closing at eight for the holiday.

"Oh, I'm sure we'll be out of your hair long before then," Carl assured her in his measured way. "You deserve to have Christmas Eve off, too."

She flashed a grin, then left them alone. When she'd gone, Carl turned his attention to Noel, who was studiously examining the still-quivering surface of his coffee.

"How did you know I was here?" Noel asked.

"A father always knows."

Noel levelled a dry look at his dad, and Carl smirked.

"I was leaving the post office and saw you walk in. From the way you made the sidewalk shake with every stab of your crutches, I figured it wasn't a business appointment. Thought I'd come check on you."

Noel gave a soft snort. "Thanks."

He took a sip of his coffee. Just having his dad there had helped calm him a little, and he knew he would be truly grateful later that Carl had shown up before Noel had done something epically stupid. The fact that he'd almost backslid after four years and seven days of sobriety rankled. And for what? Because Maddie wouldn't forgive him? How needy was he becoming?

"So, are you going to tell me why you're in here, or am I going to have to drag it out of you?" Carl kept his steady gaze on Noel as he took a sip of his coffee.

Noel drew a few long breaths and took a couple sips of his own before he answered.

"You know Madeleine Kennedy, right? The girl I dated in high school?"

"Rose's daughter? Of course I do. Your mother mentions her on occasion, and she was in my class for a couple of years. She's a hard worker, that one—earned every A she got. And she seems to be doing a fair job for herself over at Pearl's." Carl frowned. "Does whatever this is have to do with her?"

"Yes. And no." Noel sighed, his anger still beating a rapid rhythm against his eardrums. "She's as stubborn now as she was then, but that hasn't been my problem for ten years, so this can't be about that."

He wished he could articulate what it *was* about.

Carl seemed to sense his need to work things through for a minute and waited quietly, sipping his coffee. When the silence stretched, he said, "Your mother tells me you've been spending a lot of time with a new girl. What's her name? Cecily?"

"Stephanie. Stephanie Neufeld."

"Stephanie Neufeld?" He frowned as though searching his memory. "Right, I remember. Tall girl. Dark hair. Quite the looker."

Noel's chest warmed. Of course, *he* thought Stephanie was gorgeous, but the impressed look in his father's eye felt like an endorsement of some kind.

"So does this have anything to do with *her*?" Carl asked.

Noel stared toward the bar. The thirst for alcohol was fading, but the feeling that had precipitated the craving lingered. It was a feeling he'd come to recognize—vulnerability.

He hated that feeling. But ever since he'd met Stephanie, it had been poking his edges until they'd started to fray, ever so slightly. He hadn't felt that way for a long time . . . he'd made sure of it. But being with Stephanie, he found himself *wanting* to see if there was something besides sharks and pirates beyond the walls he'd built around his heart.

Caleb had been right a few weeks ago when he'd said Noel was afraid to see where things might go with Stephanie. And Noel abruptly realized he still was.

"Yeah, you know, it just might." He turned to his dad. "Things ended badly between Maddie and me, and I think I'm afraid it's going to happen again."

"Hmph. You must really like this girl if you're worried about that."

Noel thought of Stephanie—her caring, steadfast heart, her fiery spirit, the way she made him laugh, the way she grounded him. There were times he wanted to wrap her in his arms and never let her go.

He nodded. "That might be an understatement."

Carl eyed him. "Have you talked to her about your concerns?"

Noel shook his head and frowned at the table. "I haven't. Things are good between us right now, and I don't see much sense in rocking the boat in calm waters. I'm no storm-chaser."

"But if a storm is already brewing on the horizon?" Carl, said raising his brows.

Noel pondered that. "Who says it is?"

Carl tilted his head toward the bar, indicating their surroundings, and Noel nodded sheepishly.

"Okay, yeah. I get it."

Carl took another sip of coffee, then set his cup down and looked at it as he spoke, as though he were telling it a story. "Did I ever tell you about the night I met your mother?"

Noel rolled his eyes. Carl and Violet's meet-cute was so much a part of their family lore that it was practically a legend. "About a million times. You met at some dance club your college friends dragged you to. You thought she was the most beautiful woman you'd ever seen, fell instantly in love, and you two were inseparable from then on."

"Ah," Carl said, smiling, "but I haven't told you all of it."

Noel looked at him, intrigued.

"You may not believe this, but I've never been much of a dancer."

Noel chuckled, despite himself. "Why wouldn't I believe it? I haven't seen you dance once."

"Okay, you have a point. But I *did* dance once, and the first time was that night. You see, when I saw your mother, I was thunderstruck. After some 'encouragement' from my friends, I finally worked up the nerve to go talk to her. By *encouragement*, I mean that they basically set me up and left me standing in front of her alone."

Carl chuckled at the memory.

"Anyway, after my friends left me stammering like a ninny with my face on fire, your mother—being the gracious woman she is—asked me to dance. I must have looked like a frightened calf, because she said, 'You dance, right?'" He shook his head at the idea. "Of course I didn't dance! But I definitely didn't want to tell her that my idea of a good time was a night cozying up with the encyclopedia. So I said I did, then prayed all the way onto the dance floor."

Noel laughed, picturing his embarrassed father trying to impress a much younger Violet.

Carl continued. "God answered my prayer, because the next song was a slow dance. So instead of embarrassing myself, I got to hold your mother in my arms as I kind of leaned back and forth." Carl demonstrated by holding up his arms as though holding a partner and shifting his body this way and that. "You know what I'm talking about, right?"

Noel nodded. "Yep, sure do. The 'sway' has saved many an awkward young man, including me."

Carl let his arms drop. "Anyway, after the song was over, I asked her out for coffee, and we hit it off. Soon, we were spending all our free time together. But she kept bugging me to go out dancing again, and I was too embarrassed to tell her I didn't know how, so I kept making excuses. One night, she handed me a brochure. I took a look, and it was for a couples' beginning swing dance class. She said, 'I figured it would be fun to learn some new moves together.' That's when I knew she'd figured out my secret—and she didn't care. Not only that, she was right. We had a blast at that class."

Carl chuckled, shaking his head.

"I'm still not much of a dancer, but I figured one thing out—I wanted to spend the rest of my life with a woman like your mom. And so far, I'd say it's working out okay." He smirked. "But I can't say I'm a fast learner, at least in matters of the heart. Even now, I still need the occasional reminder that, even though I think I should know all the answers, your mom loves me whether I do or don't."

Noel smiled back, picturing his parents young and in love and giggling through a swing dance class. "Okay, I hear what you're saying—that I should talk to Steph about what's going on. But this is about something a bit heavier than not knowing how to dance. If I tell Steph what happened back then, it could be over between us." His jaw tightened at the idea.

Carl tilted his head. "If this girl can't handle the truth about something that happened ten years ago, this relationship was never meant to last in the first place. And wouldn't you rather find that out now than in another six months? Or six years?"

Noel had to admit that his dad had a point.

"Besides," Carl continued, "the real point of my story was this—she probably already knows something's going on. Lasting relationships are built on openness and trust, not mystery and secrets. Keeping it from her could be the very thing that pulls you apart. Wouldn't you rather it ended because you were brave enough to tell the truth instead of too afraid to take a chance?"

Noel's entire body tensed at those words, and he clenched his fists to contain another surge of anger. But even though his dad's words hurt, it was because they carried the sting of truth. His relationship with Stephanie was only a few weeks old, but there had already been several instances where he'd brushed off questions that got too close to this tender part of his soul, and the resulting hurt in her eyes had pushed the knife deeper. If they were going to continue to build something that would last—and he sincerely hoped they could—he was going to have to face this fear with her and let the chips fall where they may.

He drew a long, deep breath, and then gave a nod. "You're right. As per usual."

Carl chuckled. "It's a gift that comes with experience. Sounds like you're about to get some of that yourself."

Noel laughed dryly. "Sooner than later," he said, thinking of the evening he was about to spend with Steph—and a few dozen of their closest friends. "You and Mom and Jenny are coming to the party after the Christmas Eve service tonight, right?"

He knew Carl's idea of a good night was drinking tea and reading a good book, but since Violet's hand bell choir was performing at the St. John's Cathedral service, Noel hoped his dad would make the night a double header of socializing. And since Noel's sister was home from university, he'd invited his whole family to attend the party. His only regret was that he would miss the service himself, but seeing Steph's face when she found out about the party would be worth it.

Carl gave a long-suffering sigh. "We'll at least put in an appearance. Your mother would have my head if we don't." His indulgent smile belied his words. "Besides, you know how your sister loves a party."

"Awesome." Noel drained his coffee, then checked the time on his phone. "Shoot. I was supposed to be home to meet Steph ten minutes ago. Say, would you mind driving me so I don't have to call a cab?"

"It would be my deepest joy and honour." Carl said it with a straight face, but he couldn't hide the twinkle in his eye.

Shaking his head at his father's humour, Noel left some cash for the coffee on the table. Hauling himself to his feet, he followed Carl outside to his four-door sedan.

On the short ride to his apartment building, Noel sent Stephanie a text to apologize for being late, but she didn't respond. When they got there, he was surprised that her little silver CR-V wasn't already waiting outside. Thanking his dad, he went up to his apartment, poured himself a glass of water to wash the taste of coffee from his mouth, and then tried calling her. Again, no answer.

Frowning, he decided to give her a few minutes before trying again. Maybe she'd gotten caught up doing something. He exchanged several texts with his sponsor to explain his near miss at the Trading Post, and Mark's encouraging words, along with his Christmas and birthday wishes, reminded Noel how blessed he was with the calibre of people he had on his team. Pausing, he sent up a prayer of thanks for his dad appearing when Noel needed him most.

Noel puttered around for a few more minutes, gathering the things he wanted to take to the party, which wasn't much. He'd sent the bulk of Ryker's decorations over to Cool Beans with Caleb earlier that day. The kid had still been pretty shook up and downright exhausted after what had happened with Jordan the night before.

After they'd left the hospital, they'd spent an hour at the police station so Ryker could make his statement. Noel felt a pang for Vic Olson, who'd sounded completely shell-shocked when they'd spoken a few hours earlier. Jordan had been arrested, but Vic said that since it was a first offence, the system would likely go easy on him. Noel just hoped it would be enough for the kid to turn his life around. He made a mental note to keep the family in his prayers and to look for other ways to support them going forward.

As far as Ryker's party commitments, though, the teen had been as good as his word. He'd finished everything he'd promised, including a bunch of little signs for the party snacks.

Noel wished he could say the same for the jewellery box he was making Stephanie. Despite what she'd said about leaving it unfinished, he'd wanted to protect the wood so it would last for many years, so he'd used a homemade beeswax polish to allow the natural tones of the material to take centre stage. He was quite pleased with the resulting vibrancy of the wood grain. He hoped Stephanie would like it too. While he waited, he decided to glue in the jewels.

He'd just carefully placed the last one when his phone buzzed, and he unlocked the screen with a flick of his thumb. But as he read Steph's text about not feeling up for a date and her plans to stay in, his gut clenched, and he hit the dial button.

She didn't pick up, and he let out a grunt of frustration. Her change of heart must have something to do with the anniversary of Melody's passing. He should have planned for this possibility. Not for the first time, he cursed the clumsiness that had left him with a casted leg. Maybe he should hop in his truck and go to her anyway. His foot had healed enough that he thought he could do it.

Then the voice of reason—the voice that had actually learned something since falling off that roof—encouraged him to think of another way. Especially since he knew how peeved Steph would be if he drove against doctor's orders.

Instead, he called Autumn. When she picked up the phone, she sounded flustered.

"You almost here?" she demanded.

"No, unfortunately." He filled her in about Steph's text, then said, "Of all the things that I thought might go wrong, this wasn't on the list."

"I'll take care of it," Autumn said, and hung up.

A few minutes later, she called back. "I talked to Steph and convinced her to come out for 'coffee' here at the shop. She'll be here in half an hour or so, she said. It wasn't easy—she sounded a little shaken up. Did something happen?"

"Not that I know of." Noel hadn't spoken to Steph since he left the hospital with Jared and Ryker the night before, but he didn't think that the incident would have kept her from their date. "Could it just be the anniversary?"

Autumn sounded thoughtful. "Maybe. She doesn't usually get that torn up about it anymore, and with all the progress she's made this year, I thought she'd be completely okay. Maybe I was wrong?" She sighed, then gasped and shouted away from the phone, "Julien, don't touch that, please. Mom, can you grab him?"

Noel blinked in surprise. "Sounds like I better let you go. I'll get there as soon as I can. Steph was my ride, but I'll get Jared to bring me over instead."

"Okay. See ya soon." She ended the call.

Tucking his phone in his pocket, he surveyed the wooden jewellery box, inspecting his work. He also thought it strange that Stephanie had suddenly changed her mind about tonight—and that she was willing to go see her sister, but not go on the date she'd agreed to with him. It bothered him that she didn't trust him enough to tell him what was bothering *her*.

An uneasy feeling gnawed at his gut—the feeling that Stephanie was keeping something from him or was even outright blowing him off. That she wasn't being honest so she could hurt him behind his back.

He blew out a breath. Steph wasn't Maddie. And if he didn't want this relationship to end the way that one had, he knew what he had to do.

He tucked the jewellery box into a simple paper shopping bag and let out a long breath.

"Time to learn to dance."

Chapter Twenty-One

STEPH STOOD IN FRONT of the full-length mirror in her bedroom, smoothing her red velvet dress and checking the details of her outfit. Why had she let Autumn talk her into going to this stupid party? She didn't want to see Noel. She wasn't ready to talk about what she'd learned at Pearl's Petals just yet and wanted more time to think about it before confronting him.

On the other hand, waiting would only prolong the dread. Maybe she should call him now and get it over with on the phone. Then she might not even need to go to the party. If Maddie's accusation about his history with drinking was true—not to mention defending a drug dealer, apparently—she would need to end things with him immediately. She hadn't seen Noel drink anything stronger than plain eggnog since they'd been together, but he wouldn't be the first alcoholic to hide his dependency. And drinking was an absolute no-go on her list.

Her eyes watered, and the salt stung cheeks still raw from crying. She didn't want to break up with Noel. If her worst fears proved true, would she be able to go through with it? She suddenly gained a smidgen more empathy for why it took her mother so long to leave Eddie behind—some ghosts were harder to exorcise than others.

After sliding her earrings into her lobes, she took a step back and admired the effect. If tonight was the night she ended their fledgling relationship, at least she'd look fabulous doing it.

Her doorbell rang, and she frowned. Had Noel come to see her instead? Her stomach flipped as she bustled down the long hall of the mobile home and opened the door.

But, instead of Noel, she was greeted by the sight of Eddie Bell awkwardly holding a paper shopping bag in his gloved hands.

"Hi, Steph," he said stiffly. Fresh snow dusted the shoulders of his black dress coat and the rim of his black fedora. "May I come in? I won't take much time."

Stephanie almost said no, but something about his uncertain posture made her think twice. *I can at least see what he wants.*

Wordlessly, Steph stepped back and let her father through the doorway that led directly into her little kitchen. She moved across the room, turned to face him, and leaned against the counter—both for support and to put a slight distance between them.

"I didn't expect to see you after you no-showed the other day."

Her tone was cold, but she didn't care. She was tired of being yanked around by this man. After he'd disappointed Julien, the dim spark of hope she'd allowed herself that Eddie might have really changed had been extinguished. She *had* to stay cold, or she'd be disappointed again too.

"Yeah, about that." He shifted on his feet. "Would you tell Autumn I'm sorry for skipping out on her and Julien? I didn't mean to upset the little guy."

"Then why did you?" Steph crossed her arms.

Eddie drew a breath. "What you said at the hospital made me think. I'm . . . not a good role model. I know that. And as much as I want to get to know Autumn, and Julien, and you . . ." His gaze met hers, then skittered away. He cleared his throat, but his voice still trembled. "You were right. I should stay away. You'll all be better off without me."

Steph's gut twisted. Could he be truly sorrowful for his past? And, if he *had* changed, did Steph want to be the one who stood between him and a chance to make things right? A yearning tugged at her heart—to see if, after all these years, she could make peace with the man who'd caused her so much pain. She felt her resolve weakening.

"Why did you come here, then?" she asked, but the iron was gone from her voice.

He licked his lips and held out the bag. "I got this for Julien. I was hoping you'd pass it along for me." When she made no move to take it, he took a step sideways and placed it on her dining room table. "Tell him it's from you—I didn't wrap it or put my name on it. I just want him to have it."

Curious, Steph hesitated, then walked over to the table and looked in the bag. Nestled in the bottom was a large, brightly coloured plastic truck, still in the packaging.

"Autumn mentioned he likes trucks," Eddie added.

"He does. They're his favourite," she said, her throat tight.

Once again, she remembered the Christmas morning her father had surprised her and her sisters with their special engraved bracelets. He could be extremely thoughtful when he wanted to be. He'd given them more than a few special gifts like this when they were kids. Back when things were okay. Looking up into his steely grey eyes, she saw the unspoken longing there—a longing she recognized. A longing for forgiveness, for peace.

"Look," he said, licking his lips, "I understand why you hate me. Can't say that I blame you, either. I always swore, growing up, that I'd never turn into my old man, but . . . in the end . . ." His voice cracked, and he turned away. "I'm not making excuses. But I sure do wish I could go back and change a few things."

Steph's mouth went dry, and she swallowed. Apparently, Autumn had been right about Eddie's remorse over not only what had happened to Melody, but to all of them. What he'd done to their family. She drew a long, shaky breath, looking him over.

His outfit registered with her as odd. "Why are you all dressed up?"

"Oh. Um, . . ." Eddie looked down at himself, as though he was surprised to find he was wearing a dress coat and slacks and shiny dress shoes. "I'm, uh, performing tonight."

"You're what?" Steph wasn't sure she'd heard him right. She thought of the ancient acoustic guitar Eddie used to play when he was in a melancholy mood or on the few occasions when he'd get together with a few of his friends to jam. "Do you still play guitar?"

"I do, but, uh . . . okay, don't laugh. I'm playing in the hand bell choir for the Christmas Eve service at St. John's Cathedral."

Steph nearly choked. "You are?" She didn't know which surprised her more—Eddie playing hand bells or attending a Christmas Eve service. "What prompted that?"

Eddie straightened. "I ran into my old friend Violet Butler not long after I came back to town last month, and she invited me to join. Do you know her?"

Steph gave a strangled laugh and nodded. What were the chances?

"You know," he continued, "I'm not even sure why I said yes, but I'm glad I did. It's been fun. I've even gone to church at St. John's a couple of times." He glanced down, blushing, and pulled his phone from his coat pocket to check the time. "I should probably go, actually."

Steph's mouth had dropped open, and it took her several seconds to find any words. When she did, the last thing she expected to say was, "Would it be okay if I come and watch?"

He glanced up in surprise. "Yeah. That would be more than okay." A small grin quirked his lips. "I'd like that."

She nodded, something passing between them that she hadn't felt in a long time. A softening, like they might be taking the first step toward a new beginning.

She glanced away from the intense eye contact, her sinuses prickling. "I'll see you down there. And I'll make sure Julien gets this."

"Thank you." With a final nod and a genuine smile, Eddie turned and let himself out the door.

As chill air from the closing door wafted over her, Steph glanced down at the bag and wiped away the moisture trailing down her cheek. She pulled out her phone and sent a group text to Noel, Autumn, and her mother.

Going to watch Eddie play hand bells at the St. John's service. Will come to party after.

As she dropped her phone back in her purse, part of her accused her of delaying the inevitable confrontation with Noel. But another part of her felt that this was something she *had* to do. She had to see with her own eyes that Eddie Bell had changed. Because if Eddie could change, maybe anyone could. Including Noel.

And herself.

With her heart in her throat, she remote-started her car, put on her winter things, picked up the bag with Julien's present, and headed out the door.

Noel sat in the comfy chair near the fireplace in the corner of Cool Beans and stared at his phone, trying to make sense of the text Stephanie had just sent. He'd been starting to wonder if Steph had decided to ditch her "coffee date" with Autumn when his phone had buzzed. Now he was trying to figure out if the *Eddie* in her text was who he thought it was. But that wasn't the most surprising piece of information in the short message.

He looked up at Autumn, who was sitting at a nearby table with Julien and her parents. The little boy's upper lip had a whipped cream moustache from his hot chocolate.

"Did Steph know this was actually a Christmas party?" Noel asked.

Autumn started, turning slowly to look at him. "Um, yeah. I might have let it slip. Sorry. How did you find out she knew?"

He held his phone toward her to show her the text just as her phone buzzed. She pulled her device from her back jeans pocket and stared at it with a quizzical expression that quickly melted into surprise, then a happy smile. She looked up at her mom, who'd pulled out reading glasses to peer at her own phone.

"Mom, could you watch Julien for an hour while I go to the Christmas Eve service?"

Angelica put her phone down and gave Autumn a motherly smile. "Don't you think he should go with you? It's only an hour—he shouldn't get too rambunctious. And I can't think of a better day for him to meet his papa. We'll hold down the fort here in case anyone else shows up in the meantime."

Autumn flashed her mother a grin. "Thanks."

"Wait," said Noel. "What's going on?"

"We're delaying the party for a bit, that's what," Autumn said. "Half of our guests are already at the Christmas Eve service anyway." She hurried over to where the band was doing sound checks on the low stage that had been set up near the piano and explained the delay.

The red-headed and -bearded Doug Crawford gave a wide grin when he heard the news. "That means I can go watch Ainsley play. Excellent." He put his enormous string bass on its stand and went to retrieve his coat. Angelica was already helping Julien into his winter things, and Autumn quickly went to get hers.

Noel shook his head in confusion, trying to catch up. Then he shrugged. He hadn't wanted to skip the service, but this party had seemed the higher priority this year, for Stephanie's sake. Now he could do both.

He sent a quick text to Steph to ask her to save them a seat. As he followed a bundled Autumn and Julien out the door, he hoped his earlier misgivings had been unfounded, or this could be a very awkward evening.

Chapter Twenty-Two

B Y THE TIME NOEL, Autumn, and Julien parked on the packed street up the block from St. John's Cathedral, it was just past seven, the service start time. Jared and Ryker would already be inside, having come to watch Ryleigh play. Noel imagined his own mother's delighted smile when she saw that he'd managed to come to the performance, despite having bowed out earlier due to his other plans.

They hurried up the several concrete steps to the door of the quaint historic plaster-and-beam church and let themselves into the small drafty vestibule. The hinges let out a squeak, and Noel cringed, knowing the noise would echo into the sanctuary. The sound of the congregation singing "Joy to the World" to a piano and organ accompaniment filled the small space, despite the closed wooden doors between the foyer and the sanctuary beyond.

An elderly lady sporting a platinum-blond-dyed pixie cut greeted them with a smile from behind a narrow table covered with a dark green cloth. She picked up two white taper candles from a collection on the table and handed them to Autumn and Noel. The candles had been inserted through fluted white paper wax-catching trays that reminded Noel of tiny paper plates.

"For the finale," the woman whispered. Then she turned to Julien. "I even have one for you."

Autumn's eyes widened with alarm, and she looked about to intervene in the transaction when the woman handed the little boy a chunky plastic battery-operated toy candle. Julien's face lit up, and he poked at the unlit rigid orange cast-plastic flame, then held the candle up to show Autumn with a gleeful grin.

"Look, Mommy!"

"I see," she said with an indulgent—and relieved—smile.

"Keep it safe, young man, and remember to leave it here on the table afterwards," the grandmotherly woman said, pointing at the spot. "Your daddy can help you turn it on at the right time." She looked at Noel. "There's a button on the bottom."

Julien just nodded, distracted with trying to slide the switch he'd found on the bottom of the candle, but Autumn's face turned red.

Noel cleared his throat and decided it wasn't worth clearing up the misunderstanding. "Thanks."

He nudged Autumn and took Julien's hand to guide them into the sanctuary, where the congregation stood singing carols together with gusto. As they worked their way around the outer edge of the room to where Steph stood, he caught Autumn wiping a tear from her eye, and his heart squeezed. It had only been about two years since Denis had died, and he could imagine that this season was especially hard on her. He hoped, when she was ready, she'd find a good partner. Someone like her deserved to be happy. A moment later, Autumn was smiling at someone they passed—not covering up her grief, but responding with genuine affection to her friend's greeting in spite of it.

It occurred to Noel how differently Steph and Autumn each reacted to loss. He'd thought Autumn was quick to forgive, quick to let go, and seemingly quick to move on, but now he could see Autumn wasn't ignoring or squelching her grief—she just didn't let it interfere with enjoying the blessings in her life. Steph, on the other hand, kept her loss close as a wall of protection. She was fiercely loyal, even to the dead, and she'd worn her memories like armour for years to protect her from future pain.

How lucky was he that she'd allowed him a peek behind that armour and a space inside her heart? Knowing she'd let him into her inner circle made him want to protect what they had—protect her—with every ounce of his being.

But when he leaned his crutches against the wall next to the aged wooden pew where Steph stood and then limped over to stand beside her, the guarded look she gave him made him think twice. First, she tried to bow out of their evening plans, and now this? What had happened since he'd seen her last night? It must have something to do with Eddie. He wrapped an arm around her waist and kissed her temple, but she stiffened. Frowning, Noel dropped his arm and faced forward. Whatever was going on, now wasn't the time to talk about it. Autumn slipped into the pew next to Noel and set Julien on his feet on the bench beside her, snugging him to her hip with her arm to keep him contained and safe. As Noel and Autumn joined in on the song, Julien fiddled with the toy candle and looked around in curiosity.

When the hymn finished, the song leader standing in the pulpit instructed them to have a seat. As Noel eased himself down into the ancient, creaky wooden pew, using the back of the one in front of them for support, Reverend Olowe got up to pray. The squat man in black prayed a blessing over the remainder of the service and the people there, then gave a wide grin and introduced Violet and her musical ensemble, the Peace Country Ringers. About a dozen people in black semi-formal wear from teenagers up to seniors—including Ryleigh and the tall man Noel had seen talking to Steph at the hospital—rose from the front pews and filed toward two oblong tables that had been arranged before the chancel, one behind the other. On the tables, evenly spaced red cushions cradled several gleaming brass hand bells each. The bells were arranged in ascending size and had been laid on their sides with the bell end toward the congregation. Lights from a Christmas tree off to the side near the vestry next to the pulpit blinked cheerfully, adding ambiance to the scene.

As the audience clapped, Violet floated to the front, the gold threads of the marble-like pattern woven into her flowing black dress shimmering in the warm lights of the hanging chandeliers high above them. Noel smiled. His mother always seemed to carry her own light, but on nights like this, she shone, her love for the people of their community emanating from every word and gesture.

Violet introduced their group again, gesturing toward them with a broad smile as she talked about the hard work they'd put in to prepare for this event. Behind her, the performers found their places, put on white gloves, and waited patiently.

"We'll start by performing 'I Heard the Bells on Christmas Day,' a song based on a poem by Henry Wadsworth Longfellow," Violet said. She spotted Noel, who grinned, and she smiled a little wider. "Longfellow wrote this poem on Christmas Day in 1863, during the American Civil War, after several years of great personal loss. His wife had died in a fire two years earlier, and in March of that year, his son, Charles, had gone to war against his wishes. In November, only a month before this poem was penned, Charles had been severely wounded, ending his career as a soldier. It's no wonder Longfellow's melancholic pondering that Christmas revolved around the symbolic peace the bells of Christmas represent. At the time, he was living in a nation at war with itself. Sometimes when I look around today, I wonder if much has changed."

Quiet murmuring and titters of agreement floated through the packed church. Noel noticed his dad, Derrick, and Jenny sitting in the third row, now with an empty seat next to Carl where Violet had been. In the row behind them sat the Richardsons, Ryleigh's foster family—Cate and Rick, her husband, and their three teenage girls and preteen son, Micah. Cate kept glancing surreptitiously across the centre aisle to where Ryker sat next to Jared, the teenager giving his sister his full attention. A few rows behind them, Doug Crawford had slipped into the pew next to his wife, their red heads like a pair of matching flames.

In the front row of bell ringers, Ryleigh looked anxious but pleased. Behind her, Eddie's expression was neutral and determined, his eyes fixed on some point at the back of the church. Noel overheard Autumn whisper to Julien, who sat on her lap, that his papa was on the stage, and then she quietly pointed Eddie out. Julien's loud return question was less subtle, but everyone in the sanctuary must have been used to small children in the service, because the only reactions were a few indulgent smiles from those sitting nearby. Monica Toews, Caleb's ex-wife, sat about halfway back with Emma beside her. Caleb and Delanie had gone to the service at Peace Crossing Christian Assembly, promising to meet up with them at Cool Beans later, and it was obviously Monica's night with Emma. Noel noticed a thickening around the woman's middle and a brightness to her complexion and remembered Caleb telling him that she and her most recent ex were having a baby. He wondered how Monica was doing. It couldn't be easy looking forward to becoming a mother for the second time without her partner.

Emma saw him looking and gave an energetic wave and a grin. He smiled and gave a more subtle wave back. She wrinkled her nose in acknowledgement, and then she returned her attention to her colouring.

"As you listen to this rendition of the carol," Violet continued, "set to music by Johnny Marks, I pray that you'll also remember that 'God is not dead, nor doth he sleep. The Wrong shall fail, and Right prevail, with peace on Earth, good will to men.' May every bell that rings remind us that, no matter how dark the night, God is with us, offering peace to every heart."

She turned toward her music stand and picked up her baton, and the bell ringers picked up two bells each, holding them against their shoulders to dampen any errant reverberations. Noel waited with bated breath along with everyone else in the small church as his mother raised her arms. With her first downbeat, the silence was broken with the clarion chimes of the bells.

Noel listened to the melodic strains of the hymn, transported to music-filled Christmases of his past, his throat tightening with the meaning and memories the piece evoked. He glanced at Steph to see her reaction and was surprised to see tears streaming down her face. Instinctively, he took her hand and squeezed it. She gave him a tight-lipped smile and dabbed at her tears with her other thumb. But as soon as the song was over, she pulled her hand free and stood, excusing herself as she made her way past the elderly couple on her other side to get to the aisle.

At the front, Violet bowed at the applause. Straightening, she launched into the intro for their next number. Noel glanced over at Autumn in confusion, hoping Steph's sister might know what was going on. Autumn watched her sister disappear through the back doors of the sanctuary, but when she saw him turned toward her, she made a shooing motion with her hand.

"Go!" she whispered, as though it were the most obvious choice in the world.

As Noel tucked his candle into the hymnal rack on the back of the pew ahead of them, Autumn stood and moved into the aisle to allow him space to leave. He heaved himself to his feet, retrieved his crutches from the wall where he'd leaned them, and hurried as quietly as he could out to the aisle and through the back doors of the sanctuary.

The greeter from the vestibule must have found a seat, because the small foyer was now empty, and much cooler and fresher-smelling than the crowded sanctuary. Not stopping to fasten his coat buttons, Noel eased his way out the squeaky door and stood on the lit stoop in the chilly air, looking around to see which way Steph had gone. Through the thick flakes of falling snow, he spotted her next door, leaning against the railing on the wheelchair ramp at the rear entrance of Mackenzie Hall. Her back was toward him, her head down, and her shoulders shaking.

Proceeding carefully down the icy steps, he made his way toward her.

"Hey, Steph," he said when he got close enough. "How can I help?" He closed the last few steps between them, intending to wrap his arms around her and buttress her against whatever pain she was feeling.

But before he could, she stiffened and turned her head sideways so he could see her profile. Her tear-tracked face was stony.

"You can finally tell me what really happened with you and Maddie and Jackson back in high school." She stood and turned to face him. "And about the accident with Jenny."

Noel froze, staring at her. How had she heard all that?

As if she'd read his mind, she said with a trembling voice, "I was in Pearl's Petals earlier when you were talking to Maddie. She said I needed to ask you for the truth. So I am. Are you prepared to tell it? Because, if you aren't, you and I are done, Noel. I can't be with a liar and a drunk."

Her flint-eyed gaze prickled with challenge and hurt and shone with unshed tears.

His mouth went dry and he gaped at her, all his vulnerabilities staring him in the face. This was what he'd been trying to avoid—a rejection, just as he'd started to feel he could open up. A false accusation of his character, just when he thought she was different from the girl who'd once broken his heart. What could he say that wouldn't make his worst fears come true?

Anger stirred in is gut. How could he have let himself believe he could trust Steph, or anyone? This was what he got for letting down his guard.

He ground his jaw and glanced away, tightening his grip on the handles of his crutches. He was tempted to tell her she could think what she wanted, but he wasn't going to wait around for her to pull the plug, because *he* was done.

Then he closed his eyes and took a breath. He wasn't eighteen anymore. And Steph wasn't Maddie. And, he had to admit, she had every reason to suspect he'd been keeping something from her—because he had. Something that needled at the very wounds that had kept her from entering into the joy of this season for far too long.

His dad had been right—she'd already known something was going on. It was up to him to be a better person than he was last time and do the right thing.

Even if his honesty cost him her heart.

But he sincerely hoped it wouldn't.

Chapter Twenty-Three

STEPHANIE WATCHED NOEL SHIFT uncomfortably on his crutches, fear and anger raging in her chest. She recognized the same emotions in him—anxiety flashed across his face, just as it had at the Andersons' after the sleigh ride, followed quickly by the anger she knew he wore as a shield. What had Noel done that was so bad he'd kept if from her all this time and was still afraid to tell her?

Snow fell softly around them, settling on Noel's broad shoulders and bare head where he stood on the snow-covered lawn. Steph's position beneath the broad overhanging boughs of a mature spruce tree next to Mackenzie Hall left her relatively sheltered in comparison. The fluffy flakes refracted light from the street lamps and the strings of Christmas lights strung through the barren trees along the sidewalk, creating a diffuse glow and deadening all sounds except their own soft landings. Steph felt as though they were standing in a snow globe, where no one else could reach them.

She hoped they could find a way to reach each other.

Noel drew a breath. Swinging himself onto the wheelchair ramp, he came and leaned against the railing beside her, propping his crutches on his other side before taking her gloved hand in his bare one. He drew several long breaths, tension plain in his jaw and shoulders. She wanted to hug him, to help him see that she was on his side, but she couldn't afford to risk it right now. It would be hard enough to break up with him as it was, if that's what this conversation came down to. But she didn't pull her hand away. Yet.

"Stephanie," Noel began, his voice low, "you're one of the kindest, most caring people I know. So I hope you'll understand that what I'm about to tell you was about a different person. I'm not that guy anymore. But I used to be."

Her stomach pinched. "This sounds worse than I thought. Did you kill someone or something?"

The grave look he gave her made her throat tighten. "Not quite. But I came close. More than once."

She waited quietly.

"In junior high and high school," he began, "I was best friends with this kid named Jackson. He was a good guy, but as we got older, he started running with a different crowd, and we hung out less often. You know how it is in school. Things change all the time."

She nodded. "I remember Jackson," she said cautiously.

"Then you probably remember what happened to him, right?"

"He got arrested. I don't know what happened to him after that."

Noel sighed, his shoulders slumping. "Yeah, he got arrested. As far as I know, he's been in and out of jail ever since. We don't talk anymore. And Maddie was . . ." He stopped and pressed his lips together, then gave his head a twist as though to wind back the tape. "I mean, *I* was the reason he got arrested in the first place." His jaw worked.

She squeezed his fingers.

"What happened?" she asked softly.

He told her how, near the beginning of Grade Twelve, he'd let Jackson convince him to go to a party some of Jackson's friends were throwing while their parents were out of town. The house was out in the country, and Jackson needed a ride. Maddie had a basketball game that night, and she'd asked Noel to come, but he hadn't had a chance to spend time with Jackson for so long that he agreed to go to the party instead.

It wasn't until after they got there that Noel discovered some of Jackson's best customers were expecting him to be there.

"He'd started dealing drugs, apparently. I had no idea."

Steph nodded, encouraging him to continue. "Maddie said something about her friend Sarah almost dying. Was she one of his customers?"

"No. But her boyfriend was. And I guess he must have shared."

Noel explained that Sarah, who was at the party, ended up overdosing. Noel found her on the back deck in convulsions in her boyfriend's arms.

"He was freaking out. I called nine-one-one and explained the symptoms, and they asked if she'd had any drugs. I said I didn't know. Jackson was listening, and I asked him if he knew, and Jackson freaked out. He grabbed the phone and ended the call. I think he would have thrown it away if it hadn't been attached to their wall. That's when I found out he was dealing."

He grew silent for a moment, staring through the snowy wooden ramp. Chill started to creep through Steph's coat and gloves, and she fought the urge to huddle into Noel for warmth. Then she realized that nothing he'd said was setting off alarms. Noel couldn't have known what would happen at that party, and it's not like *he'd* been dealing drugs.

A glimmer of hope flickered in her chest. Maybe Maddie had overreacted.

Then Steph remembered what Maddie said about Noel siding with Jackson, and she tensed again.

"Sarah recovered, I take it," Steph said. "But you didn't tell anyone about Jackson, did you?"

Noel closed his eyes against the memory, then met her gaze. "I told one person. Maddie. At the party, Jackson was upset, and somehow, he convinced me I'd be in trouble for being involved, too. I was scared and didn't know better. Besides," he said, giving her a sideways look, "I'd . . . been drinking at the party. I certainly didn't want my parents to find out about that."

Steph tried not to let her alarm show on her face. Not when he was finally opening up.

"And then?"

Her pitch was higher than normal, despite her efforts. By the look he gave her, he obviously hadn't missed that, but he continued anyway.

"I didn't know what to do, so we left before the ambulance arrived. But what had happened didn't sit right with me. I didn't want to get Jackson in trouble, but I wanted him to stop dealing and clean himself up. He got mad and broke off our friendship. I talked to Maddie about what had happened to see what she thought I should do. She promised she wouldn't tell anyone, but that I should go to the police." He snorted. "Except before I got the chance, someone called in an anonymous tip and got Jackson arrested. He blamed me, but I knew it had to have been Maddie. When I confronted her about it, she said she only did what I should have done already. I later found out she'd been calling me spineless to her friends behind my back. Long story short, we broke up. You know the rest."

Steph frowned. "So she got mad at you for not doing the right thing and you broke up with her at the dance and thought you were the victim?"

That reaction seemed so unlike the man she knew. But she remembered Noel in high school—walking around with a chip on his shoulder the size of an iceberg, always with something to prove. How much of that guy remained in the man before her?

But Noel's shoulders slumped. "Yeah, I did. I'm not proud of it. I told you I'm not that guy anymore. If I could do it all again, I would do things completely differently. Sarah deserved better. So did Maddie. And, while I'm using a time machine, why not go back a little further and help Jackson make better choices when it might have made a difference?"

Steph watched his profile. His downcast eyes seemed to look right through the snowy walkway at their feet at a time long since past.

"That's why you have such a soft spot for troubled teenagers, isn't it? Because of Jackson."

He nodded, his tortured gaze meeting hers. "There's more, though."

Steph remembered the other mystery he had yet to resolve, and gripped the railing to brace herself against what was coming next.

"The accident with Jenny," she said flatly.

Noel nodded and ran his hand over his mouth. "After what happened with Jackson, I blamed myself for a long time. That night at the party was my first drink, but, pretty soon, I was drinking every weekend. After graduation, it happened even more often. I, uh, haven't told many people this, but the reason I left the army was because of an altercation at a bar one weekend that got out of hand. I was discharged for drunk and disorderly behaviour unfitting an officer."

He cleared his throat, and Steph's chest tightened. She wanted him to skip to the end, to laugh and tell her it was all a joke, but she knew he would never joke about something like that.

"You were drinking at the Christmas party," Steph said, the memory coming back to her. She'd tasted the alcohol on his breath when their lips had met beneath the mistletoe. Somehow, the other emotions of that night had crowded the memory out. How could she have missed that warning sign? How could she have allowed herself to get this deep with him?

She hadn't caught a trace of alcohol on the man since they'd started dating, but how well did she know him, really? Her mother claimed she never knew Eddie had a drinking problem until years into their marriage. Could Steph have missed the signs?

She felt gentle pressure on her hands and looked up in surprise. Noel gazed down at her with gentle brown eyes.

"I was. I'm ashamed to admit that I didn't learn much after my discharge. And then I met you, and you made me see there was more to life than what I'd been living. You were so honest, and tender, and also bold. Do you remember what you told me that night?"

Steph shook her head. Most of what had happened that night had been dimmed by time and hurt.

"I asked you if you'd ever had a serious boyfriend. You said that you hadn't, but if you ever did, he'd be a man you could brag about to your kids someday. I couldn't get that out of my head, because I knew that, the way I was living, no one would be bragging about me to anyone. That comment also showed me that you had no intention of playing around with some guy's heart. You play for keeps."

He gave her an admiring glance, and she felt her face warm.

"You got me thinking, but God wanted to make sure I got the message, loud and clear. I ended up rolling the car on the way home due to impaired judgment. Miraculously, Jenny and I both walked away without a scratch. I knew I'd been given another chance, and I didn't intend to waste it. I haven't had a drink since that night."

He extricated one of his hands and reached into his pocket, pulling out a chip much like the one Eddie had shown her weeks earlier.

"Four years and eight days tonight," he added. "And every one of those days has been a gift."

Steph stared at the chip, her insides vibrating like a rung gong. Tears leaked down her cheeks. "How did I not see it?" she muttered to herself. "The one thing I'd promised myself I'd never accept, and I didn't see it." She pulled her hands from Noel's and covered her face, hiding her tears.

A few moments later, Noel asked softly, "Don't you believe people can change?"

She dropped her hands and stared straight ahead, sniffling, his question reverberating in her chest. "When I was a kid, Eddie would go on binges pretty often. They always ended badly, with my mom and sisters and I bearing the scars—sometimes literally. After whatever blowup came of his drinking, Eddie would always promise to change, and my mom would always believe him, and things would be good for a little while. Except, he never did change. And Melody died."

Steph thought of the broken man who had brought her a gift for his grandson earlier that night. As Eddie had played the bells during the performance, he'd looked like the father she'd known at his best, a man who had more to look forward to than his next drink. And, for the first time, she'd dared hope he *had* truly changed. That he was actually trying to do better, and he might even succeed.

If Eddie could manage that after a lifetime of addiction, couldn't Noel have done the same after only a few years?

She twisted to face Noel. "I believe that addiction is very difficult to overcome, and few ever truly do. But, if anyone could do it, I know you could. Because the man you've proven yourself to be has been kind in the face of heartbreak, and determined in the face of indifference. You've never once acted the victim or chosen to ignore the right thing to do since I've gotten to know you . . . starting that night at the party, I can finally see. That's why you 'ghosted' me, isn't it?"

"I never meant to hurt you," he said softly. "I was trying to protect you from the man I no longer wanted to be."

She nodded. "I see that now. So, do I believe that people change?"

She paused, looking up into warm brown eyes that were the most vulnerable she'd ever seen them. She pulled off her glove and laid her hand on his cheek.

"I believe you have. You've restored my belief in a lot of things, Noel. Christmas. Romance. Humanity. I owe you my thanks. And an apology, I think. For how I behaved." She glanced away, her cheeks burning. "I was only thinking of my side of things. I never stopped to think—"

"No." He put a finger on her lips. "No more apologies. I can see why you acted the way you did. But that's all behind us now." Leaning forward, he kissed her wet cheek, then straightened. "You know, I owe you some thanks, too. After so many years using shallow romances as a way to keep my heart safe, you've shown me what love is supposed to be like. This? This is nice."

Her chest warmed, and she smiled.

Through the thin walls of the ancient church, congregational singing seeped toward them, permeating the night in ethereal music. Noel pushed himself off the railing to his feet, putting most of his weight on his good leg, and limped to stand directly in front of her, holding out his hand in invitation.

"Would you care to dance?"

"To 'O Holy Night'?" She laughed incredulously.

He shrugged. "With this leg, that's about the speed I can manage right now."

She giggled and allowed him to pull her to her feet. Leaving his crutches where they were, he led her down the sloped ramp and out into the magical ever-present light diffracted by the softly falling flakes. Despite his limp, he didn't lean on her as they crunched through the thin blanket of snow onto the lawn. Stopping, Noel peered upward at the steeple with its shiny new bell, then down at the ground, as though measuring something.

"Yep, this is the spot."

Stephanie looked down, then up, then at Noel. "What spot?"

He smirked. "The spot where I fell off a roof and lived to tell about it."

She laughed. Sliding her arms beneath his open coat and wrapping them around his middle, she laid her head on his shoulder, and he enveloped her in his strong arms in return. They swayed back and forth, enveloped in the heavenly strains of the carol.

"You know," Noel said into her ear, "I've been frustrated by this broken leg for weeks, but I just realized that if it weren't for falling off that roof, you and I might not be standing here like this right now. Talk about a blessing in disguise. All this time I've been grumpy about it, but God was like, 'Noel, this is exactly what you need, so stop griping.'"

Steph giggled. "Do you think God might have been giving you a not-so-subtle suggestion to be more careful, too?"

Noel snorted. "I don't know about *that*. I'm pretty sure he knew what was up when he put my blueprint together. But I'll be sure and ask him."

Steph smiled, pressing herself into his chest and allowing his warmth to seep into her. But his next words took her completely by surprise.

"I tell you one thing, though. If falling off that roof was the only way you and I could get together, I'd do it a million times."

She swallowed and straightened, looking into his eyes. "Really?"

He gazed down at her tenderly. "You're the most amazing person I know, Stephanie Neufeld—beautiful inside and out. If I could give you the world, I would. I'll have to settle for this promise: no matter what happens, I will always strive to be the kind of man you can rely on. I have no more skeletons to dig out of the closet, and I only have eyes for you. I . . . I love you, Stephanie. I think I've loved you for four years and eight days. It just took me this long to figure it out."

She was sure he could feel her heart doing a tap dance against his chest. Noel loved her? She hadn't expected that. Not yet. But did she love him?

"I don't know if I know what love feels like," she said honestly. "All I know is that I feel safer in your arms than anywhere else.

And I believe what you said about your past and your promise for the future."

In fact, there were very few people she trusted as wholeheartedly as she did this man. She remembered the dread she'd felt earlier at the idea of losing him, and her knees started shaking again.

"Also, I'd really appreciate it if you would listen a little closer when God's trying to get your attention. I don't think my heart could take it if he has to endanger your life every time he's got something to say to you. When I'm bragging about you to my kids, I'd rather you were around for them to look up to."

She bit her lip as she registered the implied commitment in her words and kept her burning cheek pressed against his chest so he couldn't see her face.

Noel's baritone rumbled through her, solemn with an undertone of amusement. "I'll see what I can do." Then his voice became teasing. "You know, I'm thinking that you *might* love me too. It's okay, you can tell me. I can keep a secret."

She laughed, her chest warming. "Don't I know it. You're as impenetrable as Fort Knox if it were situated on the moon."

"What can I say? I yam who I yam," he said, imitating Popeye.

She giggled again and met his warm gaze. Heaving a sigh of mock begrudgment, she rolled her eyes and said, "Fine. I *probably* love you. But the jury's still out. There was that whole Stalker Santa phase that I'm still getting over. I need to make sure that doesn't happen again."

His mouth twitched at the corner. "I solemnly swear, if I ever again have the urge to shower you with secret gifts, I'll tell you first."

"See that you do. Some secrets aren't worth keeping."

They stared into each other's eyes for a long moment. Between the warm banter and his strong arms around Steph as they swayed in time to the music, she felt all warm and floaty and . . .

happy. When the song ended, they stood there in stillness, enjoying their shared warmth.

Then the church bell above them gave a loud clang, and Stephanie jumped, slipping on an icy patch beneath the snow. Noel caught her and helped her regain her balance. The bells rang out a Christmas Eve blessing, and Noel leaned toward her and pressed his lips to hers, delivering a kiss that made Stephanie feel more alive and electrified than she'd ever felt before. When they broke apart, she was surprised the snow hadn't melted into a pool around them.

Yep, she could definitely get used to that.

Chapter Twenty-Four

STEPH AND NOEL SLIPPED back into the church just as the kindly greeter turned out the overhead lights. Near the front, several volunteers lit the candles held by the congregation, and each person turned and lit the candle of the person beside them. Soon the entire sanctuary glowed softly, lit only by the candles illuminating each face and the lights on the Christmas tree as the congregation sang "Silent Night". Noel and Steph tucked in next to Autumn, and Julien proudly shoved his illuminated toy candle toward Steph.

"Look, aunty! It's Chwistmas magic!"

Stephanie chuckled. "It sure is, buddy."

He grinned back, crinkling his nose. Concentrating on his candle, he managed to hold it relatively upright in front of him—until he started looking around at the rows of tiny flames in wonder.

Glancing up at Noel, Steph twined her fingers through his. He retrieved their candles from the hymnal rack on the back of the pew in front of them, and they lit their flames from Autumn's.

Looking toward the front, Steph saw her father, who'd returned to the front pews with the other bell ringers. He looked back in their direction over his shoulder, and when their eyes met, his expression lifted with gratitude, and something else—love, maybe? He nodded at her, and she smiled back, her heart fluttering a little. Could she be ready to reconcile with Eddie—with her dad? Her nerves sang louder than the congregation.

As the final strains of the hymn faded away and the scent of extinguished candle smoke filled the air, Noel leaned close to her.

"You look stunning, by the way."

Her face warmed. "Thank you."

"So, are you ready to party?" he added, arching a brow. "Apparently, I don't get to surprise you today."

She met his gaze with a broad smile. "You couldn't be more wrong about that." Thinking of what had happened outside, her heart started racing again.

He seemed to read her mind, because he grinned rather smugly. "Good to know."

She cleared her throat, trying to regain her composure. "Anyway, I've actually been looking forward to the party. But is it okay if I invite someone?" She glanced toward where Eddie stood waiting for his pew to empty.

Noel nodded in understanding. "If there were ever a night to bury hatchets, it's this one." He kissed her temple. "I'm here to help you dig, if you need it."

"Thanks, but I'll be okay."

She released his hand and, working her way around the outside edge of the church to avoid the press of bodies moving the other direction, made her way toward her father.

Eddie saw her coming and waited, letting his fellow performers drift away. Violet Butler, standing with her family in the third row, saw her and flashed a smile, then glanced between her and Eddie and turned away politely to greet Noel, who was coming to talk to them. On the other side of the aisle, Steph noticed Ryleigh and the Richardsons talking with Ryker and Jared, and she hoped there was another reconciliation underway.

When Stephanie was only a few paces away from her dad, she stopped, her hands clammy and her stomach tight. He gave her a tentative smile, waiting in the centre aisle.

Now or never.

She took a deep breath and walked over to stand in front of him.

"Eddie . . ." she began, then faltered. There was so much to say, so many years of hurt to try and heal.

Eddie's eyes glistened, and he rubbed his nose, glancing away. Finally, he met her eyes. "Stephy," he said gruffly, "I know I've got a lot to make up for. But if you can find it in your heart to give your old man another chance, I promise I'll do right by you this time. You, and Autumn, and the little guy. I owe you all that, and so much more. It's what Melody would have wanted."

Stephanie blinked back tears. "I'd really like that . . . Dad," she added softly.

Eddie's face lit up. He opened his arms, and Stephanie hesitated only a moment before stepping into his embrace. As she rested her head on his shoulder, she felt a piece of her heart that had been missing for so long finally click back into place.

She stepped back, wiping the moisture from her eyes and straightening her dress in an attempt to quell the emotions surging uncomfortably in her chest. "Um, my boyfriend is throwing a Christmas party over at Cool Beans, and I was wondering if you'd like to come."

His brows lifted, then his face clouded. "Won't your mom be there?"

Autumn came up beside them, holding Julien in her arms. "She won't mind."

Eddie turned toward her, his face breaking open in a smile. "Hey, sweetheart, I'm glad you could make it. And are you sure?"

He spoke with a little more warmth than Steph would have expected. Then again, Autumn and Eddie had been communicating much more than Steph and Eddie had.

"Positive," Autumn replied. "I texted her a few minutes ago. I was coming to invite you, but Steph beat me to the punch." Autumn smiled at her sister. "Not that I mind."

"Mommy, who's dis man?" Julien asked, his voice as unquiet and unabashed as only a three-year-old's can be without being rude. He still held the lit candle toy in his hands, but his attention was all on Eddie.

Autumn grinned. "Julien, this is your papa. My dad."

"Isn't Gwampa your dad?" His little brow furrowed.

"Yes. But you can have more than one dad sometimes. It's complicated."

He pursed his lips in thought. "Can I get another dad someday?"

Autumn's smile faltered, then widened again. "Maybe. Say hello to your papa."

Eddie had been watching the exchange with an amused grin on his face. As Julien turned toward him, he solemnly took Julien's hand and shook it.

"Hello, young man. I've been looking forward to meeting you."

Julien shook Eddie's hand with wide eyes, then, uncharacteristically, he buried his face in his mother's neck, overcome with shyness.

Autumn shrugged. "Give him an hour. He'll warm up."

Eddie nodded, not appearing to take it personally.

"So . . . are you coming to the party?" Steph asked.

Eddie looked thoughtful. "Well, parties aren't really my thing, but how could I pass up the chance to spend Christmas Eve with my girls? I do have a condition, though."

Steph's chest hitched. Conditions already? "What's that?"

He grinned. "Introduce me to the host? I need to know who thinks he's good enough for my daughter."

She chuckled, then looked over toward where the Butler family was standing and kibitzing with each other to see Noel keeping a casual eye on the proceedings with their group. She beckoned him over.

After the introductions and some small talk, they all started shuffling toward the back of the church so they could head over to the party. As Steph turned to follow Noel, Eddie leaned toward her.

"Did you give Julien his gift yet?" he asked in a low voice.

She shook her head. "I thought it would be better coming from you. Don't you agree?"

He gave her another grateful smile, and her heart warmed. For the first time in years, she felt she knew what Christmas was supposed to be. As she made her way toward the back of the sanctuary, she glanced up at a stained-glass window depicting Christ in saturated shades of gold, purple, and peach.

"Thank you," she whispered.

Ahead of her, Noel glanced over his shoulder, his posture stooped as he gripped the handles of his crutches. "Coming, slowpoke?"

"Slowpoke? I'll show you who's slow." She giggled, speeding her pace to move past him as much as her heels would allow, but before she reached him, he turned and blocked her at the sanctuary door with his body. They were almost the only people left in the church. When she gave him a mock-put-out look, he chuckled, then bent and gave her a tender kiss.

"Are you okay?" he asked quietly, his eyes full of concern.

Steph paused, thinking about it. For the first time in years, Christmas Eve would be a joyful, happy occasion spent not only with her own family, but with Noel's, and other friends they both cared about. She hadn't felt this peaceful for a very long time—maybe ever.

Steph didn't know exactly what lay ahead, but she knew she wouldn't be facing it alone. Noel had helped her rediscover the joy of Christmas and so much more. She fully expected they'd be making plenty more memories together for many Christmas Eves to come.

With a full and happy heart, she said, "You know what? I actually am. At the risk of sounding cliché, this really is the best Christmas ever."

A slow grin spread across his face. "Well. Stephanie Neufeld fell in love with Christmas. It's a Christmas miracle."

She rolled her eyes. "Yeah? Well, bah, humbug, I say."

Noel's eyes widened in mock alarm. "Oh no! She's reverting. Quick, to the sleigh! We have some Christmas cheer to recapture. Time to rock around the tree for a while."

"I'm not sure you're in any condition for actual rocking yet," she said with a giggle and a pointed look at his cast.

"Maybe not. But I already proved I'm the master of the 'sway'. And as long as I can get you under some mistletoe, I'll barely rock with you anytime."

She leaned in close. "You don't need mistletoe anymore."

Their lips met in a kiss that promised all the happiness she'd longed for and more—no ghosts in sight. After they broke apart, she took his hand and stepped out of the church and into an unknown and exciting future next to the man she loved—probably.

No matter what came their way, Stephanie couldn't wait to find out what would happen next.

Epilogue

A T THE SOUND OF the front door chime, Madeleine Kennedy looked up from the counter of Pearl's Petals in time to see Stephanie Neufeld walk in. It had only been a few days since the woman had fled out of the shop looking as though she'd seen a ghost, and the difference in her appearance was remarkable—instead of pale and trembling, she was glowing, her step full of life. When she walked in and Maddie caught her eye, Steph gave her a cheerful grin.

"Hi, nice to see you back so soon. Are you looking for gifts or flowers today?" Maddie asked politely. She assumed Steph must have found what she was looking for last time somewhere else.

"Gifts. I'm a little behind on my Christmas shopping."

"Or you're very early for next year," Maddie joked.

"I like that." Steph gave an embarrassed laugh. "I already know where to find what I want to give to Delanie, but, um, do you have any notebooks a guy might like?"

Maddie arched a brow, thinking of the conversation that had evoked Steph's previous emotional reaction. "Same guy?"

Steph's complexion flamed bright red, and she gave a twitterpated grin and a little nod. "Er, do you?"

When Stephanie didn't volunteer anything else, Maddie turned on her customer service smile. She'd tried to warn Steph about Noel already. It wasn't Maddie's job to get the woman to see reason.

"We have some really classy leather-bound journals for men. Here, let me show you. And they're even on sale. We'd like to move them before New Year's."

"Thanks."

Maddie led Steph through the maze of shelves and display stands to the appropriate section of the store, her stomach surprisingly calm. After her last conversation with Stephanie, when it had become clear her former classmate had feelings for Noel, Maddie had been a little upset. But she and Noel had been over for so long that it wasn't jealousy over him. It was more the consternation that she still hadn't found someone who made her feel that way after all these years of looking.

And gosh, had she looked. She'd heard you have to kiss a lot of frogs to find a prince, but she was starting to wonder if all the princes had already been found . . . by other people.

The front door chimed again.

"Excuse me," Maddie said.

"Of course." Steph gave her a pleasant smile.

Maddie made her way back to the front. She suspected the other woman preferred the chance to browse without having to make further small talk anyway.

When she reached the front counter, she was surprised to see Luke Anderson standing there, looking awkward and fidgeting with a white card-sized envelope. She'd known Luke since their school days—he was handsome Heath Anderson's younger brother. Heath had been one of Noel's buddies, but there hadn't been a girl in their year who hadn't known who Heath was. Luke's good looks were more understated and dark compared to his brother's sun-kissed ones, but they both had the same strong jaw and piercing blue eyes. However, other than being Noel's friend's shy kid brother, she hadn't paid him much mind until he'd lent his muscles and impressive artistic talents to the Multiple Sclerosis fundraiser she'd organized several years ago. Since then, he'd always made sure to say hi when they bumped into each other around town. This was the first time she'd seen him in the shop, though.

"Hi, Luke! Merry Christmas and Happy New Year."

"Hi, Maddie," he said, blushing. That seemed to be going around.

She slipped behind the counter to face him fully. "What can I do for you? Are you looking for some flowers to go with that card?" She indicated the envelope he was tapping against the counter. "Something special for someone special?" she teased.

He stopped tapping it and shook his head, gripping it in white-knuckled fingers before handing it over. "Actually, uh, this is for you."

Intrigued, she took the envelope from his hands. Her name was scrawled across the front in blue ink in messily artistic but readable printing.

"Thank you. Should I open it now?"

He glanced away, looking sheepish. "I mean, sure. It's just a Christmas card. Sorry it's late." He looked at her. "Happy New Year, Maddie. I hope it's awesome. See ya around."

Almost before she could get out a return, "See ya," the door was chiming behind his exit.

Puzzled, she opened the envelope and gasped. Instead of a generic Christmas card, she was met with an impressive winter scene that had been sketched in black ink. She admired the detailed work showing a team of draft horses pulling a sleigh through the forest, then noted the signature—Luke's. The hand-printed message inside was a simple wish for her to have a wonderful Christmas and New Year, followed by Luke's name. Just *Luke*. No greeting or anything. Why on earth had he taken the time to make this for her?

"That's beautiful!" Steph said.

Maddie glanced up to see her standing at the counter, looking at the card.

"It is, isn't it?" Maddie closed the card and held it up so Steph could see the front better. "If a guy makes you a card like that, do you think it means anything?"

Steph raised an eyebrow. "It means he's an amazing artist, for a start. Is he a guy you know well?"

Maddie shrugged. "Kind of. He grew up here, too, but he's a little younger than me." She knew Steph would know who Luke was, but she wasn't sure she wanted to mention those kinds of specifics. That's how rumours got started in a town this small.

Steph looked thoughtful. "I don't know what it might mean. I think that's the kind of thing you should ask him."

"You're right." Maddie gave the card one last look and set it aside. "But I probably won't. Not my type."

Luke was nice enough, but she preferred her men to be a little more mysterious and charming. She turned her attention to the scented candle with an inspirational quote on the votive holder and the walnut-stained leather-bound journal Steph had placed on the counter. The journal cover had been embossed with a fierce-looking lion and the words *Wild at Heart*.

"Oh, Noel will like that. Good choice."

She scanned in Stephanie's items and then inserted the candle and the buttery-soft journal into a brown paper shopping bag. The lion symbol was a good fit for Noel. He'd been a bad boy when she'd dated him, and even though he seemed to have lost that surly edge, he still exuded a raw but controlled strength. *That* was the kind of man she was looking for—not the Noel she'd dated in high school, but a guy who was sure of himself, and who would stand up for her when life went sideways. Preferably someone who also knew when the time to stand up was, unlike Noel had when it really mattered. And who wasn't just trying to get what he could from her before moving on, like so many of the guys she'd dated since.

So many frogs . . .

"You know, he told me what happened between you," Steph said, as though reading her mind. She put her debit card into the machine to pay, then began pushing buttons.

Maddie glanced up in surprise. "The truth?"

"I believe so. I, uh, I just wanted to say that I understand why you were upset with him. And why he was upset with you. But after all the water that's passed under the bridge, don't you think it's time to let it go?" She pulled her card from the machine and tucked it into her wallet.

Maddie's chest tightened, and heat rushed through her. "I think it's none of your business." She snatched the receipt from the till and shoved it toward Steph.

Steph frowned, tucking the receipt in her wallet before dropping her wallet into her purse.

"You're wrong. Noel matters to me, and this matters to him. But, more than that, don't you think holding on to that mistake might be hurting more than helping you?" Steph accepted the paper cord handles of the shopping bag. "I've recently learned that the things we won't let go of tend to keep us stuck in the past. They keep us from seeing what might be right in front of us. And I think you deserve to move on as much as Noel does." She cast a significant glance toward Luke's card, then shrugged. "Your choice, of course. Happy New Year, Maddie."

With that, she turned and walked out the door, the cheerful chime of the bell an added insult to Maddie's racing heart.

Pearl, the shop's diminutive grey-haired owner, emerged from the back of the store. Spotting the card, she smiled.

"Oh, that's lovely. Is that from that handsome doctor fellow you like talking to so much?" she asked, pointing at it. "Sweet of him to drop off a card."

With her swirling thoughts, it took Maddie a second to remember who Pearl was talking about.

"Justin Ross?" Her heart skipped a little just saying his name. Justin was one of their most regular customers, and she'd be lying if she said she hadn't daydreamed about him a little—but it seemed he was always sending flowers to someone new. Despite looks and charm that made her a little queasy, even she wasn't desperate enough to take on that level of risk. "No. Just a friend. Excuse me, Pearl. Could you watch the front for a minute? I need to use the restroom."

"Of course, dear."

Maddie rushed to the back and locked herself in the tiny bathroom that doubled as a storage room for the shop's cleaning supplies. Tucking herself in the crowded space between the cracked but spotless mirror—Pearl ran a spic-and-span ship, even if the building could use a serious update—and the rack of cleaners and paper products behind her, Maddie gripped the edge of the stained porcelain sink and stared at the blue eyes of her reflection.

Stephanie's words had felt like cold water across her face. She'd thought she'd moved on long ago until Noel had shown up here a few days ago. Since then, she hadn't been able to get their conversation out of her mind. And as soon as Steph had made her precocious statement, Maddie's heart had started thundering and her hands had gone clammy. If she'd truly gotten over Noel, would she have reacted so strongly?

She sat on the closed toilet seat and put her head in her hands. Maybe Steph was right. She'd held on to her bitterness against Noel for long enough. Just because he hadn't been her prince didn't mean he wasn't somebody's—maybe even Stephanie's. And that gave her some hope that she might find Mr. Right out there somewhere too.

She pulled her phone from her pocket. She didn't have Noel's number in her contacts, but a quick internet search brought up the page for Butler Bros Construction. It was time to let *some* bygones, at least, be bygones.

She punched in the number, her heart doing a tap dance on her ribs. When Noel's voice answered, she swallowed, then, gathering her thoughts, got out the words she needed to say most.

"Yeah. Noel. It's Maddie. I just wanted to say . . . I'm sorry for what I did, back in high school when I went behind your back to report Jackson. I forgive you for everything that happened. And I think you and Stephanie are going to be great together."

"Um, thank you," he said, sounding surprised. "Apology accepted. And, hey, I'm sorry I didn't do the right thing right away back then. You were right, but I was too young and proud to see it. I wanted your respect, but I didn't behave in a way that earned it."

Her shoulders relaxed. After all these years, he'd finally seen her point. The victory felt anything but empty, like a thorn had been pulled out of her finger. "Thank you."

"So we're cool?"

"We're cool." She swallowed, absorbing the feeling of resolution filling her heart. She hadn't often experienced anything like it.

"Okay, well, thanks for calling, Maddie. Happy New Year."

"And to you," she said, then ended the call.

When Maddie emerged from the back and relieved Pearl so the elderly lady could return to arranging flowers in the floral station, her heart felt lighter than she'd thought possible. She glanced at Luke's card, considering.

Who said bad boys were the way to go? Maybe she *should* call up Luke and see why he'd made her such a thoughtful and lovely gift.

Her mind raced through the potential outcomes of that call. Unlike the one to Noel, which was an ending that finally closed an open sore, a call like that to Luke held only the potential of creating a bunch of new ones. If he was interested, what would she even do about it?

Maddie gave her head a shake. She didn't know what her Prince Charming would look like. But she was pretty sure he'd be a lot more dashing than Luke Anderson.

Tucking the card in her purse, she went back to work.

Want to read what happened at the Christmas Eve party? (Hint: When everything goes wrong, there's more than one mystery to unravel!)
Download the bonus epilogue at:
www.talenawinters.com/ebtr-bonus

Dear Reader,

I HOPE NOEL AND Stephanie's story warmed your cockles. If you loved it, I would really appreciate a review on your favourite platform to help other readers find it too. And be sure to read on to learn more about the next book in the series, *Every Rose that Blooms*, featuring Luke and Maddie. (Enjoy another heartwarming Christmas read about Trevor Harris and his brothers' adoption story in *All I Want for Christmas*.)

Addiction is an issue that has touched my life in deep and personal ways. Even as I was writing this book, I had a fresh traumatic experience with an addicted family member. And in recent years, we've seen an explosion of many forms of addiction, from substances to technology and beyond, each of them destructive in their own ways. It breaks my heart—addiction destroys families, and it destroys people.

There is hope, though. Recovery and healing are not only possible, they are within reach. And, when addicts seek healing, I firmly believe the relationships can also be healed, if people are willing.

If you or someone you love is struggling with addiction, I urge you to seek help and healing today. It's never too late to take the first step, and though the road may be hard, you don't have to walk it alone.

Shame is the prison, and addiction is the warden—but truth will set you free. And the truth is, God loves you, and he made you to live a life of freedom and abundance. Healing is within your grasp, but it requires a choice: to step into that freedom and let him guide you through the process.

If you're ready to take that first step—whether it's to break an addiction or to heal from co-dependency—reach out. Get the help and support you need, because no one recovers from addiction and trauma alone.

Like Noel and Steph experienced, having a community walking with you on this journey will make all the difference.

You are invited...

Would you like exclusive bonus content? Join my reader community, the Books and Tea League, and you'll get access to behind-the-scenes content (such as real-life inspirations for the locations in Peace Crossing), character interviews, bonus art, and even some sweet recipes inspired by the food in this book. And the best part? It's free to join!

Sign up at www.talenawinters.com/batl. See you there!

Talena Winters

August 2024

Every Rose that Blooms

Sometimes the love you long for blooms right before your eyes.

Madeleine Kennedy has always dreamed of owning the flower shop she manages. But with her mom's health concerns and the shop barely staying afloat, those aspirations feel more distant every day. Then her handsomest customer offers an unexpected lifeline that could change everything—if she can get her shy artist friend and his surprise hit floral creations on board.

Luke Anderson would love to turn his side art hustle into a full-time business, but taking the leap feels as daunting as telling Maddie how he truly feels. When she proposes a creative partnership backed by an angel investor, he thinks he'll finally get his opportunity. If only that impossibly good-looking doctor wasn't always in the way.

But as their budding venture grows into something more, a Kennedy family crisis and the discovery that their silent partner is Luke's charming rival put everything they've built at risk. With Luke and Maddie's dreams and hearts on the line, will Luke take the chance and fight for their blossoming love?

Every Rose that Blooms is the third standalone title in the Peace Crossing series. If you crave heartwarming small town stories with pining heroes, determined heroines, big dreams, and sweet Valentine's vibes, immerse yourself in a swoony story that will make you believe in happily ever afters.

Coming soon!

Pre-order now to reserve your copy at
www.talenawinters.com/every-rose-that-blooms.
Shop the entire Peace Crossing series at
www.talenawinters.com/peace-crossing.

Acknowledgements

As ever, I would like to thank my lord and saviour, Jesus Christ, for the storytelling gifts he has given me, and the privilege to be able to use them.

Thank you to my husband, Jason, who gives me a reason to write and the belief that I can.

Thank you to my support team, who help me keep perspective in this writing life: Jessica Renwick, Brenna Bailey-Davies, and Jennifer E. Lindsay (whose insightful and sensitive feedback also made this story so much better). Thank you for being writing buddies and true friends. Your support and encouragement means the world to me.

Thank you to my mom, Laurel Easton, for once again being a tireless supporter of my work, and for giving me valuable feedback on the first draft of this project.

Thank you to Melody Hilman for answering my questions about medical procedures at a rural hospital, Karl Mundt for his input on the spec house scene, and Abosede Onaba and her parents, who have often answered my strange and nit-picky questions about Nigerian culture (in this and other works). Any mistakes are definitely mine.

Thank you to the amazing people of the Peace Country, whose determination, resilience, resourcefulness, and creativity inspired this series. I'm so grateful to call Peace River (the real-life Peace Crossing) my adopted home.

Thank you to the premium members of my reader community, the Books and Tea League: Elaine Blackmon, Jenn Brierley, and Jossie Coté. Your extra support while writing this meant the world to me and kept me going on the tough days.

And thank you, dear reader, for supporting my work. You're the reason I do this.

Also By Talena Winters

Peace Crossing:

Every Star That Shines (Book 1)
Every Bell that Rings (Book 2)
Every Rose that Blooms (Book 3)
All I Want for Christmas (A Peace Crossing Story)

Rise of the Grigori:

The Water Boy (prequel)
The Undine's Tear (Book 1)
The Sphinx's Heart (Book 2)

Standalones:

Finding Heaven
The Friday Night Date Dress
Up in Smoke

More Reads:

Get more exclusive content on my website in the Books and Tea League.

Talena Winters writes page-turning fantasy, romance, and adventure novels. She's an award-winning songwriter, and her editing clients have gone on to win awards and land literary agents. She and her husband—plus a rotating cast of their three young adult sons—live on an acreage in the Peace Country of northern Alberta, Canada, with two Husky dogs and a neurotic orange cat. Her writing is grounded in a deep belief in God, love, redemption, and hope against all odds, and fuelled by an insatiable passion for stories, dark chocolate, and making the world a better place. And she would really like to know why the tea is always gone. You can find her on the web at www.talenawinters.com.

g   goodreads.com/talenawinters

▶   youtube.com/c/talenawinters

◎   instagram.com/talenawinters

f   facebook.com/talenawinters.artist